POLISHING THE DUKE

Suddenly a Duke Series
Book Three

Alexa Aston

DRAGONBLADE PUBLISHING, INC.

Text by Alexa Aston
Cover by Dar Albert

Dragonblade Publishing, Inc. is an imprint of Kathryn Le Veque Novels, Inc.
P.O. Box 23
Moreno Valley, CA 92556
ceo@dragonbladepublishing.com

Produced in the United States of America

First Edition April 2023
Print Edition

Dearest Reader;

Thank you for your support of a small press. At Dragonblade Publishing, we strive to bring you the highest quality Historical Romance from some of the best authors in the business. Without your support, there is no 'us', so we sincerely hope you adore these stories and find some new favorite authors along the way.

Happy Reading!

CEO, Dragonblade Publishing

Additional Dragonblade books by Author Alexa Aston

Suddenly a Duke Series

Portrait of the Duke

Music for the Duke

Polishing the Duke

Second Sons of London Series

Educated By The Earl

Debating With The Duke

Empowered By The Earl

Made for the Marquess

Dubious about the Duke

Valued by the Viscount

Meant for the Marquess

Dukes Done Wrong Series

Discouraging the Duke

Deflecting the Duke

Disrupting the Duke

Delighting the Duke

Destiny with a Duke

Dukes of Distinction Series

Duke of Renown

Duke of Charm

Duke of Disrepute

Duke of Arrogance

Duke of Honor

The Duke That I Want

The St. Clairs Series

Devoted to the Duke

Midnight with the Marquess

Embracing the Earl

Defending the Duke

Suddenly a St. Clair

Starlight Night (Novella)

The Twelve Days of Love (Novella)

Soldiers & Soulmates Series

To Heal an Earl

To Tame a Rogue

To Trust a Duke

To Save a Love

To Win a Widow

Yuletide at Gillingham (Novella)

The Lyon's Den Series

The Lyon's Lady Love

King's Cousins Series

The Pawn

The Heir

The Bastard

Medieval Runaway Wives

Song of the Heart

A Promise of Tomorrow

Destined for Love

Knights of Honor Series

Word of Honor

Marked by Honor

Code of Honor

Journey to Honor

Heart of Honor

Bold in Honor
Love and Honor
Gift of Honor
Path to Honor
Return to Honor

Pirates of Britannia Series
God of the Seas

De Wolfe Pack: The Series
Rise of de Wolfe

The de Wolfes of Esterley Castle
Diana
Derek
Thea

Also from Alexa Aston
The Bridge to Love
One Magic Night

PROLOGUE

Southeast of Cambridge—June 1792

PIERCE STOOD AND lifted the bucket of cold water. It contained three fish he had caught this afternoon. Mama would be so happy. She always praised him when he brought home what he had caught. She would fry the fish, and they would eat them for their supper. He liked doing things that made her life easier. She seemed sad all the time, though she tried to hide it from him. Anytime he came upon her with tears on her cheeks, she would quickly wipe them away and smile brightly at him, pretending nothing was wrong.

He understood that their life was different from most. Their cottage was isolated from others. They rarely had company. Only the tall man with dark blond hair came to visit and when he did, Mama would find chores for Pierce to do outside, saying she needed some private time with the earl. Pierce wasn't sure exactly what an earl was, only that he must be a very important person. He wore fancy clothes and rode a magnificent coal-black horse that was the most beautiful creature Pierce had ever seen. One day, he hoped he could have such a beautiful horse to ride.

Sometimes, a cart appeared. From what he gathered, it came from the closest village, which Mama would not let them visit. The same man always drove the cart and wore a surly look as he delivered supplies to them. He never spoke, only unloaded the goods from the cart and left quickly after doing so. Pierce wished he could talk to the man and learn a little about where he brought their supplies from and what was nearby.

He wished he had friends and could go to school, as he'd read about in a story. Mama had taught him to read and write, and he learned about all kinds of subjects. Still, he felt lonely, with only their chickens as his companions. He thought Mama must be lonely, too. When Pierce asked her about it once, she said they had one another and that was good enough.

He arrived at the cottage and saw the beautiful black horse tied up, which meant the earl had come calling. Instead of entering the cottage, Pierce decided to peek inside a window and see if they were in serious conversation. If not, he would go inside and show off the fish he had caught in the nearby stream.

Being June, all the windows and the door had been opened. Mama loved to catch the breeze. He moved toward a window in the front of the house and heard voices as he approached. Setting his bucket on the ground, he crept to the window and looked inside.

The earl was sitting in one chair, holding Mama's hands in his. She had tears streaming down her cheeks.

"You have to let me go, Elias," she pleaded. "You have held on far too long. You are married now, with a child on the way. A *child*!"

The earl looked in pain as he asked, "How can I do that when I love you, Amanda?"

Pierce squatted by the window, knowing he shouldn't be listening, but hoping he would hear something that would explain his and Mama's isolated way of life.

"Don't talk of love, Elias. It means nothing."

"It means everything. You know how I feel about you. And the boy."

She snorted. "What I need from you is not love and empty promises. Those days are far behind us. I want a settlement from you. I want to take Pierce and go far away. I can no longer see you, Elias. I am not part of your world. I never was."

"I cannot give you up, love," the earl said tenderly. "You know I will continue to provide for you and our boy."

Pierce froze.

Our boy?

In that moment, he understood more than he ever had. That this man who came and visited them about once a month was his father. And the earl loved Pierce's mother. Somehow, something kept them from being together. But if the earl had only recently gotten married, why hadn't he married Mama instead? Why didn't he live with them, or they with him? Why were there so many secrets that no one would tell him about?

Pierce heard Mama begin to weep. "Oh, Elias, don't you see? We must move far from here. I don't want you to know where we go. I cannot be somewhere convenient for you anymore. I must break away and start a new life. It isn't fair to Pierce to keep him from others. He should be around boys his own age. Be able to walk into the village and even take lessons. He is so very smart, Elias. I have taught him almost everything I know, and he still hungers for more knowledge."

He listened to them argue and plead with one another, finally reaching a compromise. The earl agreed to having his solicitor come once a year and give them funds for the year. Mama had wanted the solicitor to merely send the money and not see them in person. The earl was insistent, though, and Mama promised to write a Mr. Potter and share with him their final destination so he could come every year.

"I want a report on our boy and his progress. Potter will do as I have always done and quiz Pierce. See where he stands in his lessons. He can also give me a physical description of the boy."

He thought back to the earl's visits over the years and how the man would ask him about history and have him add sums in his head or conjugate Latin verbs. This solicitor would probably do the same and report back to the earl.

His father.

"You are certain you won't change your mind about this, Amanda?"

"We must leave, Elias. I will build a new life for Pierce. One where he and I will not be judged and treated as outcasts."

"If you ever change your mind—"

"I won't. I have spent too much of my life waiting around for you and stolen moments. That time has passed. I need to live for myself and my son."

"Then if this is goodbye, will you make it a proper one, my love?"

A long silence ensued, causing Pierce's curiosity to rise. He inched up and peered through the window, seeing his parents clinging to one another, a desperate air about them as they kissed.

His chest ached, as if someone stabbed him in the heart. He still didn't understand everything, only that these two loved each other a great deal and could not be together.

"Where is he?" the earl finally asked. "I must see him one more time."

"He went fishing, Elias. He loves it as much as you do."

A long sigh sounded. "I remember those days. Us sitting on the bank, fishing poles in the water. I loved you from the first time I saw you. I will always love you, Amanda. Always."

"And I you, Elias. We must part, though, before the pain becomes unbearable."

"Will you tell Pierce of us? Of me?"

"Perhaps. When he is older and can understand more. Let me call for him. I would think he'll be home soon."

But Pierce didn't want to see this man. Not now. Maybe not ever. He listened as Mama called for him, continuing to crouch on the ground.

He heard their steps outside the house, just a few feet around the corner where he hid.

"He is too far away, Elias. You must go. You know it. I do, too."

"How can I leave, Amanda? Leave you and our child?"

Pierce leaned around the cottage wall and saw his father had his arms wrapped about Mama. They both looked as if their hearts might break. Quickly, he ducked back, not wanting to be seen.

He listened as the horse's hooves began to sound, racing away from the cottage.

The earl was gone. He would not return. If he did, they wouldn't be here.

After waiting five minutes, Pierce reclaimed his bucket and went inside the cottage, doing his best to pretend that he hadn't heard and seen what had occurred within it over the last half-hour. Mama wasn't in the front room, a combination parlor and kitchen, and so he went to the bedchamber they shared.

Clothes were strewn about on the bed. Mama was folding one of her gowns.

"There you are, my darling," she said, forcing a smile upon her lips.

"What are you doing?" he asked.

"We are moving!" she proclaimed, her excitement contagious. "I have found a new place for us to live. I will open a shop, and you shall go to school with other boys."

Catching her enthusiasm, he said, "Where is this place?"

"Oh, far from here. It is a small town south of Bristol and growing quickly. We will ride a mail coach to get to it, and it will take several days to reach our destination."

Mama captured his hands and sat on the bed. "I have news to share with you." She hesitated and then said, "Not only are we leaving for a new life, but you are going to be a big brother come next February."

Pierce said nothing, dumbfounded.

She squeezed his hands. "Oh, you will be such a good big brother, Pierce. You are already such a wonderful helper for me. Do you hope it is a boy or a girl?"

He thought a moment, wondering if she had told the earl about the new babe.

"I suppose a girl. You already have a boy in me. A girl would be nice."

Mama beamed. "I think so, too. I may be a little ill for a while. Women carrying a babe often are. This child will be a blessing."

She stood. "Come and help me pack. We will be leaving the day after tomorrow."

Pierce did as asked, happy simply because Mama was happy. He supposed leaving this place—and the earl—made her spirits lighter.

The next morning, they breakfasted and were washing their dishes when the sound of approaching horses caused Mama to drop a dish.

"Oh, please. Not again," she murmured.

He thought she was upset because the earl had returned. Running to the open door, he saw a couple in a cart pulled by two horses. Mama came to join him.

And cursed under her breath.

Shock filled him. He had never heard her do so. At least he thought she had cursed. He had read once about someone being very upset in a book. The man had cursed, shocking everyone about him. The way Mama had said the word let Pierce know it was a bad one.

"These people do not love us," she told him quietly as the man climbed from the bench and helped an older, worn-out version of his mother to the ground. "Watch what you say," she warned.

The man was old, with iron-gray hair, and thin. His face looked as if he stayed angry all the time. He came toward them, the woman meekly trailing behind.

"I have come to see your mistake."

Mama stiffened beside Pierce, her arm going protectively about him. "Then you have come to the wrong place and may leave."

The man stopped in front of Pierce. "I am the Reverend Tamblyn." He indicated his wife. "This is Mrs. Tamblyn."

Pierce wanted to introduce himself but recalled Mama's warning and remained silent.

"I see the boy has no manners," the man said gruffly.

"Why are you here?" Mama asked. "You were not invited."

"*He* stopped and told us you would be leaving the area. Suggested we say our goodbyes."

"Then goodbye," Mama said. "Thank you for coming."

The woman took a step forward. She placed her hand on Pierce's head. "You are a handsome boy. I hope—"

"The Devil was handsome, Woman!" the clergyman shouted. "Get away from him."

A bit of defiance crept into her eyes. She smiled at Pierce, her hand going to his cheek. "Be good for your mother. She loves you very much." Then she leaned close and whispered, "I love you, too."

Mrs. Tamblyn straightened and smiled sadly at Mama and then stepped away, returning to the cart.

"Can you add sums? Spell?" barked the reverend.

"I can do both. I also know history and geography and Latin and Greek."

The man glared down at Pierce. "Fancy now, are you? What is to praise?

"*Laudo,*" Pierce replied. "Principal parts *laudo, laudare, luadavi, laudatus.*"

Mr. Tamblyn looked disgruntled and challenged Pierce again. "To carry?"

That was an easy one.

"Active infinitives are *portare, portavisse, portaturus esse.* Passive? *Portari, portatus esse, portatum iri.*"

"Participles?" the old man pressed.

With confidence, he said, "*Portans* and *portaturus* are active. *Portatus* and *portandus* are passive. Would you care for imperative? *Porta, portate, portato, portatote, portato, portanto.* Active. *Portare, portamini, portator, portator, portantor.* Passive."

"He is arrogant and smug," Mr. Tamblyn said. "Just as his father is."

Pierce heard Mama's quick intake of breath. "Leave," she said, her voice firm. "You abandoned me years ago and wanted nothing to do with me. I would like to stay estranged from you."

"You are a godless woman who succumbed to the temptations of the flesh," he bellowed. "*This* is the result of your iniquity."

A fierceness filled Mama's face. "Pierce is a loving, kind boy. What I thought a clergyman should be. If Christ could forgive sins, why can't you, Father?"

He winced at her words then glared at her. "It is a good thing you are leaving."

"I know of his marriage. And the babe," she said quietly. "Please. Go. I want no trouble from you."

Wheeling, he marched to the cart and sat upon the bench. Taking up the reins, Mr. Tamblyn urged the horses on.

Mrs. Tamblyn—the woman Pierce knew was his grandmother—smiled and waved.

"She will suffer for doing that," Mama said, her tone bitter. Then she pulled him to her, hugging him tightly. "When you are older, I will tell you more of those people. And the earl. For now, let us be glad that we are leaving this place. A new life awaits us, Pierce.

"A new beginning."

Chapter One

London—January 1812

Lady Nalyssa Shelbourne stared out the window, the bleak January afternoon only growing bleaker. She saw snowflakes begin to dance in the air and turned away, going to sit behind her enormous desk.

What would she do for clients?

Nalyssa was a rare member of the *ton* in that she actually had to work for a living. It had not always been the case. Once, long ago, she had been a darling of the *ton* and the daughter of the Earl of Starling. Well, she was still an earl's daughter. Papa was dead, however, and had left her close to destitute. She'd had two wonderful Seasons in which she'd had more fun than she should have, causing her to decide to wed by the end of her third Season. Just before that Season began, though, her father put a bullet through his head. The ensuing scandal, though kept out of the newspapers, became general knowledge, touching her. Painted by the thick crush of gossip, she retreated to the countryside and buried Starling in the nearby village's graveyard. The family solicitor had a long discussion with her, telling Nalyssa of the distant cousin who had been located and found to be the heir to the earldom. The man was a lowly country barrister from just outside Liverpool and had no idea of the workings of Polite Society.

That is where she stepped in for her first time, remaking the awkward man into the very image of a perfect earl.

By the next Season, the newest Earl of Starling was successfully launched into society, making a brilliant match with a marquess' daughter, who had a fat dowry. That dowry saved the new earl's entailed estate and in gratitude, he had helped set Nalyssa up in the business she had operated for close to a decade.

That business was turning unsuitable men into suitable ones, ones who might be accepted by Polite Society.

Starling had bought her a small place just beyond fashionable Mayfair, and she did her business from her home. The *ton* knew she had taken a sow's ear and made a luscious silk purse from it. She had let it be known that she was willing to do the same again for other gentlemen in need, as long as they paid her hefty fee to turn them from the proverbial frogs into princes of men.

And they did.

It surprised her how many men, some even raised within the *ton*, had no idea how to behave in it. Most of her work involved whipping bastards of noblemen into shape or working with officers returning from war because they now held a title.

Nalyssa was frugal and watched her money carefully. She had slowly been welcomed back into Polite Society's good graces, although she knew she would never receive an offer of marriage herself. One, because she no longer possessed the huge dowry which her worthless father had gambled away. Two, because she *was* a businesswoman. While still invited to *ton* affairs, she was not truly a part of Polite Society anymore. Her friends had abandoned her once it was made known what her father had done and that she would have no prospects at marriage.

It didn't matter anymore to her. She was self-sufficient. She made do with a cook and two maids, directing them about their tasks without the services of a housekeeper, which she would not have been able to afford.

Worry filled Nalyssa, however. It was the end of January. February would make its appearance next week—and she still had no clients for this upcoming Season. Usually, the months before the Season were when she did the bulk of her training, clients coming to her, begging to take the lessons she would give them in order to help them seamlessly move into the Season. No one had stepped forward this year, however. Nalyssa could make it through another Season without a client—*if* she watched her expenses. But going one Season without any might lead to a second one.

And that would spell disaster for her.

She toyed with the idea of letting one of the maids go and then realized the girl's salary was so small that it would not make a difference. She could talk to Cook, though, and see that they cut back on some meals. Even tea. Usually, Nalyssa's lessons began with and then revolved around tea. She was proud of the lavish teas her cook prepared. In the future, she would make do with a cup of tea and possibly the occasional biscuit if she had no guests.

She wondered if she would receive invitations to *ton* affairs as she had in the past. Part of her believed the only reason she was still invited to balls and parties was so that others could observe her as she launched her clients into society. If she had no clients, she feared those invitations might dry up. Then where would she be?

A knock sounded on the door of her study and she called, "Come."

Jenny, who served as both a parlor maid and Nalyssa's lady's maid, came into the room and closed the door.

"My lady, there is a Mr. Potter here."

"Is he a solicitor?"

The servant smiled. "He is, my lady."

She breathed a sigh of relief. First contact for her services almost inevitably involved a solicitor. One who alerted her to the death of someone and the name of the heir who would replace that titled gentleman.

"Show him in," she said, confidence swelling within her.

Moments later, a man of about thirty entered her study. He was already a bit portly, and his hairline receding more quickly than most men his age.

"Ah, Lady Nalyssa. Thank you for agreeing to meet with me. I am Mr. Potter, the younger. My father, Mr. Potter, sent me here today."

"Won't you have a seat, Mr. Potter?"

He took one opposite her desk, and she seated herself behind it, not rushing things by asking a flurry of questions. Experience had taught her it was best to remain silent and let the solicitor unveil the purpose of his visit.

"One of my father's longtime clients is the Duke of Stoneham," he began.

"How is His Grace?" she asked politely, already having heard the man had been in poor health for more than a year and knowing the duke had not attended the Season last year.

"His Grace is doing rather poorly," Mr. Potter shared. "His doctors give him very little time to live."

She thought a moment, recalling who the ducal heir would be. "I am not certain as to the objective of your visit, Mr. Potter. If I remember correctly, the heir to the Duke of Stoneham is the Earl of Hardwell. I have met Hardwell before and do not think him in need of my services."

Potter shifted uncomfortably in his seat. "His Grace has asked to meet with you in person, my lady."

"He is well enough to do so?" she inquired, curious about this entire situation.

"In truth, no," the solicitor admitted. "He does know of your services and asked if I could bring you to him directly. Now."

"Now?"

"Yes, my lady. Before it is too late."

His words surprised her. "He is that near death?"

"I would not be exaggerating to say the duke already has one foot in his grave." Potter looked imploringly at her. "I beseech you, my lady. Please come and meet with His Grace. I assure you that you will be compensated well for your time."

The man's words had the desired effect. "I would be happy to visit with His Grace. Give me a few minutes to collect my cape and reticule, Mr. Potter. You may wait here."

Nalyssa left her study and found Jenny lingering in the hallway. "Come quickly."

They went to her bedchamber, where Nalyssa had Jenny help her change her dress to something more suitable to meet with a duke, albeit one on death's doorstep. Then she returned to Mr. Potter and the two of them left the house, the snow coming down harder than earlier.

If she had any previous doubts, seeing the Stoneham ducal carriage awaiting them cast those aside. A footman handed her up, and she found a plush robe to throw over her lap for warmth.

"Do you know what His Grace wants to discuss with me, Mr. Potter?"

"I have an idea, Lady Nalyssa, but my father said to speak nothing of the matter with you. It is for His Grace to say."

"I see."

They traveled the busy streets and reached the duke's townhouse, where they were admitted and her cape and reticule collected from her.

The butler took them upstairs, leaving Mr. Potter in the drawing room and taking Nalyssa to the duke's rooms.

Outside the door, the servant paused. "His Grace tires easily, my lady. If he suffers from a crisis, I shall be waiting just outside the door."

"Thank you."

She wondered what crisis might occur and what ailed the dying duke as the butler opened the door and nodded for her to cross the room to the large bed on the other side of the room.

As Nalyssa approached the bed, a man sitting next to it rose, claiming her attention.

"How good of you to come, Lady Nalyssa. I am Mr. Potter, solicitor to the Duke of Stoneham."

"I would have known so by your resemblance to your son."

The man smiled. "We do favor one another quite a bit. But we should address why you were called to the duke's bedside today, my lady. He asked that I awaken him when you arrived."

"You were so certain that I would, sir?"

"I know what you do for a living, my lady. I will say this—you are about to have the challenge of a lifetime."

Potter turned to the duke, and Nalyssa saw how changed the man was from the last time she had seen him. Though she had never been formally introduced to the Duke of Stoneham, everyone in Polite Society knew who he was. Even in his early fifties, he had been a handsome man, full of life and charm.

This was no longer the case. A shell of that man now lay in this bed, looking frail and gaunt, his sickly pallor making him appear ghostly.

Potter touched a hand to the duke's shoulder and gently shook it. "Your Grace, Lady Nalyssa is here."

Stoneham opened his eyes and blinked several times, his focus on her.

"Another pillow," he commanded, in a weak voice.

She stepped forward and as Potter helped raise the duke's shoulders, she slipped another pillow behind him.

"Better." He gazed at her intently. "Tell me what you do. How you accomplish it."

She settled into the chair next to the bedside and said, "I am certain you knew my father, Lord Starling, and the man who assumed Papa's title. He was a distant relation and had never been exposed to anyone in the *ton*, coming from a small town near Liverpool. He did not know an oyster fork from a fruit fork. He had never drunk champagne, nor had he danced the waltz. I took him from being a country bumpkin to the polished earl he is today, all within a few months' time."

The duke nodded slightly. "Did you help arrange his marriage?"

"I encouraged his suit and did the same with the woman who became his countess. If you know of my father, you know the state his affairs were left in, Your Grace. Starling had to wed—and wed quickly—in order to save himself. He took to my lessons and is now one of the most respected men in Polite Society. He and Lady Starling entertain frequently."

She paused. "You have an heir, Your Grace. I know it to be Lord Hardwell. Why would you have need of my services, if I may be so bold to inquire?"

The duke's eyes closed, and he did not speak for a full minute. Nalyssa thought he might have fallen asleep again, but he opened them, seeming to rally a bit.

"It is a long, complicated tale, Lady Nalyssa. One that I have written out for my firstborn son. Not Hardwell."

Understanding filled her. "Ah, you wish for me to bring one of your bastards into society then. I have done this on several occasions, Your Grace, and I can assure you that I will meet with success."

"No," he insisted. "Not a bastard. My oldest child. My true heir. My firstborn, legitimate son."

Confusion filled her. "You were wed previously? And a child resulted from that marriage, a son?"

Stoneham nodded and then began coughing. The coughing spell went on for some minutes, as Potter handed the duke handkerchiefs which sat in a neat stack by the bedside. Nalyssa saw the blood on them and knew the duke wasn't long for this world.

After sipping water from a glass, which she offered him, he seemed to calm.

"I wed in secret, you see, many years ago, my lady. The woman was not of my class. Amanda was the daughter of a clergyman and the sweetest, kindest, most beautiful woman I had ever seen. We traveled to London and wed in a small parish church there before returning to Cambridge. I was young, barely twenty, and fearful of my father, who had beaten me for the slightest infraction as I grew up. Even being at university, I was still afraid of him. Amanda had just turned ten and seven and was also fearful of her strict father. I managed to scrape up enough money on my own to purchase a special license and then borrow more from friends of mine at university, pooling it in order to buy a small cottage for her. She gave birth to our son there."

He motioned for the glass she held and once more, she brought it to Stoneham's lips.

"We saw each other whenever I could get away over the next ten years. I was still under my father's thumb and afraid of him. Since he was a duke and the holder of the purse strings, I did not want to alienate him. He forced me into a marriage with the woman Polite Society came to know as my countess, and then duchess once I assumed my new title after my father's death."

"You were a bigamist," she said neutrally.

He nodded. "And an unfaithful husband. My new wife was a timid little thing. She gave me three children, first a boy and then two worthless girls. One died when she was young and the other married some Scottish laird and turned her back on me and England." He paused. "My boy, Edwin, thinks himself my heir. I must right the wrongs of the past since Edwin's mother passed away six months ago. I had not wanted to embarrass her while she still lived."

"You realize that your son will be stripped of his title and be known as a bastard. Is that what you wish to stir up, Your Grace? There will be no going back from this."

"Edwin cannot help the circumstances of his birth. I do owe it to

Amanda and our son to make him my rightful heir."

"Where is this son and true heir now?"

The duke motioned to Potter, who stepped forward and said, "I visited him and his mother once a year after they left the area. Mrs. Selkirk, as she called herself, wished to break away from His Grace once he married. His Grace settled a sum upon her. She and the boy, Pierce, moved to just outside of Bristol."

Mr. Potter hesitated a moment and then added, "She gave birth to another child seven months after they arrived there. Mrs. Selkirk confirmed to me that the girl was the duke's." He cleared his throat. "I, at the duke's behest, visited them in person once a year. His Grace generously provided them funds each year and I talked with the boy and gave a report to His Grace each time I returned. Pierce understands that he is a bastard child of a high-ranking nobleman. His sister has no idea of the circumstances."

"Is Mrs. Selkirk—your true duchess—still alive?" Nalyssa asked.

Stoneham nodded. "She will be upset with me for this scandal that will unfold, but her judgmental father and my blackguard one are now dead. Pierce—and Penelope—as well as my beloved Amanda, should be able to take their rightful places in society. You know, though, that will be a monumental task. Amanda and Penelope will need to be taken under your wing, but I foresee no problems in helping them acclimate themselves into a new world."

The duke paused. "It will be Pierce that will give you trouble as you try to mold him into becoming a duke. He will resist every step of the way. He has become a headstrong man."

Potter interjected, "Pierce refused to see me after he turned eight and ten. He told me that he would take care of his family in the future and that they no longer wanted the duke's financial help. I tasked Bow Street to keep a watch on him, along with his mother and sister. We receive quarterly reports of their activities."

Nalyssa turned to Stoneham. "So, my task will be to get a headstrong, supposed-bastard to accept he is soon to be a duke and teach him the ways of the *ton*? As well as taking on your duchess and daughter and doing the same. Am I correct?"

"That and helping my other boy, Edwin, to come to terms with his position. I have left an unentailed estate to him in my will. He will be able to see income generated from that. Of course, he will not live as he has and will hold no title."

Nalyssa knew what the man would hold. A huge grudge. Both against the father who had lied to him his entire life and his half-brother, who would take Edwin's place in Polite Society.

"I do not want to handle your true bastard, Your Grace," she said crisply, knowing for the sake of her business that she must keep far away from the angry son of this man who would have his world turned upside down upon the duke's death. "I take on men who must be polished to a fine sheen so that they will be able to take their place in Polite Society. That will be your heir, the man who becomes the new Duke of Stoneham. Have Mr. Potter handle the matter if you are not man enough to explain things to your other son. It is not business of mine."

Nalyssa knew she was speaking more frankly to the duke than anyone had ever dared, but she would not be a part of telling this young man he would never hold the title he had grown up expecting to be his. She must keep her distance from him. If she lost Stoneham's business, so be it.

Stoneham studied her a moment. "You are blunt, my lady."

She shrugged. "I would call it candid, Your Grace."

The duke nodded. "You are right. I have overstepped in asking you to prepare Edwin for his new role. My chief concern, however, is Pierce." He gazed at her steadily. "Are you up for such a task, my lady?"

"Do you have proof of your marriage, Your Grace?" she asked. "Its validity will need to be established before I agree to take on your case."

The duke began coughing up copious amounts of blood again. She feared he would die before her very eyes.

Once the coughing fit passed, he settled back into the pillows and motioned to Potter.

"I have seen the records at the church in London, my lady. The same clergyman who married His Grace is still serving at this church thirty years later. I have spoken with him. He is willing to testify in court, if necessary. Is that satisfactory?"

"Yes, Mr. Potter." She turned her attention to Stoneham again, who seemed even more frail than when she had first arrived. "I assume you will want your heir to be brought into society this upcoming Season?"

"Yes," he rasped. "Along with my girl, if that's possible. Focus on Pierce first. He is the one who must take his place quickly and command society's respect."

"How old are they?"

Potter supplied the answer. "Pierce is now thirty. Penelope will be twenty next month. Neither are wed, though our last report from Bow Street indicated that Penelope has a suitor. Mrs. Selkirk is in good health and owns and runs a millinery shop, assisted by her daughter. Pierce has a haberdashery, which does quite well."

"Then you must send for the three of them," she declared. "By the time they arrive in town, time will be short. The Season will be starting in a little over two months. I will have my work cut out for me."

The duke reached for her hand and took it, squeezing it weakly. "No. Not in town. Have them go to Stonecrest. Let your lessons take place in the country, away from prying eyes." He sighed wearily. "Thank you, my lady. I can rest in peace, knowing my wife and children are in good hands."

The faint pressure ceased and Nalyssa watched Stoneham's eyes slowly close. He did not move nor did he speak. She placed her hand atop his and squeezed, getting no response.

Looking to Mr. Potter, she said, "His Grace has left us. You must go at once to Bristol if we are to honor his wishes. The new Duke of Stoneham must be summoned to the ducal estate."

CHAPTER TWO

PIERCE SELKIRK WAS in an extremely good mood. He closed the ledger, satisfaction filling him, knowing he had built a haberdashery equal to none outside of London. The small town he resided in had been good to him and his family these past twenty years, ever since their arrival there when Pierce was ten years of age. Mama had rented rooms for them, telling Pierce that the sale of their cottage allowed them the luxury to do so. She also promised once she opened her own shop, they would find a larger space to live, possibly above the store itself. Pierce had gone to a day school in Bristol, first walking the five miles each way, eager to be around boys his own age. He had made friends with a boy who lived nearby and began riding in a cart driven by his friend's father, cutting the travel time considerably.

Mama grew larger and larger, finally delivering a healthy girl seven months after their arrival. She had sought his input on the name, and they had chosen Penelope, after Odysseus' wife in *The Odyssey*. Although Mama always called her daughter Penelope, Pierce called his sister Pen. Though ten years separated the two, they were extremely close.

A year after Pen's birth, Annie came into their lives. Kind, jovial, and a mother-figure to them all, Annie cooked and cleaned for them, allowing Mama to begin her millinery shop. Over the years, the shop had grown in nature and now carried not only hats but parasols and umbrellas, gloves, scarves, and tippets. Mama seemed happy running her own shop and many of the women in Bristol patronized it, saying Mrs. Selkirk's creations were superior to those in the larger city.

Pierce rubbed his chin, thinking how when he was ten and three, Mama sat him down and had a long talk with him, explaining how as a young girl, she had fallen in love with the Earl of Hardwell. She was only sixteen years of age, and her father forbid her from seeing the earl. Nevertheless, Mama had disobeyed her strict clergyman father and continued seeing her sweetheart, a Cambridge university student. She had given birth to Pierce shortly after that. He had asked why the earl had not married her and a distant look came into her eyes before she told Pierce that clergyman's daughters were not of the same social standing as that of earls and their families. In fact, her beloved was the son of a duke, a powerful duke whose favorite thing in life was to crush his son.

Mama explained how the duke would never have accepted her as his son's wife, and they had continued to see one another over the years, until the old duke demanded his son wed and provide an heir.

Frustration filled him, and Pierce raked his fingers through his hair, recalling the last day they had seen the earl. He remembered that Mama said he had wed now and had a child on the way. Mama said the earl needed to create a new life with his family, and it was best that she and Pierce leave. He had questioned why she had accepted anything from such a man, anger growing within him as the years progressed. Mama said she might be proud—but she would not let excessive pride hurt her children. That is why she had accepted the proceeds from the sale of the cottage and also a yearly sum given to them by the earl through his solicitor, Mr. Potter.

Potter came to Bristol once a year, surprised at first by baby Penelope's presence. The solicitor always spent an hour or so with Pierce, asking him about school, his friends, and if he enjoyed his life with his mother and baby sister. Pierce supposed this man reported back to the earl and thought they should cut all ties with the nobleman. Pierce had convinced his mother to do this very thing by the time Pierce turned eight and ten. The millinery shop was incredibly successful, especially with the accessories they had added. Pierce helped his mother run the business, handling the ledgers and inventory and stocking goods when they came in. Mama was the creative one, making up original hats and bonnets and getting to know the women who patronized her shop. When Potter came for that last time, Pierce told the man he was no longer welcome to visit with them. That the payments of guilt the earl sent each year would now cease. Pierce told Potter he was a man and would provide for his family in the future.

He had done so ever since.

Pierce had held a variety of jobs over the next five years while continuing to help Mama run her shop. He was good at whatever occupation he tried and was able to create quite a nest egg. His goal was to open a matching shop next to his mother's. When the previous tenant retired, he sold the space to Pierce, who turned it into a haberdashery, starting slowly as his mother had years before. He sold gentlemen's accessories, such as cravats, gloves, smalls and hosiery, and boots. The Crafty Gentleman was profitable from the beginning, and Pierce quickly added clothing to the items available. He employed two tailors and learned the business from one of them. They now sold not only accessories but coats, waistcoats, and shirts. His customers said Pierce's goods rivaled that of what they found in the best shops of London.

He had never visited London and had an itch to go there in order to study what other haberdasheries carried, especially since he was interested in expanding and starting more branches of The Crafty Gentleman in other towns. He was on the verge of hiring a manager for his store in order to free up time for him to do so and focus on other ventures. He hoped to take Mama and Pen with him on this trip, allowing them to tour the great city and see its sights. He worried, though, that Mama would turn down the trip, fearful that she might run into her former lover. Though Pierce and Pen had both encouraged Mama to see someone over the years, Mama steadfastly refused, telling Pierce in private that her heart would always belong to her beloved earl.

Hatred for the earl had grown over the years in Pierce's heart, especially when he saw how Mama had put her life on hold for a man who'd used and discarded her. Pen, of course, had no idea she was the bastard daughter of an earl. Mama had vaguely talked of a Mr. Selkirk and how he had left them long ago and Pen had been astute enough not to ask further questions. His sister assisted at the millinery shop and was being pursued by a few young men in nearby Bristol, most notably Mr. Adams, who was a clerk in a solicitor's office. Pierce wondered if his sister would wed Mr. Adams.

That led him to wonder if he might ever wed. At thirty, he was at the height of his looks and a popular man among the working class of Bristol and in their small town. Many women had chased after him, hoping he would put a ring on their finger, and they were disappointed when he did not. What he was building in his shop, however, should be left behind to someone, preferably his own flesh and blood. Perhaps it was time to think about settling down. He worried that a part of him would be unfaithful, as his father had been, and Pierce vowed never to betray his wife in that manner. He didn't believe in love, seeing what it had done to his mother.

Still, he thought he could make a good marriage with a woman and it would be successful. He would continue to run the haberdashery and perhaps invest in other businesses while she raised their children.

Pierce decided he would make the trip to London, with or without Mama and Pen, and then look for a suitable wife upon his return.

A knock sounded at his open door, and he glanced up, seeing Wilson, his chief clerk.

"We're ready to close the shop for the day, Mr. Selkirk. Anything I might get you before I leave for the day?"

"No, thank you," he told the young man. Then he said, "Wait. Come in and shut the door."

Wilson looked apprehensive as he did so and sat in the seat Pierce motioned for him to take.

"You have been a clerk here for three years, Wilson, the last two being head clerk. Do you have higher aspirations?"

The young man swallowed. "I do, Mr. Selkirk. I would like to eventually manage a store." He grinned. "Even possibly open one of my own one day. Of course, that is far down the line."

"You have a good eye when it comes to inventory," Pierce said. "You have also done an admirable job when I have asked you to update the ledgers. I am thinking of hiring a manager for The Crafty Gentleman."

The man's eyes widened. "You would step away as manager, Mr. Selkirk?"

He mulled it over a moment and then nodded. "I would. I am contemplating opening additional branches of my haberdashery and wish to devote more time to that venture. I would need to leave this original location in capable hands, however."

Wilson sat up a bit straighter. "I know I am young, Mr. Selkirk. I think you were about the same age when you began The Crafty Gentleman years ago. I believe I am up for this task. I would hope, though, that you might make yourself available to me if I had questions." He hesitated. "That is, if you are considering me for the position and I was fortunate enough to receive it."

"I would try my best to allow you to run The Crafty Gentleman as you see fit, Wilson, but I would always make time to meet with you on a regular basis and answer any questions. I would expect this shop to not only remain successful but become even more so. Are you the man to lead when I am gone?"

Wilson smiled confidently. "I am, Mr. Selkirk. I am not perfect and will certainly make mistakes, but I will always own up to any and correct them as soon as possible. As you mentioned, I have a good eye for fashion and a head for numbers. I also enjoy speaking with the customers. I believe establishing a rapport with a client will make for a happy client who returns again and again. I admire how you keep records of each of our customers and their purchases in order to have an overall picture of what they like, what they've previously bought, and what they might need in the future. I would most certainly continue that practice."

It was one Pierce and Mama had started when she first opened her millinery shop two decades ago. Mama had a page devoted to each woman who bought a hat, listing her name, a description of the hat, and when it was purchased. It gave Mama leverage, knowing what a lady had in her wardrobe and allowed her to suggest ways to supplement it. Pierce had continued the practice at his haberdashery and found it valuable.

"I will be going to London soon, Wilson, probably in the next few days. I shall turn things over to you then. Your first task will be to hire a new clerk to replace you."

"I would like to promote one of our current clerks into my position, Mr. Selkirk. I think it is wise to grow leadership within a business, no matter its size. I think I will have Mr. Ford take my place. He and I together will interview for a clerk to replace him."

Pierce smiled broadly. "Your words let me know that I have already made the right decision in elevating you to store manager, Wilson."

He stood and offered the former clerk his hand, and they shook.

"Congratulations, Mr. Wilson. Not only will you receive a new title, but you will also be compensated fairly, reflecting your new position."

He named the monthly salary and saw Wilson was more than

pleased.

"Tomorrow, we can share this news with the other employees. That will allow you and Mr. Ford to start interviewing for a new clerk."

"Thank you for this opportunity, Mr. Selkirk. I promise that I will not disappoint you."

The young man left Pierce's office with a spring in his step. He couldn't help but chuckle. He rose and locked his office, leaving the haberdashery and going next door, where Pen greeted him. Pierce went next door to dine with his mother and sister each evening, Annie still cooking their nightly meal. He did retire to his own set of rooms above The Crafty Gentleman each night, preferring to have a bit of privacy, especially when entertaining comely widows.

The moment he entered the shop, he saw the heightened color in Pen's cheeks.

"Has something exciting happened, Pen?"

His sister said, "Something very mysterious, Pierce. A man showed up a quarter of an hour ago, just as we were closing, and asked to see Mama. She was busy in her office and so I inquired of his name and went to tell her that she had a visitor. Mama looked as if she might actually faint! She did go out and greet this man, though."

Anger boiled within him. "Was his name Potter?"

Pen's brows knitted together. "Yes, how did you know, Pierce? I had never seen nor heard of him before today." She frowned. "At least I don't think so. He looked vaguely familiar, but I do not recall where I might have known him from."

"Lock the shop doors and go upstairs, Pen," he ordered, his tone firm so she did not question him. "I will go see Mama and this Mr. Potter."

Pierce wound his way through the displayed goods and turned, going down a corridor. At the end sat his mother's office, and he entered without knocking.

Mama sat behind her desk, tears streaming down her cheeks. Her appearance led him to suspect why Potter had come after so many years of staying away. Knowing he should comfort her first, Pierce instead turned his wrath upon the man seated in front of the desk.

"What in bloody hell are you doing here, Potter?" he demanded. "You were told a dozen years ago never to darken our doorstep again. I want you to leave immediately."

He turned to Mama and went behind the desk as she rose. Pierce embraced his mother as she began sobbing.

"Mama, Potter will leave now."

"I do not want him to, Pierce," she said quietly. "Mr. Potter has things to discuss with our family."

She pushed away from him and pulled a handkerchief from her pocket, wiping her tears. "Mr. Potter, would you care to dine with us this evening?"

"I will not sit at the same table as this man," Pierce said through gritted teeth.

Mama turned to him, color flooding her face. "It is *my* dinner table and I will invite whomever I choose to sit at it," she said evenly. "Mr. Potter has something important to share with all three of us, and we will hear him out."

"This man represents everything that made you unhappy, Mama. Look at the state you are in now. I will not have him upsetting you."

Anger sparked in her eyes, the first time Pierce had ever seen her this way. "You will come to dinner, Pierce. You will listen to what Mr. Potter has to share. Is that understood?"

"I have never gone against your wishes, Mama, but I must do so tonight. Nothing this man could say or do would make me change my mind."

"Tell him," Mama said tersely to Potter.

The solicitor's brows arched. "Are you certain?"

Mama nodded, determination filling her face.

Mr. Potter cleared his throat. "I am here because your father has passed away."

His instinct had been correct. "I don't give a bloody fig if the man is alive or dead," Pierce said. "He abandoned Mama and me—and Pen—twenty years ago. He tried to buy away his guilt by providing us with money. Well, we didn't need him in our lives. As you can see, we have done quite well on our own. If the earl has left us money in his will, we don't want it. We have made our way in the world without his interference."

Pierce crossed his arms over his chest and glared at Potter.

"I cannot change what happened in the past," the solicitor said apologetically. "But you have a new future ahead of you, Your Grace." He looked to Mama. "Your Grace, I would be happy to dine at your table this evening."

Her chin raised a notch. "Shall we go upstairs then, Mr. Potter?"

She swept by Pierce, who was trying to make sense of Potter's words.

Your Grace.

Potter had addressed both Pierce and his mother as *Your Grace.*

"Oh, bloody, bloody hell!" he roared.

Chapter Three

PIERCE FOLLOWED THE pair upstairs, his mind whirling. Pen awaited them, a questioning look on her face, but he shook his head, avoiding meeting her gaze.

Potter had addressed Mama and him as Your Grace. But how could that be? Pierce knew from the little his mother had said about his natural father that the earl had been the heir to a duke. Since so many years had passed, it was natural to assume that the old duke had given up the ghost, allowing his heir to inherit. That made the earl a duke.

Since the duke had died, his eldest son should inherit, not a bastard. Unless the man had all girls. Would a title pass to a bastard in that instance? Pierce had no working knowledge of titles among the *ton*. Yes, he knew what they wore because he sold it to them. Members of the *ton* who lived in Bristol and the surrounding area patronized The Crafty Gentleman and Manda's Millinery Shop. His family had sold their goods to the *ton* for years now. He had seen how they dressed and made certain his tailors could sew the latest fashions which would appeal to his clients. He heard how these clients spoke and behaved and had learned, to some extent, to even imitate their speech. But as far as the inner workings and inheritances went, he hadn't a clue.

Deciding to keep his mouth shut for the moment, Pierce went to the dinner table Annie had set and seated Pen while Potter did the same for Mama. Annie brought in the meal, with Mr. Potter raving about how wonderful everything looked and smelled.

Mama introduced Potter to Pen, telling her that he was a solicitor who had offices in London. His sister had always been curious about the great city, one of the reasons Pierce thought to take her there, and she asked Potter several questions about London. He obliged and talked at length of the city.

All while Pierce stewed.

He ate his dinner without contributing to the conversation. He supposed Mama had decided they would not speak of the business at hand until the meal had been completed.

In turn, the solicitor asked about the millinery and haberdashery and mentioned how the town had grown since he last visited here. Mama spoke of several of her more prominent customers and some of the designs she and Pen had created. His sister had a talent for art and had started drawing pictures of bonnets and hats at a young age. Pierce and Mama had encouraged Pen in this endeavor, and she now created more than half the designs of Manda's Millinery Shop.

Annie came in to clear the dishes, and Mama directed them to the parlor. Once the door was closed, they settled themselves, Pen coming to sit beside him on a settee.

"Do you know what is going on?" she asked under her breath.

"I have a vague idea. Let's see if I am right," he told her.

Mama looked to her children. "Penelope, you are going to hear a few things that may surprise you, things that Pierce is already aware of." She paused. "Some details, though, will also be new to your brother. I ask that you listen to what I have to say and then hear out Mr. Potter and what he has come to tell us."

Pierce knew that last remark had been directed toward him.

Briefly, Mama told Pen of how she had fallen in love with the son of a duke when she was even younger than her daughter, explaining how she had given birth to Pierce and years later, Penelope. He could sense his sister's shock.

"One thing your brother never knew, though, is that your father and I wed in a small church in London."

Stunned, Pierce's jaw dropped.

"We never lived together as husband and wife," Mama continued. "His father, the duke, was a wicked man who was a terrible father. He would never have accepted the daughter of a clergyman as his son's countess, much less a future duchess. Because of that, we kept our marriage a secret.

"Until now."

Potter took up the tale, explaining how the earl had wed another woman because the old duke had demanded the marriage between his heir and an old friend's daughter.

"But . . . Papa was already married to you, Mama," Pen protested.

Pierce hated that she called the man who had sired them *Papa,* but held his tongue.

"He was," Mama agreed. "It was a painful time for us both. And yes, that made him a bigamist since he was already legally wed to me." She sighed. "I was not of his class. I would never have fit into his world. I loved him enough to let him go. It is why Pierce and I moved west. We made a new start and you arrived soon after, Penelope."

Potter cleared his throat. "The earl, and eventually duke, had three children from this marriage. Edwin, known as Lord Hardwell, was his firstborn in the marriage. Another daughter came a year later. Four years after that, his last child was born. Unfortunately, she died when she was four." The solicitor paused. "Hartwell believes himself to be his father's heir but in truth, Pierce Selkirk is now the Duke of Stoneham."

Penelope turned to Pierce, her eyes wide. "You . . . are a duke? Oh, Pierce. Oh, my goodness."

"Since your mother was legally wed to the duke, she is the Duchess of Stoneham. And you are Lady Penelope."

Pen shook her head. "This is too much!" she cried, fleeing the room.

He rose to follow, but Mama said, "Let her be, Pierce. It is much for her to take in."

"And you don't think it is the same for me?" he said angrily. "You lied to me all these years, Mama. A lie of omission. You never told me of your wedding. Pen and I are not bastards."

"I didn't want you to be a part of such an artificial world, Pierce," Mama said apologetically. "We had one another. We made a good life for ourselves. Never in my wildest imagination did I think this would become public knowledge. I thought a certain sum might be given to us upon his death, but . . . not this." She shook her head, tears spilling down her cheeks. "Dear God, not this."

Potter withdrew three letters and handed one to Pierce and the other two to his mother. Pierce saw Pen's name scrawled on the top one.

"These are from His Grace. He wrote one to Edwin, your half-brother, as well."

Mama asked, "Have you seen Edwin? Does he . . . know?"

"No, Your Grace. He is a student at Cambridge. It was His Grace's wish that I come to you first. I will next go to Cambridge and summon Mr. Selkirk home to Stonecrest, where we are to bury His Grace." The solicitor hesitated. "He is to be given his letter once he reaches home."

"He will hate us, you know," Mama said, looking to Pierce. "You most of all."

He didn't care about some spoiled lord learning he was a bastard, half-brother or not. What Pierce worried about was what would now become of him—and his family. If Mama had worried all those years ago about not being good enough to be a part of the *ton*, even with the man she loved by her side, then what would become of her and her children now? They would be interlopers, staking claim to something many would believe them not worthy of. They would also have to contend not only with the vicious gossip that would surround them but the sympathy this Edwin would receive.

And Edwin's wrath.

The young man would experience the greatest betrayal of his life. Everything he knew to be real would be swept away. Moreover, he might become a threat. Pierce could handle any danger Edwin might pose. His mother and Pen would be fragile, though. He would do whatever it took to protect them.

"Lord Hardwell—that is, Mr. Selkirk—" Potter amended, "will not be destitute. His Grace's will generously provide funds for Mr. Selkirk to complete his university education. Also, an unentailed estate will be given to him, one in Somerset, so he will have some income."

"What in tarnation is unentailed?" he demanded.

Not that he cared if an estate of the duke's went to this half-brother. In truth, it was a good thing that Selkirk would be provided for. If their father hadn't done so, Pierce would have settled a sum upon the young man.

"You now are in possession of five estates, Your Grace. They are entailed, meaning that they can only pass to the ducal heir," Potter explained. "An unentailed estate is one in which you, as the Duke of Stoneham, can leave to anyone that is not your heir." Potter hesitated and then added, "I believe His Grace bought this estate several years ago so that he could bequeath it to Mr. Edwin Selkirk."

Pierce's thoughts swirled until he couldn't think. It was too much. Too much.

"I suggest that you and Her Grace read your letters," Potter said, rising. "Then we can speak again, perhaps tomorrow."

"No, you aren't going anywhere," he growled. "Sit. I may have questions that I need answered once I have read the contents of this . . . letter."

"Of course, Your Grace."

He wanted to scream at the man for continuing to address him as

Your Grace, but knew it was a courtesy. Potter was now *his* solicitor, or would be as long as Pierce decided to employ the man. A part of him wanted to fire Potter on the spot. That would be rash, though. If anything, Pierce would need Potter in the coming weeks and months. If it were as the solicitor said and he owned five estates, he would have much to learn. Potter, having been employed for decades by the duke, would be able to answer those questions.

Mama rose. "I would like to read my letter in private. I will say goodnight. Will we see you tomorrow, Mr. Potter?"

Potter responded, "Not only should I see you, Your Grace, but you should be ready to leave for Stonecrest tomorrow."

"Leave?" Pierce asked sharply. "Tomorrow?"

"Yes, Your Grace," the man said to him. "I arranged to have the duke taken back to Stonecrest for burial. His Grace wished for you to come and attend the burial and take the reins at Stonecrest immediately. He was in ill health for much of the past two years. You will need to—"

"We have businesses here," he said. "They do not run themselves."

"Then I suggest you find someone to run them for you, Your Grace. You are free to keep them, of course, but the day-to-day management must fall to someone else. You must take your place in Polite Society and your seat in the House of Lords when they next meet. You have hundreds of tenants to care for on your various estates. And your father expected you to come to town for the Season this spring, Your Grace."

"The Season?"

Pierce knew what it was because he sold plenty of goods and clothing for it. His clients talked of nothing but the Season once the new year was rung in. They wanted to be in their best finery for their time in London. He sold quite a bit of goods in the months leading up to the Season. Still, going and taking part in it?

Out of the question.

"Yes, Your Grace. The Season is a series of social affairs which—"

"I know what the Season is," he growled.

Potter stood his ground. "Then you know it is a time when couples make matches. His Grace wanted you to attend this year's Season and find a bride so you might carry on your ancestral line and provide an heir for the dukedom. He also wanted your sister brought out. He knew this might be overwhelming for her, and if you and Her Grace think it is too much for Lady Penelope to make her come-out this Season, she could wait until next spring. That would give her time to adjust to her new position in society."

"Penelope will wait," Mama said firmly. "I will see that she is properly prepared. Potter is right, Pierce." She came and placed a hand on his forearm. "You are a duke now and responsible for our family, both now and its future generations. That means finding a wife. She must be one with a pristine reputation, as there will be plenty of gossip surrounding you being named Stoneham's heir. The right young lady will provide a stabilizing effect."

"What if I don't wish to marry a woman of the *ton*, Mama? You didn't think you would fit into this world. Now, you are shoving me into it and demanding I wed a woman from it?"

She smiled sadly. "You are a man, Pierce. Man enough to accept what has happened. Mature enough to handle it with grace and aplomb. You must also think of Penelope. She will marry into this world. Your wife could help guide your sister in this, as well as you."

Mama brushed a lock of his hair from his brow. "I am so proud of the man you are, Pierce, but you have many challenges ahead. You are up for each and every one you will encounter. I know you will make me proud. Though I know next to nothing of the *ton*, I promise I will accompany you to events. You will not be alone."

"Thank you, Mama," he said quietly, knowing what it would cost her to attend these affairs. Gossip would occur, not only behind her back, but possibly to her face. She loved him enough to be by his side.

Pierce must live up to be the man she thought he could be.

"Your Graces, I do have one other thing to add," Potter said. "His Grace knew it might be difficult to ask you to navigate the waters of Polite Society with no knowledge of it. Because of that, just before his death, he met with someone who will teach you all that you need to know in order to take your place comfortably among the members of the *ton*. Lady Nalyssa Shelbourne will be waiting for you at Stonecrest. She will spend the next two months seeing that you are prepared to make this transition."

He frowned. "Who is this woman?"

Potter said, "Lady Nalyssa makes the impossible happen, Your Grace. She takes men who have no understanding of the *ton* and teaches them all they need to know in order to be successful."

Pierce already didn't like this Lady Nalyssa.

And nothing would change his mind about a woman who tried to remake him into something he wasn't.

"I will say my goodnights, Your Graces, and be back in the morning. I came in the ducal carriage and you will take it to Stonecrest. I will make my way to Cambridge in a rented vehicle and collect Mr. Selkirk. We will all meet at Stonecrest and bury His Grace."

Pierce made a decision. "You may go ahead, Potter. We will need tomorrow in which to pack and prepare our employees for our departure. We will leave in the provided carriage the following day."

He could tell Potter wanted to argue with him but held his tongue, and found he liked the man just a tad for doing so.

"Very well, Your Grace. Your coachman knows the way to Stonecrest. It will take you two days to arrive. The staff knows you are coming and will have rooms prepared for you. I will hire a coach and collect Mr. Selkirk and make certain we arrive after you do. I believe it would be best for you to already be at Stonecrest and known as the duke. Until then, Your Graces."

Potter departed, leaving Pierce with Mama, who still looked slightly bewildered.

"I have much to think about, including my shop," she told him. "There is so much to be done. And Annie must come with us. I cannot leave her behind."

"Annie is family. Of course, she will come with us," he told her. "I have already asked Wilson to become my manager," he shared, telling her of how he had thought to travel to London and visit various haberdasheries.

"I had planned to open another branch of The Crafty Gentleman," he revealed. "Those plans will never come to fruition, I'm afraid."

Mama smiled gently. "They can if you wish them to, Pierce. You are a duke now. You can do anything you want. You have enough wealth to launch a haberdashery in every city in England if you so choose." She paused. "I think you will have other things on your mind, however. I am off to talk with Penelope. This will have hit her hard. I will give her the letter her father wrote to her and then I will read my letter. I suggest you do the same."

She paused. "I know you have stored anger in your heart, Pierce. It has built for years. But you should know that despite everything, your father was a good man. He loved you a great deal."

His anger would never abate. And Pierce thought his father was the ultimate coward for not standing up to his own father and Polite Society.

"Goodnight, my son." She kissed his cheek and left the room.

Pierce decided he wanted total privacy and returned next door to his own rooms. He poured a hefty amount of brandy and sat, breaking the seal and opening the letter. He noticed it was dated six months ago.

Pierce –

I wanted to address it to my dear son—but we both know you are already angry as you read this and such a salutation would increase your ire. Yes, I know you, Pierce, more than you think I do. I, too, carried much of that anger within me. Anger at a father who never loved me. Who beat me for the slightest infraction, based upon arbitrary rules he set forth for me, rules which always seemed to change according to his whims. I may have been an absent father to you, Pierce, but better absent and loving than present and spiteful.

First and most important of all, you must know how much I loved your mother. That love extended to you and your sister. You will think me weak and gutless because I did not stand up to my own father and acknowledge the marriage I had made. Bring your mother home with me to Stonecrest and make her my countess. But, my son, I feared my father would harm my sweet Amanda and by harm, I mean murder her. He wanted my total obedience and devotion. Once, I played on the floor with my dog, a better companion than any human friend. The duke saw the happiness I took from my furry companion and shoved me aside. Drawing a knife, he told me that I was to only love him. He slit the poor creature's throat and I watched the light dim from its eyes.

I was six years old.

He was a cruel man and I fear he would have had your mother killed, especially if he learned she carried my child. I will admit I was weak, Pierce. I should never have become involved with Amanda. But she was pureness and light and filled my soul with hope. I stole what moments I could have with her, savoring them as the best times in my life. I may have been tempted by her beauty and kindness, so much that I married her, but I did my best to keep her—and you—safe from the monster I came from.

I did wed another woman, one who was meek and barely spoke to me during our marriage. I never really knew her and had little to do with her. She is gone now, put into the ground today, which is why I am writing to you. I know I must right the wrongs of the past three decades. Upon my death, you are to be acknowledged as my heir and the new Duke of Stoneham. My darling girl will finally be the duchess she deserved to be. My daughter will be a lady.

It will not be easy, Pierce, but I have faith in you. You are strong, both in mind and body. You will be the duke I never could be. You will have to deal with Edwin, your half-brother. He will be resentful of you assuming what he thought would always be his. I have provided for him, though, so he will not be entirely without means.

Take care of your mother. She will not care for the material wealth, but give her every luxury because she deserved the world placed at her feet and I could not do that for her. Make certain your sister weds a worthy man, one who will love and honor her all the days of his life.

And you, my dearest son, whom I have loved from afar all these many years—my greatest hope is that you will do good with the fortune you will receive and be just and kind. That you will care for your tenants and be respectful of them. I pray you will have the wisdom to make the best life you can. I hope that life will include finding a woman you can love as much as I have loved your mother.

I grow weary now. My health is gone and the doctors say I will not last another year. I am only sorry I could not see my loved ones one final time. Know that I carry you in my heart. Always.

Your father,
Stoneham

Pierce read the letter a second time. And then a third. Part of him wanted to forgive the man who sired him, even as the rest of him resented the duke more than he ever had. He wondered if he would ever be able to reconcile his feelings.

When he had awakened this morning, he was Pierce Selkirk, haberdashery owner, son, and brother.

Now—and forevermore—he would be known as the Duke of Stoneham.

CHAPTER FOUR

PIERCE GAZED OUT the window at the Sussex countryside. Based upon what the coachman had told him at the last stop, they would reach Stonecrest in the next quarter hour. It was possible he was already looking at land he owned.

It would become truly real once he disembarked from this ducal carriage. True, he had been referred to as His Grace these past two days as they journeyed east in two carriages, one for him and his family and the other, only slightly less grand, carrying what they had brought with them.

In the end, the Selkirk family had taken very little with them, merely clothes and a few prized possessions. Pierce had gotten little sleep the night Potter left and had gone early the next morning to speak with Mama. Together, they had decided it was best to walk away from the businesses they had created. Mama decided to shutter her shop. Since she and Pen designed all the hats that were sold, no one would be able to take her place. Annie had volunteered to remain behind and oversee the closure of the shop. Every last bonnet and pair of gloves would be sold and then the shop itself, Pierce many years ago having purchased the space of Manda's Millinery Shop and The Crafty Gentleman, thinking it wise to own instead of renting.

He had then left Mama and gone to his own place of business, finding Wilson already there. He'd taken his new store manager up to the office, looking about it a final time, a wave of sadness washing over him. He kept their conversation brief, telling Wilson that circumstances had changed since their previous discussion. At first, Wilson thought Pierce had changed his mind about turning over the store's management to him. Pierce quickly cleared up that misunderstanding, gifting the store outright to the young man, who was in his early twenties. He told Wilson The Crafty Gentleman was his to not only run but own, as well, and that Wilson could move into the rooms above the store the next day since Pierce was vacating them. He also told the new owner that he could expand into the space being vacated by Manda's Millinery Shop. Explaining things had radically changed in his life, Pierce shared that he had unexpectedly inherited a title and would need to move to the property he had inherited.

He did not tell Wilson that he was now a duke.

The former clerk had been flummoxed at first, but he quickly regained his senses and profusely thanked Pierce. Together, they had gone downstairs when the rest of the staff arrived and shared the news. It would be difficult for him to walk away from a business he had built from the ground up, but Pierce knew he was leaving the place in good hands. Though he longed to encourage Wilson to write to him, Pierce realized it was best to cut all ties. Perhaps he would come and visit in a few years and see what Wilson had done with The Crafty Gentleman. If it were running as well as he believed it would be, he might consider investing a sum with Wilson to bring the shops to other towns throughout England.

That, however, was far in the future. Right now, Pierce needed to concentrate on the present.

And that frightened him beyond measure.

He was going into the unknown. A world which had barely existed to him before. Yes, some of the *ton* had come and patronized The Crafty Gentleman, so he knew how a few members dressed and spoke. But he feared treacherous waters lay ahead.

His first concern would be to learn everything possible about Stonecrest, his ducal seat. Potter had also spoken of other properties Pierce had inherited. He would want to learn where they were located and visit them all once he had gotten a solid grasp on Stonecrest. He needed to learn how an estate ran. Meet his staff and tenants. See what needs were being met and which ones still needed action taken.

As far as entering the glittering world of the *ton* and becoming swept up in its social affairs, he was less concerned about that. Yet he knew it would be vital to step into it for Mama and Pen's sakes. He would even need to become a leader among its members. Few dukes existed in society, and they were looked upon as the chosen leaders of the elite. Pierce would need to become more aware of political, economic, and social issues that might be presented in the House of Lords since he would be voting on the bills put forward.

He would also need to choose a wife among them, a thought almost repugnant to him. His mother was the best woman he would ever know. If she had felt unworthy to enter such a society, he doubted it was one he would approve of, much less enjoy. Pierce must step up and make certain that Mama and Pen were treated with the respect due them, the widow and daughter of the Duke of Stoneham.

Mama had discussed some of this with Pierce after Pen fell asleep at the inn last night. The innkeeper had fawned over them as if they were royalty, giving them the best rooms. Pierce hadn't been able to sleep and had been pacing his room when Mama knocked softly at his door. They talked until the wee hours of the morning, deciding that she would accompany him to social affairs and that he would definitely take a bride by Season's end, one with a sterling reputation, which would help solidify his own. That wife could help launch Pen into Polite Society next year when the Season began.

Already, his sister was both anxious and resentful of being yanked from her old life and thrust into a new one. Pierce had confronted Pen as she grumbled, asking if this was about Mr. Adams and if she cared for him. Even if she did have feelings for Adams, he knew he could not allow his sister to wed a lowly clerk. Daughters of dukes did not do such things. Pierce was determined to honor their father's wishes and make certain that Pen made a brilliant match, almost choking on the irony, knowing it was this very thinking which had torn his parents apart. He must do what was right for Pen, though, and see that she wed someone of her own class.

Yet what eligible lady of the *ton* might wish to wed a former haberdashery owner turned duke?

Pierce finding the right bride would influence how Pen and Mama would be treated. Frankly, he didn't care whom he wed, as long as her reputation was pristine and she could help advance his family's social standing and quell the gossip that would surround them. While his parents had expressed their undying devotion and love for one another, Pierce had no intentions of ever falling in love. He would be respectful of the woman who became his duchess, but he did not care to get to know her, in part to protect himself. He would always be viewed as an outsider, despite his lofty title. He did not need to be judged as inferior in his own marriage, thus he would keep a set distance between him and his wife. She would be present in his life to provide him an heir and secure the approval he needed so that Mama and Pen would be accepted.

The carriage slowed, making a wide turn and continuing up a lane. His heart began beating faster, knowing he would soon be at his new home.

Home . . .

He doubted the grand place could ever seem like a home, not after the modest way he had been brought up. He valued that upbringing, knowing Mama had instilled in him the proper values and not the artificial ones of the class he now belonged to. Sympathy, verging on pity, filled him for his mother. Her own father had cast her from her family, judging Mama for giving birth to Pierce. He still remembered

Reverend Tamblyn, filled with hate and wrath, and could see the man's meek wife, Pierce's grandmother, who looked beaten down and weary. Because of her judgmental father, Mama had lost the link with her own world, that of humble working people. She had been cast out from that society and was astute enough to know she would never belong in the world of her husband. No wonder she had wanted them to go far from Cambridge and make a fresh start.

They had, thanks to Mama's forbearance. She had taught Pierce and Pen what was important and instilled in them values that would transcend the world they now entered.

"Oh, my," his sister said, awe in her voice.

The carriage stopped, and Pierce saw the grand stone edifice, so vast that he could not begin to imagine the number of rooms contained within it. It would take a staff of dozens to keep the place running.

And all for three people.

The door to the vehicle opened, a footman having placed stairs beneath it so they could descend. He left the carriage first, seeing two lines of servants now awaiting them. Pierce turned and handed down Mama and then Pen.

"Do not gawk," he quietly told his sister. "Hold your head high. You are a duke's daughter."

Pen nodded, determination filling her eyes. He glanced to Mama, who looked as regal as any queen.

"Shall we?" he asked, offering each of them an arm and escorting them to a couple who stood apart from the others. He assumed them to be the butler and housekeeper. They would be the ones who ran his household.

As they moved in that direction, another woman stepped forward, catching his attention. This woman was no servant.

She was a goddess.

She stood taller than every woman present and most of the men.

Her figure was remarkable, causing his blood to heat. She had a commanding presence, as if she could lead England's soldiers into battle and best Bonaparte and his men with a single charge. As they reached her, he noted her sapphire blue eyes and the auburn tint to her hair, which was pulled away from her face, allowing her bone structure and beauty to shine.

Dipping into a deep curtsy, she finally rose. "Your Graces. Lady Penelope. I am Lady Nalyssa Shelbourne."

Her voice was cultured. Pierce saw the intelligence in this woman's eyes. He realized she was the woman Potter had spoken of, the one who was to take him in hand and make him acceptable to others. He had disliked the idea of her to begin with.

Now, he wanted to fall at her feet and worship her.

Finding his voice, he said, "Good afternoon, my lady. May I present to you my mother, the Duchess of Stoneham, and my sister, Lady Penelope Selkirk?"

Mama offered Lady Nalyssa her hand. "Mr. Potter spoke of you, my lady. It is thoughtful of you to greet us."

Lady Nalyssa smiled. "I am here to make your transition flow easily, Your Grace." She released Mama's hand and took Pen's. "Delighted to make your acquaintance, Lady Penelope." Turning to Pierce, she said, "Your staff eagerly awaits you, Your Grace. Might I present them to you?"

"Of course," he said briskly, tamping down the lust he felt.

Pierce told himself this was a woman, just like all the other women he had bedded over the years. She might be a member of the *ton*, but she was no different from anyone else. With her looks and age, she was no doubt married. He drew the line at that. His own father had been unfaithful to his mother and pretended to wed and live with a woman for decades. Pierce had a simple rule, one which kept him from women who already had a husband.

Thank God for that rule—because even having it, he might have fought—and lost—his heart to Lady Nalyssa Shelbourne.

She led him to the couple. "Your Grace, this is Mr. and Mrs. Pugh. They serve as Stonecrest's butler and housekeeper."

They bowed and curtseyed to him and then his mother and sister.

"We are here to serve you, Your Grace," Pugh said formally, his words neutral, but his tone conveying slight disapproval. "Mrs. Pugh and I are at your service."

Pierce studied the pair a moment and then quietly said, "I know I am not who you expected in this position, yet I will expect not only good service from you, Pugh, but your loyalty, as well." His own tone conveyed his own expectations. He knew these two could make or break whether he and his family were able to make Stonecrest a true home.

His gaze met that of Pugh's and the butler's slight nod spoke volumes. "My father and his before him served the Duke of Stoneham. I am, and always will be, your faithful servant, Your Grace."

He nodded his own approval and looked to the housekeeper. "Mrs. Pugh, I would like you to take us on a tour of the house tomorrow morning."

"Certainly, Your Grace. There is much of it to see."

"For now, let me meet my staff."

Pierce did his best to stand erect and look solemn, thinking that is what these servants expected. He listened to the multitude of names and knew he might never learn all of them, particularly those he would have little contact with. Then he decided he would get to know them all, as well as the names of the tenants who resided on his lands. It was the least he could do, given that he had worked for a living, much as these people did.

They reached the end of the line, Pierce and his family having met everyone from parlor maids to grooms from his stables, and Lady Nalyssa appeared again. He had been conscious of her presence nearby. He had always had a weakness for beautiful women.

She said quietly, "Address them as a group," and then stepped back.

Going to stand so that all could see and hear him, Pierce said, "My family and I are happy to have come to Stonecrest," his deep voice carrying. "I want you to know that I appreciate each one of you and will be meeting individually with everyone present, in order to get to know a bit about you and how you came to be at Stonecrest."

A slight murmur and shuffling occurred, letting him know this was highly unusual.

"I value hard work and loyalty. I know I am responsible for you all and will do my best to live up to your expectations, as I hope you will live up to mine. Thank you for welcoming us today. You are dismissed."

No movement occurred for a moment. Then a few of the grooms fell out of line, heading toward the stables. His coachman returned to the carriage and took up the reins, driving it away.

Lady Nalyssa came toward him. "Well done, Your Grace. I see you are a man who knows his own mind." She paused briefly. "I do hope, however, that you will be openminded enough to take in and use the lessons I will give you."

"Potter said that you remake men so that they are acceptable to the *ton*. I am my own man, Lady Nalyssa."

She smiled, melting his heart. "Then you are already more a duke than most who acquire the title, Your Grace. I believe you will be wise enough to take what I tell you to heart—and still remain your own man."

Lady Nalyssa turned to his mother and sister. "Tea is to be served in the drawing room, Your Grace. Shall we go inside? The day is quite chilly."

Pierce fell into step behind the trio of women, entering the foyer and following them up the stairs to the drawing room. His drawing room. His house.

His new life.

Chapter Five

NALYSSA BELIEVED IN that moment that she should have been an actress on the stage because she had thoroughly disguised the reaction she had to the new Duke of Stoneham.

He was breathtaking.

His clothes were of a better quality than she would have expected from one coming from the working class. Stoneham was dressed as a country gentleman, passable for now, but his wardrobe would be one of the first things she would need to work on with him. She could teach him the manners needed to play the part of a duke, but clothes did make the man—and a duke's wardrobe needed to be elegant and fashionable. It would be the first thing others saw about him, the manner in which he dressed. Every coat, every cravat, every stickpin must be immaculate.

There would be no disguising his size, though. The new duke was a couple of inches over six feet, with a commanding frame. Nalyssa suspected he had done physical labor, which had hewn the muscles that clothing barely disguised. Stoneham had the look of his mother about him, most notable the dark blond shade of hair. His eyes were blue as hers, though his were a startling ice blue in nature.

He did, however, have one feature that marked him as the son of the previous duke. That was the small cleft in his chin, which Stoneham's father had also sported. The feature was unusual and would be noted. It—more than a certificate of marriage—would tell the *ton* that this man was the duke's issue.

She led the new Selkirk clan into the drawing room, where a fire burned cheerily in the grate. Lady Penelope, who favored her mother with the same shade of hair and blue eyes, as well as the peaches and cream complexion, started to take a seat.

The lessons—for all of them—would now begin in earnest.

"Lady Penelope, wait a moment if you would," Nalyssa said. "Polite Society focuses on rank. Your mother, being a duchess, should always sit first, followed by you. Then the men will take their own seats, by rank, of course."

The young woman bit her lip. "I am sorry, my lady."

"No need to be," Nalyssa said carefully, realizing Lady Penelope was most likely the most fragile of the three. She made a quick decision, believing the duke and duchess would support it.

"I know there is much to be learned. Some of the rules can be quite silly. Even annoying. But they are rules you must adhere to. Your father wished for you to take your place among the *ton*, but you need to be comfortable in doing so. I think it will be enough to see Their Graces take their place in Polite Society this Season. We will give you a bit longer and have you make your come-out next Season."

She looked to the other two. "Would that be acceptable, Your Graces?"

The duchess nodded sagely. "I believe that to be a wise idea, my lady. Your focus should be on my son, naturally, but I realize you will have things to share with me. Penelope can sit in during those times when you are teaching me. It will give her time to grow accustomed to her new role and also allow you to concentrate on making certain His Grace manages to integrate himself into Polite Society."

Lady Penelope blew out a long breath. "Thank you, Mama. This has been so sudden. If I had to go about all those men and women in society before I was ready, I might die of fright. I would appreciate the extra time." She smiled at her brother. "Papa wanted you to be the one to wed this Season, Pierce. Lady Nalyssa can help you do so and then work on helping me become a lady."

"You are already a lady," Nalyssa said quickly. "I can see from your speech and the way in which you carry yourself that your mother has taught you well. Good manners go beyond whatever class we are born into. You only need a bit of confidence. If His Grace does wed, the new duchess can help prepare you to make your debut."

"Won't you help me, though?" Lady Penelope pleaded. "Papa wanted you to launch all three of us into society."

She saw the irritated look cross the duke's face and knew it was because his sister referred to their father in a familiar way. She couldn't blame the duke. Their father had let them down disgracefully, keeping his wife and children hidden away while he had a second family. The scandal was going to be huge, even though these two children were legitimate. Still, Stoneham was a duke. Somehow, Polite Society always seemed to forgive dukes for practically anything, especially circumstances not of their own making.

"We will focus on His Grace," she told the young woman. "He will find it incredibly easy to find a bride and the new duchess will help launch you. I can also help, of course."

She paused, not wanting to bring up her fees. She had already been paid by Mr. Potter from the deceased duke's estate and would spend these two months exclusively at Stonecrest. If she were to return next year, however, she would have to charge additional fees for her services.

"You don't do this for free, do you, my lady," the duke said.

"No, Your Grace. I do not. I am paid to teach others how to assimilate into the *ton*."

"That seems unusual," Her Grace said. "But I can see my daughter has already taken to you, Lady Nalyssa. My son will see that your fees are paid. Launching Penelope into Polite Society means sparing no expense."

"We will definitely cross that bridge when we get to it, Your Grace. And I would be happy to work with Lady Penelope." She paused. "Ah, here is the teacart."

She waited until the maid left and said, "Usually, the hostess would pour out, but I will do so today. Please watch carefully, Your Grace, as you will be doing this in the future. You, as well, Lady Penelope. It is a skill we will work on daily over the next two months."

"Why two months?" His Grace asked, his voice a low rumble.

"Because that is when the Season will begin," she explained. "Have no fears. I will attend events with you both, at least in the beginning. We will go over everything you need to do and say on the way to a social affair and discuss how it went on the carriage ride home. Once you are comfortable, you and Her Grace may arrive on your own. I will usually be in attendance myself and will watch carefully and be available in case you have need of me."

Those ice-blue eyes bored into her. "Won't your husband demand your attention, Lady Nalyssa?"

She felt color fill her cheeks. "I have no husband, Your Grace, and no intention of ever marrying."

Surprise filled his eyes, but he quickly shuttered them again. "Then begin your lessons, Lady Nalyssa."

Nalyssa took a calming breath, not wanting to be rattled by this handsome man. She looked at the teacart, knowing she was in her element.

"Notice the cups and saucers are at one end, while the teapot, milk, sugar, and lemon slices are at the other. Cook has also sent a pitcher of hot water because some individuals prefer their tea to be weak after it is steeped."

"I have never seen that before," Her Grace said. "How interesting."

"You will pour each cup of tea for your guests, Your Grace,"

Nalyssa continued.

"Mama knows how to pour a cup of tea for visitors," growled the duke. "We may not have frequented drawing rooms of the *ton*, but we are not heathens."

"Hush," commanded the duchess. "I must get every move down pat, Pierce. I will have eyes upon me from now on whenever I am with others. They will want to pick me apart. It might be behind my back, but I do not want to give them fodder for their gossip."

"You must refer to your son as Stoneham, Your Grace," Nalyssa said. "Even around family."

"I can no longer call him Pierce?" she asked, looking stricken.

Giving a little, Nalyssa said, "Only behind closed doors, Your Grace. With no servants present. That would be the exception to the rule. Even then, I do not recommend it. It will be too easy for you to slip. My suggestion is to refer to him as Stoneham from now on. At breakfast, with footmen looking on or at tea and especially in public—he must always be called Stoneham by you and Lady Penelope. If you practice it that way, it will become habit."

"Why?" Lady Penelope asked.

She shook her head. "I wish I could tell you, my lady. It is the way of Polite Society. They have many unwritten rules which you will learn and adhere to. It is my task to teach them to you so that they become a part of your lives without you having to think about it. Begin now and please refer to His Grace as Stoneham in conversation."

"Stoneham," Lady Penelope said, trying it out, her nose wrinkling. "Oh, I do not like it one bit, Lady Nalyssa."

"Liking it is not a factor, my lady. Simply do it." She paused. "Back to our lessons. You will always ask how your guest takes their tea, Your Grace."

She taught the duchess and her daughter the correct order in which to add anything to the tea, once poured, making certain milk was the last element placed into the cup, pointing out that they must never take lemon and milk together in the same teacup.

"You must stir gently and noiselessly. Move the teaspoon in a small arch back and forth in the center of the teacup. It is considered ill-mannered to touch the sides of the cup with the spoon. We will practice this together in the coming days. Now, how to hold your saucer."

"It's a bloody saucer," the duke said, frowning. "Believe it or not, my lady, we heathens of the working class drink tea and know—"

"I will not have you interrupt me, Your Grace," Nalyssa said calmly, though her heart was racing at having to correct a duke. "You are to forget everything you know—or think you know—because we are starting from the beginning. Your mother is right. Your every move will be scrutinized. I want you to move and act without thought because we have practiced the correct way of doing things so often that it becomes second nature to you. I am the expert here. Not you. Is that understood?"

"Yes, my lady," he said begrudgingly. "I apologize for my interruption."

"Your apology is accepted. But a true gentleman learns from his mistakes, Your Grace. Do not make that one again," she warned.

She lifted a saucer and said, "Place your saucer in the palm of your left hand, locating it so it rests on your four fingers. Spread them slightly apart so they nicely balance your saucer. Keep it steady by resting your thumb on the saucer's rim."

The three did as she demonstrated, and Nalyssa continued. "English teacups have handles. You will hold this handle with your index finger slipped through the handle, your thumb just above it in order to support your grip. Add your second finger below the handle for balance."

She checked each of their fingers and grip. "Good. You can see how your other fingers follow the curve. And under no circumstances do you allow your smallest finger to rise. That is an affectation which will mark you as someone trying to impress. Now, let us drink."

They sipped their tea, and she added a few more tidbits, such as telling them never to swirl their tea around the cup.

"That is for wineglasses—and another lesson."

She then pointed out the various food items on the tea tray, noting that some hostesses fixed a plate for their guests while others enjoyed having their guests choose what they wished on their own.

"It is a personal preference, Your Grace. The same is true for sandwiches. While everyone in the *ton* has their cooks cut off the crusts, the shape is also left up to you—triangles, strips, or squares. You will need to let your cook know your preference. As to sandwiches, I had Cook prepare for you today the usual fare. Beyond the sandwiches, there are biscuits, seedcake, and fairy cakes with butter icing."

"Is there a certain order in which we should eat our food, my lady?" Stoneham asked.

Nalyssa didn't know if his question was a genuine one or merely sarcastic, testing her. She politely replied, "You may eat whatever you wish, Your Grace, although once you start a sandwich, I advise finishing it before moving on to a scone or biscuit."

"Thank you," he said, his tone clipped.

Oh, he would certainly make for a good duke because he already thought himself so above her.

"Will we be subjected to the same type of lecture at dinner this evening?" he asked.

"Stoneham!" said Her Grace. "I raised you better than this."

"My apologies, Mama, but I was merely inquiring of Lady Nalyssa if our lessons would extend to dinner."

"You know they will, Your Grace," she said tersely. "You are an intelligent man. Do not waste my time or ours by asking a question you already know the answer to. Or think you know the answer to. I am being paid a good deal of money to live in the house for the next two months, money your father earmarked so that you and Her Grace would be comfortable enough to move into Polite Society seamlessly. Do not dishonor the deceased duke's memory or override his wishes. He wanted you to succeed. I was with him when he passed."

She bit back the edge in her words. "His last thoughts were of you entering society. He knew he had wronged all of you terribly by not acknowledging you. It was his last wish to make it up to you by hiring me. He asked me to bring you here, to Stonecrest, away from prying eyes so that we might have these lessons in private. I intend to do my part in honoring his wishes. You need to see that you do yours, as well, Your Grace."

"I owe him nothing," the duke said angrily. "He set us aside. Sent money to try and buy our affection or silence or God knows what. I insisted we quit taking it. We learned to stand on our own."

She heard anger in his voice—but also hurt. Nalyssa doubted the duke even knew how hurt he had been by his father. She wondered if this man had even seen his father or if the previous duke had done everything through the Potters.

"You may feel as if you owe him nothing," she said quietly. "It is for you to decide how you do or don't feel. But you owe your mother and sister the best of you, Your Grace. The impression you make upon Polite Society will be reflected upon them. Her Grace will have a trying time as it is, assuming her title among a group of people who knew another woman held it for many years, even though she was not the true duchess. You owe it to your sister, who will follow in your footsteps and make her come-out next year. Everything you do and say this Season will affect her next Season."

Nalyssa paused. "I believe you love your mother and sister a great deal. If that is the case, then you must take my lessons to heart. Become the duke your father never was. Care for and protect your loved ones in a way he never did. Are you up for that task, Your

Grace? If you aren't, I can leave immediately."

Their gazes met and no words were spoken. Silently, she saw they came to an understanding.

"I will learn your lessons, my lady," the duke solemnly said. "I would give my life for Mama or Pen."

Then he smiled, a smile that took Nalyssa's breath away.

"I suppose learning how to hold a teacup is a small price to pay in order to give those I love the life they deserve."

Chapter Six

When tea ended, Pierce thought he would slip away to his new study for a few hours, but Lady Nalyssa had other ideas.

"I think it would be best if you two ladies had a bit of a rest after your long journey from Bristol," she told Mama and Pen. "I have instructed maids to unpack for you and since neither of you have a lady's maid, we will need to see about hiring one for each of you."

Mama and Pen glanced at one another, and Mama said, "My daughter and I have always aided one another in dressing, my lady. It won't be necessary to—"

"Of course, it will be necessary," Lady Nalyssa said smoothly, acting as if she had not interrupted a duchess. "It is a requirement that you both have one. I have a special relationship with an employment agency in town and can write to its head today. Do you have any specifics you might require in your lady's maid?"

Mama looked perplexed. "I have no idea what I should ask for, Lady Nalyssa."

"Then you may leave it to me, Your Grace. Until you have hired help, I will lend the both of you Jenny, my lady's maid. She is quite good with hair and has a fine eye for fashion. We can go into Brighton, which is about fifteen miles southwest of Stonecrest, and see to a few items for your wardrobes. The bulk of it must come from a modiste in town, however. Though Lady Penelope will not be making her come-out this Season, she will still require an extensive wardrobe. You will be entertaining at your townhouse, and she will meet guests there. She will also want to get out and about and see the great city's various sites. In fact, it would be best if we went into town in a week or so and meet with a modiste. I also have a special relationship with one of the best in the business, and she will handle both of your wardrobes. Your Grace, you will need numerous ball gowns and day gowns, as well as slippers and hats. I have experience in these areas and will be able to help you choose wisely.

"In the meantime, why don't you both lie down and rest until dinner is served at seven. Country hours are earlier than town ones. That is why dinner is so early."

Mama and Pen rose, and Pierce did the same, ready to escape.

"Not you, Your Grace," Lady Nalyssa said brightly. "We still have a few matters to address."

Mama and Pen left the drawing room, and he sat once again, depressed at the upcoming lecture he was to receive.

"You, too, will need a new wardrobe, Your Grace," Lady Nalyssa informed him.

Resentment flooded him. "Why would you say so, my lady? My ensemble today is perfectly adequate."

She cocked her head and pursed her lips, studying him a moment. A flicker of desire ran through him. He wanted to kiss those plump lips.

"You do wear clothes well, Your Grace, but you are not suitably dressed as a duke should be. You look like a well-dressed shopkeeper, and that will never do. At least as far as a duke goes," she amended, picking up on his mood. "I think you should accompany us to town, and we will visit an exclusive tailor, shirtmaker, and bootmaker. You will need at least three dozen shirts and a couple of pairs of boots, as well as shoes. Numerous coats and waistcoats and pants. And I know you are not in possession of black evening clothes. Every *ton* affair held during the evening, from balls to routs to card parties, will mean fine evening wear."

"I had actually planned to travel to London myself this month," he told her. "You see, I *was* a shopkeeper in my old life. I owned a haberdashery before the dukedom was thrust upon me. The Crafty Gentleman was its name. I began by carrying accessories and expanded it to gentleman's wear. Men from Bristol and beyond frequented my haberdashery, many of them telling me that it held items as fine as any shop in London."

"Call it town," she suggested. "You will rarely, if ever, hear a member of the *ton* call it anything but town." She paused. "If you carried such fine items, why are you dressed as you are?"

"What is wrong with the manner of my dress?" he asked, his simmering anger beginning to boil over.

"Oh, I see," she said, nodding her head sagely. "You did not want to dress better than your clients who purchased clothing from you. You do dress well—but not above your former station. That was smart on your part, Your Grace, but you will need a much better and more extensive wardrobe. Clothes for the country and for town. The Season has an incredible number of events and you will be changing clothes several times a day. Do you ride?"

"No," he said flatly. "Neither do I dance."

"A pity, but I will assume you are a quick learner. I can teach you both to ride and dance while we are at Stonecrest. Many gentlemen ride mornings in Rotten Row, which is a long lane in Hyde Park, the most fashionable park in town. It is the closest park to your townhouse in Mayfair. I shall write the people I need to and tell them we will be in town in a week's time and ask that they set exclusive appointments for us. I would like to go with you, as well as Her Grace and Lady Penelope, so we will designate different days and times."

"I am not six years of age, my lady," Pierce said haughtily. "I know enough to pick out my own wardrobe myself. In fact, I could even sew a new wardrobe for myself if I wished to do so. And it would be grand, grander than anything you have ever seen."

Interested sparked in her eyes. "Ah, you have tailoring skills?"

"I do. I worked several jobs, saving money before I opened my own haberdashery. One of the two tailors I hired taught me how to measure, cut, and sew."

"You will not need your sewing skills any longer, Your Grace. Your valet will handle that for you."

"My valet?"

"Yes. Not only have you inherited a title and lands, but you also have a valet. Wattleby was your father's valet for the last ten years or so. Wattleby is quite good at what he does."

Pierce eyed her with suspicion. "Exactly what does a valet do, my lady? Sew on a missing button?"

"Why, Wattleby will take care of all your needs. He will handle your wardrobe and make any repairs necessary. He will polish your boots and shoes. Bathe you. Shave you. Dress you."

"I am not an infant," he said, more loudly than he should have and thought to temper his volume and tone. "I can do all of those tasks for myself, my lady."

"Of course you can, Your Grace," she said genially. "However, you are a duke. It is expected that these things are to be done for you. Look at it this way—you are helping a man be gainfully employed and at the same time, allowing yourself to be freed up for more important affairs. It is the same with your estates. They are managed by stewards, but you naturally have the final say-so in any matter."

"I can run my own bloody estates," Pierce declared.

"You have several of them," Lady Nalyssa pointed out. "You cannot be all across England at each one of them at the same time. That is why you do have someone to manage them in your absence. Now, most of your time will be spent here at Stonecrest, your ducal seat, when you are not in town. You will get to know Mr. Dixon, Stonecrest's steward, quite well. You seem to want to have your thumb in every pie. I am certain once you learn about estate management, you can make your wishes known to Mr. Dixon."

Lady Nalyssa had a point. He could not be all over the place at the same time. Even if he could, he didn't know the first thing about how to run a large estate. Or even a small one.

Sullenly, he said, "I do want to get to know my tenants here."

"I find that most admirable, Your Grace. Many gentlemen never bother to visit their tenants. I think not only would it help you learn more about Stonecrest, but it would help you earn their respect. Usually, though, it is the duty of the lady of the house to visit tenants, bringing them baskets of food and checking on them once babes have been born." She paused. "That means finding yourself a duchess, Your Grace."

"I know I am obligated to provide an heir," he said testily. "You are teaching me everything else. Are you to pick out my wife for me?"

"I think you would prefer doing so yourself, but I will discuss suitable candidates with you. The ones you grow interested in as the Season progresses. I have been in Polite Society for a good number of years now and know—or know of—most everyone. You will need to decide what you want in your duchess. I can then steer you in the proper direction. I need to warn you, though."

"Warn me of what, my lady?"

"You are a duke. A single, eligible gentleman in need of a wife. You will be a prized commodity this Season since it is rare that a duke is looking for his duchess on the Marriage Mart. Every mother worth her salt will try and ingratiate herself with you, thrusting their daughters in your path. I won't ask you what you are looking for in a wife now, Your Grace. That will take some time and consideration on your part. It would be helpful if you decided the age of the woman you wish to be your duchess."

Her statement puzzled him. "Is age an important consideration?"

"Well, there are advantages and disadvantages to different ages in a bride. For instance, you might want to choose one of the new girls making her come-out this year. She will be unsullied and young. Young means pliable, Your Grace. It is easier to mold a very young lady than one who is older."

"Such as yourself, Lady Nalyssa?" he asked, cocking an eyebrow.

"You would not want someone of my age," she told him, her tone conveying how displeased she was at the question.

"Why? How old are you?"

She frowned at him. "It is never polite to ask a lady's age, Your Grace. Since we have a different type of relationship, however, I will share that I am nine and twenty. Considered on the shelf."

He looked at her blankly. "*What* does that mean?"

She laughed, a deep, throaty laugh, sending a ripple of lust through him. He wanted to be the one who made her laugh more often. She softened as she laughed.

"On the shelf means that I am much too old to be considered for marriage. Now, if you are not interested in a young, green creature, you could choose a girl who has already been out for a Season or two. She will have been through events and have experience about her. She would also be young enough for you to get an heir off her, as well as your spare. That is the goal of marriage, Your Grace. Getting heirs. Now, if you were only a viscount or an earl, we would be looking for more in a marriage than an attractive, sweet woman. We would be looking to improve your social standing. That is another goal of marriage within the *ton*. You form a union with another person—and his or her family—in order to improve your position in Polite Society. Since you are a duke and at the very top rung of the ladder, we will not need to consider that. From what I understand, you are also as wealthy as Midas, and so financial considerations will not be necessary."

She paused and then added, "Many marriages are made simply on the basis of finance, Your Grace. An impoverished gentleman seeks an eligible woman with a hefty dowry to refill his family's coffers."

"You are telling me then that looks do not matter? A person's manners or way of speech are not to be considered."

"They will matter to you, Your Grace. As I said, you have a lofty title and a firm financial footing, so you will not need to wed merely for money or to improve your social standing. Unfortunately, because you do possess those two things and you are quite handsome, every eligible young lady of the Season will be after you. It could grow quite tiresome. Even exhausting."

She cocked her head again, and Pierce realized she did so when she was thinking. It pleased him that she thought him handsome, which was absurd. He had no interest in this woman. Yes, he had been attracted to her upon first meeting her, but her lessons had already grown tiresome.

"Now, you could wed a young widow. That is to be considered. It would solve everything. She would be seasoned enough and know how to handle Polite Society. She would have been introduced to . . . marital relations . . . and not have to be trained as to what her marital and household duties include. If you choose a widow in her early to mid-twenties, that might work out best for you. In fact, I have a few ladies in mind for you already."

Frustration continued to build within him. "It is good you have a few women in mind, but widows in their twenties? How often does that occur?"

Lady Nalyssa paused and then said, "You see, oftentimes in Polite Society, marriages of conveniences are only convenient to men. Especially old men seeking a young wife. Every Season or two, there are at least one or two widows who fit that bill, women who did their duty to their family and wed a much higher-ranking man in order to better their family's social standing. Occasionally, one of the old codgers will get an heir off a young wife. Many times, they are not able to . . . shall we say . . . perform their marital duties."

"It sounds as if women are *sold* into marriage," he noted, not liking the idea one bit.

"I would not put it quite so frankly, but yes, Your Grace, it could be viewed in that manner."

"Did you not have a father who wished for better social connections, Lady Nalyssa? Or a mother who wanted to push you up the societal ladder?"

She stiffened, hot color flooding her cheeks. "We are not here to discuss me, Your Grace. I am here to do my duty to the Dukes of Stoneham, both your father and you. By the beginning of this Season, I will have you entirely knowledgeable regarding all social graces. You will know what is appropriate in a conversation. How to ride and dance. You will have decided on what you want in your duchess and I will help you find her. If you are pleased with the results of my work, regarding both you and Her Grace, I hope you would also consider me to help prepare Lady Penelope for her own come-out next Season. She will, of course, sit in on the lessons I give your mother and may not even need my help by then, especially if you do wed as planned. Your duchess would be the one to help launch your sister into the *ton*. My specialty is helping the unsuitable become suitable, productive members of Polite Society."

Lady Nalyssa rose. "I have those letters to write, Your Grace. You should go to your rooms and ring for Wattleby. It is time for the two of you to get to know one another."

"Where are my rooms?" he asked, resentful at this woman's bossiness and yet still feeling the pull of attraction.

"Oh, you have not had your tour of Stonecrest. I had forgotten." She rose. "Follow me, Your Grace."

She took him to a suite of rooms, pulling the bell cord, and said, "The first is a sitting room and waiting room of sorts. Most every time, you will meet your guests in the drawing room or your study. On a rare occasion, you might have a friend come to your rooms. It would be appropriate for him to wait here."

"What if it is a female friend?" he asked slyly.

"That will not happen within the walls of Stonecrest," she chided. "We will discuss at a later date how you are to conduct an affair and if you wish to visit those houses which specialize in . . . entertaining."

Once more, Pierce noted the blush on her cheeks, making her very appealing.

"We do not need to discuss such private matters, my lady."

"We most certainly will," she corrected. "I will not have you going to the wrong type of place. And there are definitely rules for having an affair within the *ton*. But that is for a later discussion. Come along, Your Grace."

She led him to the next room, which she said was a private study.

"You have another study for business affairs on the first floor and will see it tomorrow. You also have a wonderful library if you wish to take advantage of it. This room is for you alone. To read. To think. No interruptions."

Lady Nalyssa opened the next door, and Pierce's jaw dropped.

It was the largest bedchamber he had ever seen, with the most enormous bed on the far side of the room. A bed he wished he could climb into now.

Taking Lady Nalyssa Shelbourne with him.

She continued moving, though, and he caught up to her.

"This is your bathing room. You will be shaved in that chair. Beyond this is your closet."

Pierce followed her and stepped inside it, shocked at its size. "You think I will fill this entire space with my clothing? An entire family could live within these walls."

She smiled indulgently. "You will fill it to the brim, Your Grace. Each Season, you will replenish your wardrobe, only keeping a few favorite pieces. Everything else will be new."

"What a waste," he uttered, knowing what she said was true since he had catered to some of those very people, a class he now belonged to unwillingly.

"Actually, it helps many others. Every time you purchase a new shirt or cravat or a new pair of boots, someone gets paid." She paused. "That was going to be another lesson, but I will give it now. Many men in the nobility, especially the ones of highest rank, are the most pitiful when it comes to paying their bills. I urge you to have your secretary pay on time, at the end of each month."

He nodded. "As a former shop owner, I understand this principle. I was pigheaded enough not to let a single piece out of my shop if a client had not paid his previous month's bill. It caused resentment on the part of some. I even lost a few customers. But the majority understood that the haberdashery was how I made my living and that I had employees to pay, as well as myself. I will pay every bill on time, my lady. That is a guarantee."

A throat cleared behind them. "You rang, Your Grace?"

Pierce supposed this was his valet. "Wattleby, I assume?"

"Yes, Your Grace. I was valet to His Grace before you and hope you will consider keeping me on."

"His Grace will give you two weeks in which to prove yourself to him," Lady Nalyssa said. "If the two of you do not suit one another, a letter of reference will be given to you, reflecting the service you did for the previous Duke of Stoneham." She looked to Pierce. "I will leave you and Wattleby to become acquainted, Your Grace."

Turning back to the servant, she said, "He will need a bath and a shave. His clothes unpacked. You are to explain to His Grace what you do since the duke has never had a valet before."

The servant's eyes widened in shock, causing Pierce to cover his mouth with his hand to keep from laughing. If his own valet thought him a heathen, what would the members of the *ton* make of him?

For a moment, he was pleased that he did have Lady Nalyssa to tutor him in all the social graces and beyond, even if she was a bit overbearing at times.

"I will see you at dinner, my lady," he said formally.

Her eyes twinkled with mischief as she said, "Enjoy your time getting to know one another. And Your Grace? This will be the last time I visit your rooms."

Lady Nalyssa left, hips sashaying.

If Pierce had anything to do with it, she would be back.

Chapter Seven

NALYSSA AWOKE, ALREADY tired before setting a foot out of bed. Usually, she was a heavy sleeper, dropping off shortly after her head touched her pillow each night. Last night had been an exception.

It was all because of the Duke of Stoneham.

She had her hands full with him. He was certainly going to be the challenge which the deceased duke promised her. Arrogant. Headstrong. Irritable. Questioning everything she said. It would take as much patience as she could gather to turn him into a civilized gentleman acceptable to Polite Society.

He had all the makings. His arrogant attitude alone would mark him to be the son of a duke. He also cut a fine figure in his clothes and had been educated well enough. She had learned that the duchess herself had taught both children and then sent each to a day school when they were older. Both the duke and his sister had then gone to work for a living, the duke trying several occupations, while Lady Penelope had assisted her mother.

It had been interesting to learn that Her Grace had been the owner of Manda's Millinery Shop and that she and her daughter created all the hats sold from the shop prior to them coming to Stonecrest. Nalyssa was even familiar with a few of their designs, having been drawn to them, asking the hats' wearers where they had purchased them. She felt the duchess would be easy to work with in building a wardrobe for herself and her daughter since she had such impeccable taste. Already, the duchess expressed excitement at getting to journey to town and see the shops, especially the millineries.

As for the duke, once she had him dressed appropriately for his rank and station, no one could question he was a duke merely by his appearance. It was disappointing, though, that he did not know how to ride or dance. After dinner last night, they had gone to the drawing room and talked for an hour, where Nalyssa learned more about the trio. She had asked Lady Penelope to entertain them on the pianoforte, wanting to assess the girl's musical skills, but she had never had a music lesson in her life. That was something that Nalyssa could easily remedy. Every young woman needed to be accomplished in music, whether by playing an instrument or singing. They should also have experience with tasks such as painting or embroidery.

Lady Penelope had laughed when Nalyssa mentioned these two things, saying that her brother was the one who was the best at sewing in their family, not her. Nalyssa intended to teach the young woman what she could of embroidery and also start her on music lessons. She could certainly tutor Lady Penelope in the basics since Nalyssa herself was an accomplished pianist. She would teach the newly-minted lady how to read music, what the keys were, and basic chords. They could progress to simple songs until they returned to town shortly before the Season began. Lady Penelope would have time on her hands while her mother and brother attended social affairs, time in which she could practice her pianoforte.

She had enough to work with, finding all three of her charges interesting and delightful conversationalists, if a bit unorthodox by the topics they selected. She had discussed with them subjects which would be most appealing to other members of Polite Society in everyday conversation. The duke had rolled his eyes like a naughty boy at her recommendations, but she knew he would come around and take her suggestions.

What she didn't know was how long he could keep his hands off her.

She had seen a look in his eyes several times the previous day, a look that told her he found her desirable. He seemed to be a man no one said no to, least of all a woman. Nalyssa figured she would be the first.

The only problem was that she had felt certain urges she had never felt before merely looking at the duke. His powerful physique. Those large hands with their long fingers. She could imagine them cupping her face as he brought his lips to hers.

She thought his kiss would be divine.

Nalyssa had been kissed many years ago, on more than one occasion. She'd had her pick of any gentleman among the *ton* during the first two years she had entered society. Regret coursed through her at not being mature enough to wish to settle down and make a marriage. If she had, she would be wed now, with children and a husband to care for. Instead, she had let her popularity go to her head, thinking she had plenty of time to enjoy herself. She had foolishly believed she would find love, which was why she had not accepted any of the numerous proposals she had received. Her father's subsequent suicide had ruined Nalyssa's place in Polite Society. She was barely respectable enough to be invited to *ton* events, and she certainly wasn't going to jeopardize herself and find herself ruined all because of an infatuation with the Duke of Stoneham.

Even if he did have designs on her.

She did wonder, though, what a kiss with him would be like. She had kissed half a dozen men during those years long ago. Two of the kisses were slobbery and distasteful. Another two had been brief but interesting. The final two men she had kissed showed her there was more than only touching lips together, and she had seen the potential that lay in kissing.

Nalyssa pushed aside those thoughts. She was in no position to kiss a client. She needed the funds she had been paid and was determined to make this duke, his mother, and his sister into the elites their titles told of.

Rising, Nalyssa rang for Jenny. The maid arrived soon after.

"Good morning, my lady," Jenny said. "I see you are up early this morning."

"I have much to do today and in the weeks to come in order to mold His Grace into being acceptable to Polite Society," she declared. "Once you finish helping me dress, I would like you to go to Her Grace's rooms and then Lady Penelope's and help prepare them for the day."

"They haven't had a lady's maid, have they?" the maid guessed.

"No, they have not. This is going to be a different experience for them. You will have to exercise patience with the pair. You will teach them as I will, showing them what services you will provide for them and helping them as you always have me. I hope it will not be too much work for you, taking care of the three of us while we are at Stonecrest."

Jenny laughed merrily. "I would much rather take care of three ladies in this manner than my tasks back home," she told her mistress. "It is better than scrubbing floors, beating rugs, and washing bed linens. Yes, I will be busy, but the work will not be nearly as physically taxing."

Guilt flooded Nalyssa. "I have asked a lot of you, Jenny, and I am sorry of that. You do an excellent job when you serve as my lady's maid. Her Grace and Lady Penelope will need their own lady's maids. They should not share one, so two will be hired." She paused. "Would you like to be considered for one of those positions?"

Jenny grew thoughtful. "It would mean leaving you, my lady. You know I am loyal to you."

"You always have been. I could not do what I do without you. But you have earned the right to be in a better position, however. Why don't you consider the idea of becoming a lady's maid for either Her Grace or Lady Penelope? If you are amenable, I will broach the topic with the pair."

"What would you do, my lady?"

"I would survive—as I always have."

Once she was dressed, Nalyssa dismissed Jenny and told her to go to the duchess first. She made her way downstairs to the large breakfast room and saw Pugh standing there.

The butler said, "Cook has prepared a buffet as you requested, my lady."

"Thank you, Pugh. We will try this for a few days and then we will also have Cook prepare individual breakfasts for the others once we can ascertain their likes and dislikes."

"You have a world of patience, my lady," the butler said in confidence.

Nalyssa knew he referred to dinner the previous evening. Her charges had all been surprised at the number of courses which came out from the kitchens. She had explained the order, as well as discussing which forks and spoons to use as they ate. Lady Penelope had mentioned that their cook, a woman named Annie, set everything on the table at once, and they served themselves from it. Nalyssa actually did the same when she was by herself and not training any outsider ready to take his place within the *ton*, eating simple meals.

She had told the three they would have a lesson after breakfast so that they might become familiar with all the cutlery at various meals.

A footman seated Nalyssa, while another one brought her tea. She added her own milk and sugar and stirred, sipping on the hot brew as the duke entered.

"Good morning, Your Grace," she said, rising to curtsy to him before seating herself again. "It is good to see you this morning."

"I suppose you will be in my company all day today, Lady Nalyssa?" he asked, faint disdain in his voice.

"For a good portion of it, Your Grace. The four of us will tour the house with Mrs. Pugh and the grounds nearby after our breakfast lessons. After that, it will be time for your first riding lesson."

He frowned at the mention of that. "I had thought to meet with my steward today and possibly go out and introduce myself to some of my tenants."

"Horseback is the easiest way to reach almost anywhere in the country. That is why it is important for us to begin your riding lessons as soon as possible. You move with an innate grace. I believe you will take to the saddle with ease."

"A compliment from Lady Nalyssa? Will wonders never cease."

The duke scowled when a cup of tea was set before him. "I prefer coffee in the morning," he told the footman.

"Yes, Your Grace," the footman said, taking the cup and saucer away.

Pugh stepped up. "I am sorry that I did not ask Your Grace his preference. It will take some minutes to brew the coffee. Might you like to have the tea until then?"

"I suppose so."

Pugh motioned for the footman to return with the cup and saucer, and he placed it before the duke. The duchess and Lady Penelope arrived then and were seated, doctoring their tea as they liked. She noticed they took care in stirring, feeling pleased her lessons were already taking with them.

Nalyssa said, "Different households have their own customs. We will start the next few days with a buffet at breakfast. You may go through the buffet yourselves and select whatever pleases you. We can discuss with Cook your preferences, such as how you like your rasher of bacon cooked and the way you enjoy eating your eggs. A buffet is easiest when you have guests, as many can be fed in a short amount of time. For now, we will do a buffet at the morning meal. If your preference instead would be to order something each morning, we can decide if you wish to place that order the night before or when you arrive at the breakfast table each day."

Pen chuckled. "This will be a treat. We merely ate what Annie put in front of us each day."

Nalyssa rose. "Shall we?"

They moved toward the buffet and Stoneham gestured for his mother to go first.

"Very good, Your Grace," Nalyssa praised. "Your mother is the highest-ranking lady present and should be served first. You may go next if you wish."

"Not before you ladies have served yourselves," he said.

"Ah," she said, giving him a smile. "It seems I have a diamond in the rough and you do possess good manners."

"Mama may not have been a duchess all these years, but she drummed into me how to behave decently. Especially where women are concerned."

His words said one thing—but his gaze said something quite different as his eyes swept up and down her.

"Go ahead, Lady Penelope," Nalyssa urged before turning back to Stoneham. "Good manners involve not ogling your guests," she said lightly. "Although I may be your tutor, I am also a guest in your home. You will treat me respectfully in front of both your family and the servants. Is that understood?"

"Ouch," he said, a playful smile on his sensual lips. "I apologize, my lady. However, you do have an uncommon beauty. I was merely wishing to acknowledge it."

She arched her brows. "Then pay me an appropriate compliment, Stoneham. You may compliment my gown. My hat if I were wearing one. And keep your eyes on my face and not my bosom," she ordered sternly.

He chuckled. "I have been chastised enough, Lady Nalyssa, and am ravenous. Go ahead and choose what you wish because I will come behind you and most likely put the rest of everything on my plate."

"You will do no such thing, Your Grace," she told him. "You are not to heap your plate like some famished coal miner who has been laboring for sixteen hours. Put a decent amount on your plate. If you wish for seconds, you may have them."

"Aye-aye, Captain Shelbourne," he said cheerfully.

After that, breakfast went well. Once the dishes had been cleared from the table, Pugh had the footmen lay three different place settings on the table.

She went to the first one and said, "This should look familiar since it is a place setting you just experienced. One for breakfast."

Nalyssa pointed out the various items and how they were to be used.

"The center one is for times when you choose to serve luncheon. It is something which is coming into fashion and you may be invited to a luncheon during the Season."

Once more, she went through the names of all items in the place setting and how they were to be used.

Finally, she turned her attention to the dinner place setting. "As you can see, there are many more forks and spoons present here."

She walked through the use and order of each one and reiterated how footmen served and the way to take items from the plate a footman offered.

"This is so much to learn," Lady Penelope said.

"It will become second nature to you soon, my lady," Nalyssa promised. "Shall we take our tour of the house and grounds now?"

"I must say that I am eager to see the house," Her Grace admitted. "My suite of rooms alone is staggering in size. It is the size of the rooms we all lived in before we came here."

"I hope you have been pleased with them, Your Grace," she said. "There is a separate series of rooms set aside for you once your son weds. You will need to vacate the duchess' suite at that point, but I can promise you, there is another suite, quite beautiful, that is waiting for you. We will stop by it today so you can see it for yourself."

"I don't know," the duchess said. She looked to her son. "Will you even want me around once you marry, Pierce?"

"Stoneham, Your Grace," Nalyssa reminded the woman, tilting her head toward Pugh, who stood at attention observing them.

"Stoneham. Yes, that is correct," Her Grace amended.

The duke said, "Mama, this house is so large, I will probably get lost in it for the first year. Of course, I want you here. Pen, too. I want as much time with you as possible."

"But what if your wife does not wish us to be here?" the duchess insisted.

"I am the Duke of Stoneham. If it pleases me to have my mother and sister in residence, then that is what will be."

"Stoneham," his mother said gently, "we may be your family for now. We always will be. You will now build a new one. You must realize a wife will have her own opinions."

"My wife will have *my* opinions," he declared boldly. "I would not wed a woman who did not want you and Pen around."

"Very well, then," Her Grace said quietly, turning back to Nalyssa. "Shall we tour Stonecrest now, my lady?"

The duchess left the room, closely followed by her daughter.

The duke glared at Nalyssa.

"What did I do?" she asked. "Your anger is obvious."

He shook his head. "You did nothing, my lady. You are just the recipient of my anger. I want no rift between my family and the wife I choose." He paused. "I think you were correct in saying that I should wed someone who is making her come-out. I need a bride I can tell what to do and not one who believes she can order me about. The younger, the better. I would have no patience for anything else."

Stoneham strode from the room.

Chapter Eight

Mrs. Pugh was waiting for them in the foyer, and Pierce heard Lady Nalyssa ask a passing maid to retrieve the ladies' shawls and have them waiting once the house tour ended, and they went outside.

As Mrs. Pugh took over, she led them to the top floor, indicating a door to the attics.

"I don't really know what is up there, frankly, Your Graces," the housekeeper told them. "I have been at Stonecrest since I was a little girl and my mother was housekeeper before me. I can't recall in all that time if anyone has ever been in the attics."

"Perhaps it is something we can explore at a later time, Mrs. Pugh," Pierce said. "Let us start our tour."

The servant led them first into the nursery, and he couldn't help but think of his father's other children and how they had been brought up here. He recalled Potter saying one of the girls had died when quite young. He couldn't imagine the hurt that might have caused his father. For the first time, Pierce was beginning to think of the deceased duke as his father. The anger which he had held for the man over the years still simmered just below the surface, but he was beginning to understand what an impossible position love had placed the duke in. Already from the many rules Lady Nalyssa had spouted, Pierce could see that Polite Society was a strict, unforgiving body of members. It seemed as if his paternal grandfather had been an impossible man. It saddened him that his father hadn't had the courage to stand up to his own father and bring the woman he loved—his wife—into this very household.

Pierce had never known weakness because his mother had always been strong and raised him to stand on his own two feet. How ironic that she had been the strong one in their marriage and had finally told her husband she was walking away from him so that he could live the life he was meant to live, the one the Duke of Stoneham now wanted his older son to have.

Gazing about the room, Pierce realized that his own children would be raised within its walls.

Mama must have been thinking the same thing for she said, "Just think of the happy hours you will spend here, Stoneham. Your children will be raised for the most part at Stonecrest, although you will most likely wish them to visit your other estates at some point in time."

Lady Nalyssa said, "It is quite unusual for a duke to visit a nursery, Your Grace. I know mothers of the *ton* do so on rare occasions, but usually the nursery is the domain of the nanny."

Mama looked baffled. "People of the *ton* do not come up to see and play with their children?"

Lady Nalyssa flushed, looking uncomfortable. "Perhaps I am speaking from my own experience, Your Grace," she said apologetically. "I lost my mother when I was but two years old and I know my father never once visited the nursery. From what I have gathered speaking to friends, it is not common for parents to haunt the nursery, especially for a duke and duchess. Babes and children are brought downstairs to them."

"Well, I think that is ridiculous," Pen voiced. "When I have my own babe, I will certainly be in the nursery, rocking him or her. And looking upon them when they sleep. I believe Polite Society is missing out by not going to visit their own children in the very place they spend most of their hours."

Pierce spoke up. "I agree with you, Pen. I remember being around you when you were born. I know our circumstances were different, but I do remember Mama letting me hold and rock you. I would gaze down at you, thinking how perfect you were. How you were all ours and how fiercely I loved you."

Pen smiled. "You always have been protective of me, Pierce." Then she let out a squeak, and her hands flew to her mouth, knowing she had made a mistake. Her hands fell from her face and she said, "Stoneham, I mean."

Pen looked to Lady Nalyssa, who said, "It is fine, my lady. I know it will take some getting used to since you have addressed your brother by his Christian name your entire life."

Mrs. Pugh led them across the hall to a schoolroom, which had a long wooden table and benches on both sides of it. Cabinets held a few slates and some books. Pierce looked at the table and walked the length of it, seeing at the far end of it that initials had been carved into it, thinking of some long-ago Selkirk who had sat there and done so.

Lady Nalyssa moved to him and saw the initials. She touched her fingers to them. "Ah, it seems as if a naughty boy sat here." She smiled. "I can see him now, watching his governess or tutor, surreptitiously using a penknife to make his first mark in the world."

Her gaze met his. "You would have been that kind of boy, I surmise."

"You think I would be one to destroy furniture?" he asked haughtily and then chuckled.

They toured the rest of the floor, which had rooms designated for a governess and children. The housekeeper turned them back toward the staircase and his mother asked, "What is down that wing?"

"That is the servants' wing, Your Grace," Mrs. Pugh said.

"Might we peek inside a room or two?" Mama asked. "I don't wish to invade anyone's privacy, but I would like to see how our servants are living. That is, Stoneham's servants," she corrected.

"No, Mama. They are your servants, as well. Until I marry, you are mistress of this house. You will run it and give your orders to Mrs. Pugh and Pugh."

His mother's eyes widened. "I don't know if I'm up to such a task, Stoneham."

Lady Nalyssa gently touched his mother's arm. "You ran your own business, Your Grace, along with raising two fine children. That takes a woman of both vision and backbone. Running His Grace's household will be simple compared to all you have previously done. I will be meeting with you separately to talk about your concerns and how a household this large should be run. For instance, you will meet with Cook weekly in order to set the menus. I have already done so with Mrs. Pugh before your arrival so that you would not have to take up that task immediately. But we will do so together in the next few days."

Mama smiled gratefully at their tutor. "Thank you, Lady Nalyssa. Your guidance in these matters is most appreciated."

The housekeeper showed them a couple of the servants' rooms. Pierce noted there were two cots to a room, with a washstand and not much else. He made a note to himself to talk with the Pughs and his mother to see if they might be able to provide more and brighten the rooms for the people who waited upon them day and night.

They went down a flight and looked at various bedchambers. Mrs. Pugh must have seen him growing restless and told them that most of them looked the same and that she could spend more time with Her Grace and Lady Penelope at a later date.

"These bedchambers have not been touched in many years," Mrs. Pugh explained. "They are cleaned and aired periodically, but Her Grace might wish to refurbish them."

"No," Mama said. "That will be a job for my son's wife. I would not want to put my touch on things, only to have my new daughter-in-law not like or appreciate what I had done. Continue on, Mrs. Pugh."

They visited all of the rooms the family would use when entertaining guests and beyond. Pen was taken with the library, declaring that she would set a goal to read every book within it, teasing Pierce that she might never wed and simply stay at Stonecrest the rest of her natural days, reading. His sister had always enjoyed reading. Pierce had not picked up a book to read for pleasure once he left school. He had been too busy trying to earn money and establish himself. Now, of course, he would live a life of leisure and have time for books.

He hoped he would not grow bored in this new life.

They went to a ballroom, the room so large and grand. He had never seen anything quite like it and said so.

"Why would I even have a ballroom in the country?"

Lady Nalyssa supposed the answer. "Members of the *ton* do entertain outside of the Season, Your Grace. You can see how vast your estate is. You would have plenty of room to invite others and hold a ball here. Some members of the nobility even hold country balls."

"What are those?" asked Pen.

"They are for everyone who lives near your country estate. His Grace would invite your neighbors. Members of the neighboring village. Even his tenants and servants would come. A country ball is when all these people mingle together."

"You mean I might dance with a scullery maid?" Pierce asked. "That is, if I knew how to dance."

"Exactly," Lady Nalyssa said with a smile, a genuine one which caused his heart to skip a beat. "Some estates hold a celebration once the autumn harvest is brought in. You might consider making that a new tradition if it is not one that already exists at Stonecrest."

"Did your father hold to such traditions?" he asked, curious to know more about her.

Her lips thinned. "No. Starling was not one to mingle with his tenants." She turned to Mrs. Pugh. "Let us see the rest of the house if we could."

"Of course, my lady," the housekeeper replied and took them to parlors and sitting rooms, the study, the billiards room, and even to a conservatory. Mama and Pen raved over the existence of something of this nature and both seemed eager to return to it soon.

By the time they had seen the entirety of the inside of his new residence, two hours had passed. Lady Nalyssa dismissed Mrs. Pugh, telling the housekeeper that she would guide their party outside the house. Fortunately, the day was milder than usual, with bright sunshine greeting them.

They spent another hour going about the buildings outside. Lady Nalyssa pointed out the gardens, which looked vast.

"I have not walked them myself, but we must take time to do so before you return to town for the Season. You may have instructions for your gardener."

He snorted. "Or you might have those instructions, my lady. I know nothing about shrubbery and flowers."

"I would be happy to walk the gardens with you and give you advice, Your Grace."

As they passed by the stables, Lady Nalyssa said, "We will visit inside the stables this afternoon at our first riding lesson so let's save that for another time." She looked to Pen. "His Grace has told me that he does not ride. I assume you do not either. Is that correct?"

"It is—and I have no intention of getting upon the back of a horse," Pen declared. "They are far too large and I would fall off immediately."

Pierce said, "Pen was bitten by a rather large dog when she was but three years of age. It has left her with a fear of all dogs and other animals, such as horses."

"Horses can be very gentle beasts, Lady Penelope," Lady Nalyssa said. "I am to teach your brother how to ride. If you change your mind, I would be happy to extend those lessons to you, as well."

Pen blew out a frustrated breath. "Mrs. Pugh is not here. Could you please stop calling me my lady and Lady Penelope? It has grown quite wearing. I don't feel like a true lady at all. I hate all this formali ty."

"I tend to agree," Mama added. "We are alone now. Might you address us as Amanda and Penelope?"

Lady Nalyssa grew thoughtful. "It is a great honor to be asked to do so in private. This is usually reserved for your closest of friends. I am but your tutor, preparing you to take your place within the *ton*."

Mama smiled. "Then I will pull rank on you and demand that you call my daughter and me by our Christian names. We shall call you Nalyssa. It is a lovely name." Mama's eyes flicked to Pierce. "I know it would be inappropriate for you to call my son anything but Stoneham. Among us ladies, however, I insist upon informality when we are alone."

"Thank you for bestowing such an honor upon me, Amanda. It has been a long time since I have had a friend."

"You don't have friends?" Pen asked, puzzled.

Pierce watched the rueful smile form on Lady Nalyssa's lips as she said, "My status in Polite Society is a precarious one. Due to the nature of my father's death, I was subjected to quite a bit of gossip. I doubted the scandal would die down and I thought to retreat to the country, assuming I would spend the rest of my life ruminating there. Instead, I decided to cross the Rubicon on my own and took the reins myself, steering my future destination and that of my distant cousin, who had inherited the title. He came from the north and knew nothing about Polite Society."

"So, he was your first client," Pierce noted.

"Yes, Lord Starling was exactly that. Fortunately, he was thrilled with the opportunities his new life provided and eager to assume his place among the *ton*. He took to my lessons quickly and became such a success story that it helped my reputation to grow. Nowadays, when someone needs grooming to enter Polite Society, I am the one called upon to put that bit of town polish on them. I am the rare person who belongs to Polite Society and yet I earn my own living."

Lady Nalyssa sighed. "I am fortunate to be invited to *ton* affairs, but I remain on the periphery of Polite Society. The friends I had, both before and after my come-out, abandoned me due to the gossip which surrounded me. They had all made their matches and were beginning to start families of their own. This was something I would never do, and so we had nothing in common anymore."

"That's shameful," Pen said. "I don't understand why you would be blamed for whatever it is your father did. What was so terrible about it?"

Lady Nalyssa looked stricken, and Pierce quickly said, "Some things should remain private, Pen."

His sister apologized at once. "Forgive me, Nalyssa. I did not mean to pry into such personal matters." She hesitated. "I hope you still wish to be my friend."

Lady Nalyssa bit her lip, the first time Pierce had seen a chink in her armor.

"I will be frank, Penelope, and tell you that while I appreciate your friendship now, as well as Amanda's, we must keep our distance from one another once we return to town. It would not bode well for you to be known as my friend. I would never be considered your equal. Yes, I can take you about the various shops and help you create your wardrobe, but once that has been accomplished, we should not see each other socially. Your mother will already have to withstand quite a bit of gossip as she enters society, and you will be making your own come-out next year. I would never jeopardize either of your chances."

"We will not abandon you once we return to town, Nalyssa," Mama said sternly. "You are not simply teaching us ways we must learn. You have been a breath of fresh air as we explore about a world so unfamiliar to us. Yes, our shops have catered to elite members of the *ton* at times, but we have never been a part of this society. Penelope and I will be proud to call you our friend."

Pierce saw the doubt in Lady Nalyssa's eyes, and he wondered at how lonely she had been after her friends dropped her because of the fear their own reputations might be tainted by their association with her. He did not want to think he was a member of the very society which had mistreated this lovely woman, all for something her father did many years ago. He supposed that was why she had mentioned that she would never wed. The stain of scandal still must color her after all these years. It seemed so unfair. She was beautiful. Thoughtful. Generous. Why would the *ton* shun her?

A thought came to him, one which he tried to quickly shove away, but the seed had been planted and quickly flourished.

What if he didn't need to take the time searching for a woman to be by his side, wasting his time attending events he had no interest in and meeting people he did not care to befriend? What if the answer to his biggest dilemma stood right before him?

Turning his attention to her, Pierce thought Lady Nalyssa Shelbourne would make for a wonderful duchess.

His duchess . . .

Polite Society be damned.

Chapter Nine

Nalyssa decided to suggest one more stop. "Would you like to see the dower house? It is about a half-mile away. We could always save it until another day if you are tired."

"What is a dower house?" Pierce asked, curious that his ducal estate might have a second house on it.

"It is a small house reserved for the widow of the title holder," she explained. "Your mother is the Duchess of Stoneham until you wed. At that point, she becomes the Dowager Duchess of Stoneham. Oftentimes, the new wife wishes to run her household as she sees fit without her mother-in-law's presence. A dower house allows the dowager duchess to move to it, while still being a comfortable distance from the family home."

"Where is this dower house?" Mama asked. "I would be most interested to see it now."

"Me, too," Pen declared. "Mama and I love to walk and always did so when we had a bit of leisure time." She grinned at him. "Stoneham, on the other hand, only walks when he has a destination in mind. He can be quite single-minded," she teased.

Yes, he could be single-minded. Especially when he wanted his way about something. Stubborn to the point of obstinacy.

And his heart and mind told him that pursuing Lady Nalyssa and making her his duchess would be a grand idea. She already got along famously with Mama and Pen. She was cultured and intelligent. Quite lovely to look at. True, she was on the outs with Polite Society—but marrying a duke could fix that significant problem. He had a feeling that once she became a duchess, the *ton* would suddenly embrace her as one of their own again, and she might become a leader.

Yes, his mind was made up—even though he knew she was not the pliant young woman he had thought to make a match with. Nalyssa Shelbourne had opinions. Strong opinions. But Pierce believed he would rather take her as a wife and enjoy the challenge of taming her than any other woman. She would be hard to convince, though. She saw herself in a certain way and persuading her to become his wife would be a monumental task.

He grinned to himself. He had never backed down from a challenge in his life. Besides, how hard could it be to sway one woman to become a duchess?

"It may be cool, but there is no wind to chill us," he said. "I would like to see this dower house. Not that Mama will ever live in it, but I want to become familiar with everything at Stonecrest."

"It is this way," Lady Nalyssa said.

Pen looped her arm through Lady Nalyssa's, and they started off. Pierce offered his mother his arm, and they followed.

"You seem pensive," Mama said as the young ladies moved at a quicker pace and were soon out of earshot.

"I have reached a decision, one that I wish to share with you in confidence."

"It concerns Nalyssa, doesn't it? You wish for her to become your duchess."

Pierce shook his head. "Am I that obvious?"

"No," she said, smiling indulgently at him. "I just know you well. I couldn't agree more. Nalyssa is bright and charming. She would be a tremendous asset to you."

"But?" he asked. "I hear something in your voice."

"She has been hurt, Pierce. Terribly hurt. I think it has shaken her confidence, the way the *ton* has treated her. She won't see herself as worthy of you."

"Then I will have to make certain she does."

"Do you love her?" Mama asked.

He snorted. "Not in any form or fashion. I barely know her. Even when I do know more of her, I have no intention of falling in love, Mama. It caused you a world of grief. I don't need to borrow that kind of trouble. It will be enough to like and respect my wife. Love simply does not factor into my plans for the future."

Mama brought them to a halt. "What if Nalyssa desires love?"

"She will be grateful to have the opportunity to be a duchess. She doesn't want love."

Her lips pursed. "I wouldn't be so sure about that."

They begin walking again, increasing their pace so that they caught up to their companions by the time they reached the dower house.

"It's beautiful," Pen exclaimed. "May we go inside it?"

"We did not come all this way to merely view the outside," Lady Nalyssa teased. "It is open. We can go in."

"Why isn't it locked?" Mama asked as they crossed the threshold.

"Because it is on His Grace's property," Lady Nalyssa explained. "No one would dare enter it, much less take anything from it."

The furniture was covered in sheets and Pen lifted a few, peeking under to see what things looked like. They wandered through the ground floor, and Mama said she wanted to see the bedchambers upstairs. Pen went with her.

Leaving Pierce alone with Lady Nalyssa.

"If you have any questions, Your Grace, please feel free to ask them," she said. "I will do my best to answer them."

"You have done a fine job showing us about," he said, his voice lower than usual.

She had gone to gaze out the window and turned, a questioning look on her face. He closed the gap between them, standing close enough to smell the soap on her skin.

"I would have thought a woman of the *ton* would wear perfume. Or her bath water would be scented with oils."

"Most do," she said, her gaze lifting, meeting his. "I am a practical woman, however. Perfume can be costly. It is not a necessity. I run a business, Your Grace. I can forgo little luxuries that others believe are necessities."

She turned slightly, and he caught her elbow, turning her back to him. He saw the blush rising on her cheeks. His fingers tightened slightly.

"You may release my arm, Your Grace," she said in a deliberate fashion. "Just because I am not one who chooses to waste her money on perfume, it does not mean I am begging for unwanted attention."

Pierce continued to hold her elbow and brought his free hand to cup her cheek. "I don't think you would beg for anything. Not even a scrap of bread if you were starving."

She smiled ruefully. "You are correct about that. I learned long ago that I can only depend upon myself." She paused. "Let me say this. I know you are a duke. You already exhibit the arrogance of one. But you need to remove your hands from my person. Even dukes cannot always have what they want."

Instead, Pierce brought his other hand up to frame her face. "And you believe I want you?"

"You have made it obvious enough, Your Grace. You aren't a man to hide your feelings. I have seen a certain look in your eyes. I may have been paid to tutor you in the ways of the *ton*—but I am not for sale. Nor do I seek to have any kind of personal . . . relationship with you."

She took a few steps back, bumping into the window seat behind her He closed the gap and took her face in his hands again.

"Have you ever been kissed, Nalyssa?" he asked softly.

"Several times," she said sharply.

"Did you like it?"

"A few times," she admitted. "Yet I have no intention of allowing you to kiss me, Your Grace. You are my client. And I am not your plaything."

Pierce smiled. "The best laid schemes o' Mice an' Men gang aft agley."

Surprise filled her face. "You are quoting Burns to me?"

"Does it surprise you that I know any poetry at all?"

"I suppose not. Your mother did a fine job educating you. Now, I will say it again, Your Grace. Please take—"

He did not allow her to finish her sentence. Instead, he lowered his mouth to hers.

Paradise . . .

Her lips were even softer than he had imagined, just as her face was as smooth as porcelain, feeling fragile beneath his callused fingertips. His thumbs stroked her cheeks as he held her in place, softly brushing his lips against hers. He had feared she would push him away and was grateful when she didn't. She didn't kiss him back—but she didn't stop him, either.

Pierce continued with the soft kisses for a time and then pressed his mouth harder against hers. Need shot through him. She was right. He had been eyeing her, his interest obvious, and she was mature enough to know what it meant. He wouldn't push her too far, however. His plan was simple.

He had to make Nalyssa Shelbourne want him as much as he wanted her.

He felt her clutch at his lapels and couldn't help but smile. Knowing his mother and sister might reappear any moment now, he needed to end the kiss.

For the first time in his life, though, he didn't want to do so.

Pierce stroked her cheeks a final time, wishing his tongue might stroke hers, but wisdom prevailed. He broke the kiss, his mouth hovering above hers for a moment, then he lifted his head, seeing the dazed look in her sapphire eyes. His hands dropped to his sides, and he turned away as he heard movement on the staircase.

A moment later, Pen appeared. "This house is marvelous. I would be happy living here."

"Well, you won't," he told her. "I am selfish and want you and Mama with me."

But he did have an idea how the dower house could be put to use. Servants were everywhere, and he wanted no gossip about Nalyssa. Pierce thought the dower house would make the perfect spot for a tryst. He would make love to her leisurely, without fear of interruptions. When she saw how he could make her feel, not to mention the title he would bestow upon her, he had no doubt that she would accept his offer of marriage.

"I must agree with Penelope," Mama said, joining them again. "This house is quite lovely." She paused. "I would be most happy living here after you wed, Stoneham."

He went and embraced her tightly, whispering in her ear, "If you think that will convince Nalyssa to marry me, you are wrong." Leaning back, he took her hands and kissed them. "You will never live here as long as I am the Duke of Stoneham, Mama."

She eyed him, her brows raised a notch. "It might not be for you to say, Stoneham. I would think your wife would have a say in the matter."

Knowing he had a twinkle in his eyes, he said, "My future wife will adore you." He turned and smiled at his sister. "And Pen, of course."

"Well, I hope we will like her," his sister said jokingly. She looked to Nalyssa. "Please tell me you will find an accommodating bride for my brother."

By now, Nalyssa's face had returned to normal, though a bit of color remained in her cheeks.

"I am no matchmaker, Penelope, and should not be mistaken for one. I will do my best, however, to recommend certain ladies who would be suitable to become a duchess."

Pen giggled. "It might take more than a matchmaker to find my brother a bride. It might take a miracle."

Nalyssa nodded. "I have worked a few of those in my time. I helped rid a young man from the gutter of a Cockney accent. We practiced speaking for weeks, with him repeating after me until he could talk easily in cultured tones."

"I might think poetry would be good for those kinds of lessons," Pierce said, seeing if he might get a rise out of her. "Perhaps Burns?"

"No," she said, shaking her head. "Too much of a Scottish brogue in Mr. Burns' work. When working on diction, I try to rid a client of his dialect, as I did Lord Starling. His thick, northern accent made him hard to understand when he first arrived in town."

"But you broke him of it?" Pierce asked.

"I think broke is a harsh word, Your Grace. I suppose it is fitting, as one who breaks a horse. You can still allow a horse to be spirited and yet have it learn to tolerate a saddle."

"Am I a horse to be broken then?" he asked, a mental image of Nalyssa atop him, naked in bed and riding him hard forming in his mind.

"You already are haughty, Your Grace," she said lightly. "An arrogant streak is almost expected in a duke. What you will need to do is learn the ways of Polite Society. The rules."

His gaze met hers. "I have usually made my own rules in the thirty years I have walked this earth."

She sniffed. "Then I shall help you unlearn some of those and replace them with rules of the *ton*."

Knowing his smile usually had women grow weak at the knees, Pierce used it now. "I look forward to those lessons, my lady. More than I thought I would."

He hoped he affected her, but she was too strong to show it.

"We will work on some of those lessons later this afternoon, Your Grace. For now, we should return to the house. I think it is time you had your first dance lesson, followed by a riding lesson."

"I look forward to both, my lady."

What Pierce looked forward to was being able to touch her. He knew some dancing involved touch. Right now, he was itching to put his hands on her. He must show some restraint, though. He remembered he wanted to make her desire him. He couldn't seem too eager, yet he must do enough to tempt her.

They left the dower house and headed back to the main house. When they arrived at the front, he saw a carriage coming up the lane. Dread filled him because he knew who rode in the vehicle.

"I believe we are about to meet the former heir to my title," he told the three women.

CHAPTER TEN

NALYSSA QUICKLY ASKED, "Will Lord Hardwell have been told of the change in his status?"

"No," Pierce said. "Potter said he would merely retrieve the young man from university and give him the letter his father wrote once they arrived at Stonecrest. I am certain he will question our presence and wonder about our identities the moment he sets foot out of the carriage."

"I should be the one who speaks to him," the duchess said. "It might be easier for him to hear, coming from a woman, and not the man who has replaced him."

"No, Mama," Pierce said quietly. "He is a man who has been entitled his entire life. He will not take to the news well, especially coming from the woman who was his father's true wife. I won't have you being abused by him and his wrath. Go inside, now, the three of you. Tell Pugh to have all the servants clear out from the foyer and beyond. I will take Mr. Selkirk to my study and allow him to read his letter there."

Pierce was only glad he knew where his study was.

"I think His Grace's advice is sound," Lady Nalyssa told the others, ushering the other two women to the front door.

He watched them enter the house and then turned his attention to the approaching carriage. He had always been a confident man, but doubt seeped through him. He forced it aside, knowing he must be strong now and stand his ground with this man.

His half-brother.

The vehicle came to a halt and a footman bounded from the back of it, placing stairs upon the ground so the occupants could descend. The footman opened the carriage's door and Edwin Selkirk climbed from the coach.

His eyes flicked up and down, assessing Pierce. It made him realize Lady Nalyssa was correct and that he needed to begin dressing according to his station in life.

The young man walked toward him as Potter descended the stairs.

"Who are you? Is Dixon no longer Stonecrest's steward?"

"I am not the steward of this estate. We must talk." Pierce's eyes flicked to Potter, who joined them.

The solicitor pulled a letter from his coat pocket. "This is for you," Potter said, handing his traveling companion the note, cleverly not addressing the young man. "It is a letter written to you by your father about six months ago."

"Why am I just now receiving this, Potter?" Selkirk asked, clearly annoyed with the solicitor. Then he paused. "That was at the time of Mama's death."

"I suggest that you read this in private," the solicitor recommended.

Pierce said, "The study is ready for you. You might read your letter from His Grace there. Then it is imperative that we speak."

"Of course," his half-brother said dismissively, not bothering to inquire who Pierce was as he started toward the door to the house.

Pierce and Potter followed the young man and paused in the foyer.

Selkirk asked, "Where the bloody hell is everyone? No servants to greet me." He turned to Pierce. "Have someone bring in my luggage. I will read this letter and then go to my father."

The young man walked off in the direction of the study, and Pierce waited until Selkirk was out of earshot.

"I supposed I don't have to confirm that he has not been told of the duke's death—or his new status within the family," Pierce said dryly.

"No, Your Grace. I will admit that I have taken the cowardly way out. Young Mr. Selkirk is about to see his world shift immeasurably." The solicitor paused. "I see you have had the servants vacate the area."

"I did not think it would be wise for him to hear them address me as Your Grace, much less him as Mr. Selkirk and not my lord. Find Pugh and have your luggage and that of his brought into the house. Have Pugh place Selkirk in his old room. He will need familiarity about him as he tries to come to grips with his new position in the world."

"At once, Your Grace. Will the funeral be held tomorrow morning then?"

Pierce nodded. "Now that you and the duke's son are here, I see no reason for delay. Would you be so good as to notify the local clergyman? I will leave those arrangements in your hands since mine will be full with my half-brother."

"I wish you good luck, Your Grace. You are going to need it. Selkirk will be a handful." Potter sighed. "He always has been. Even before he began the drinking."

Potter left the foyer and returned outside as Pierce walked slowly to his study. He lingered outside its door a few minutes in order to give Selkirk time to finish reading the letter. Then he entered without knocking, closing the door behind him. He observed his half-brother, who held the letter from his father in his hands. The color had fled the young man's face, making him appear as white as a ghost. He favored the deceased duke, down to the cleft in his chin, similar to the one which Pierce sported. He remained silent until Selkirk dropped the page, and it fluttered to the floor.

His half-brother's gaze met his. Pierce saw hatred in his eyes.

He went and took the seat in front of his desk since Selkirk had seated himself behind it, already certain of his position.

"You are Pierce," the young man said, his voice laced with anger.

"I am—and our father is dead."

Pierce deliberately used the word *our*, emphasizing it so that this blood kin to him would begin to comprehend his circumstances.

"When did he pass?"

"It was a week ago."

Something flickered in Selkirk's eyes. "I am just now being told of his death?"

"Mr. Potter and I thought it best that you wait to be informed of His Grace's passing until you returned to your home and familiar surroundings."

"Home?" the young man asked harshly. "Apparently, Stonecrest never should have been my home because I and my sister are bastards," he spat out. "And my mother was never married to the old man. Did he tell her of this? Is that what put her in her grave?"

"I cannot answer that, but I doubt so. The duke kept the secret from her and only wrote these letters after her death, when I have been told he was in poor health himself. I did not learn of his death until Potter arrived to inform us."

"Us? Us," Selkirk echoed harshly." You mean the duchess, the heir, and my half-sister. Oh, this is rich."

"From what I gather, and I suppose our father wrote to you, you were loved, Selkirk. You and your sisters."

The young man flinched at the mention of his siblings. "Thank God one is dead and the other wed and lives far away in Scotland. Not that Eliza ever intended to return to England, but now she cannot. How could she? My sister is a proud woman. It would be hard for her to hold her head high, knowing how our father betrayed us and our mother so deeply." He paused, his eyes narrowing. "He writes of you, your mother, and *your* sister. How he loved your mother more than anything in the world. I don't care what he said. She is a whore."

Pierce sprang to his feet, holding back from slamming his fist into his half-brother's nose, knowing the young man was hurting and trying to get a rise from him.

"My mother is the Duchess of Stoneham and you will treat her with all the respect due her," he said evenly. "I understand how hurt you must be—"

"You understand nothing! I was raised to be the Duke of Stoneham. What is to become of me now? How can I go back to Cambridge? My friends will soon learn the news. They will drop me faster than a scullery maid drops a hot potato. I am nothing now. I have been stripped of everything."

"No, your father provided for you in his will. He purchased an estate in Somerset for you, near Taunton. He also set aside funds in order for you to be able to complete your university education. True, you will no longer be Lord Hardwell, but you will have an estate and income generated from it and be able to live as a country gentleman."

"I will be a pariah. I will never be able to show my face among Polite Society again. Not that I will be invited to any events." He sneered at Pierce. "*You* will be the one taking my place. You have the land. The wealth. The ducal title. You will move about the *ton* and find a woman who will take you, merely because of that title. She will do so not because of who you are as a person, but because you can elevate her to be a duchess. I will never come to a *ton* event again," Selkirk lamented.

"You are not being turned out," Pierce insisted. "Your father has generously provided for you. You will not attain the station you once thought you would and will be called Mr. Selkirk, but no one can take away these first twenty years of your life." He paused. "I would never shut the doors at Stonecrest to you. It is your childhood home. You will always be welcomed here."

His half-brother laughed harshly. "Oh, so you are telling me that we are to be the best of friends? That I am to come and sit at your table at Christmastime and smile as if nothing were wrong? Meanwhile, the servants will look on, and I will see the pity in their eyes. No, I won't have it. You may be the new Duke of Stoneham, but you are more vile than the scum covering a pond."

Pierce knew this young man could spread vicious gossip and so he needed to put him in his place. His voice authoritative, he said, "I will never speak an ill word about you, Mr. Selkirk. I expect the same consideration in return. When you return to Cambridge, you are to say nothing to blacken my name or that of my mother and sister. If you do so, I will destroy you."

He paused a moment, letting his words sink in.

"You are a bastard. There is no getting around it. Our father did us both a disservice when he kept my mother and his marriage secret, and he wed your mother and lied to you all these years. We must make the best of this situation, however. I am the duke and I will use my title for good—unless you cross me. Then I will make certain to ruin you. Do you understand what I am saying, Selkirk? You have been given money and lands. A way to generate income for yourself for the rest of your life. You will be able to marry the daughter of a gentleman and live a life in the country far better than most. You must do so with a smile on your face, never maligning my family. I, like you, have a sister and want her to wed as your sister has done. Nothing and no one will ruin her chances of making a desirable match. We can part on friendly terms if not friends. You are always welcome at Stonecrest, but I would understand if you chose not to return. Our father's funeral will be held tomorrow morning. I expect you at it."

"I am to mourn a man who betrayed me and those I love?" Selkirk asked incredulously.

"I don't care if you mourn Stoneham or not—but you will attend that funeral. We will now go to the drawing room and have Potter read His Grace's will. You will meet my mother and sister, along with Lady Nalyssa Shelbourne, and you will be nothing but gracious to them. Is that understood?"

His half-brother studied him for a moment. "You may not look much like him—except for that cleft in your chin—but you have all the haughtiness he possessed. Yes, Stoneham, I will keep my bitterness to myself. I will be gracious to those now living here. I suppose Lady Nalyssa is going to try and work her magic and make a gentleman out of you." Selkirk snorted. "Well, I have heard she has done it for years now."

Selkirk rose. "Let's get on with it. The will. I want to hear Stoneham's words for myself."

His half-brother moved away from the desk, and Pierce asked, "Don't you wish to take the letter your father wrote to you?"

The young man glanced at where it lay on the ground. He picked it up and moved to the fireplace, tossing the parchment into the fire. "May Father rot in hell for his actions."

"Then let us go to the drawing room," Pierce said.

Selkirk stormed from the room, and Pierce followed at a slower gait, coming across Pugh hovering in the corridor.

"Have Mr. Potter bring the will to the drawing room," he told the butler. "We will be having the former duke's funeral tomorrow morning. Please inform Mrs. Pugh and the servants of this." He hesitated. "What is called for in these circumstances, Pugh?"

"You will go to the village church for the funeral service, Your Grace," the butler explained. "You will then accompany the body to the graveyard for burial. It is custom for the family to entertain mourners afterward."

"Then that is what we will do, Pugh. I leave everything in your hands and those of Mrs. Pugh. I am grateful to have you. Thank you for sharing custom with me."

He went to the foyer and told the two footmen there to summon his mother, sister, and Lady Nalyssa to the drawing room.

"The ladies are already there, Your Grace," a footman told him.

"Lady Nalyssa had them go there to wait for you."

"Thank you." He paused. "Charles, isn't it?"

The footman looked pleased that the duke knew his name.

"Yes, Your grace, I am Charles." He indicated the other footman. "This is Peter."

"Thank you," Pierce said again, heading up the stairs.

When he turned the corner, he saw his half-brother standing outside the drawing room, his shoulders slumped in a moment of privacy. Then the young man's head went up, and he thrust back his shoulders and entered the drawing room. Pierce did have to give Selkirk his due. He had received the worst news of his life, news which changed the trajectory of the rest of his entire future. He would need to keep that in mind and be as supportive as possible.

With that in mind, Pierce entered the drawing room himself and saw Lady Nalyssa was making introductions. He joined the group and after all had met, an awkward silence blanketed them.

"Why don't we have a seat?" Lady Nalyssa asked. "Her Grace could ring for tea."

"No, thank you," Selkirk said in a clipped tone. "Potter is coming to read the will to us."

"Then we should all take a seat and make ourselves comfortable as we await Mr. Potter," his mother said graciously.

They did so, and Pierce informed them the duke's funeral would occur the following morning.

"I am deeply sorry for your loss, Mr. Selkirk," Mama told their guest. "You look so like him," she said wistfully.

Selkirk turned bright red. Whether in anger, humiliation, or embarrassment, Pierce could not say.

Fortunately, Potter entered the room with his satchel and joined them.

The will was read and after the solicitor reached its conclusion, Selkirk stood.

"If you will excuse me, I will retire to my room." Then a stricken look crossed his face. "That is, the room Her Grace has assigned to me," he said stiffly.

Mama smiled gently. "You have the room you have always had, Mr. Selkirk. That has not and will never change."

"Thank you, Your Grace," Selkirk said stiffly. "I have had a long journey and the news of my father's death has greatly upset me. I will take a tray in my room tonight and see you tomorrow morning at the funeral."

With that, Selkirk stood and left the drawing room.

"Excuse me," Pierce said, hurrying to catch up with the young man. When he did, he said, "Thank you for being so gracious, Selkirk. I know the situation was awkward for you."

His half-brother glared at him. "I met those women and put a pleasant expression upon my face so they will never know how much I hate them. And you, Your Grace, the man who usurped my position?" Selkirk's eyes narrowed. "I always felt a distance between me and my father. Something I could never quite put my finger on. Now, I know why. *You* were his firstborn son. The one who received his love and are now blessed with all his worldly possessions.

"Between you and me, Stoneham, will be as it was between Eve and the serpent. Enmity will lie between us always. You will try and crush my head—and I will strike at your heel. I will keep silent simply because you are the one with all the power."

Selkirk smiled, a twisted one that left Pierce cold. "I will have my revenge upon you. When you least expect it."

"Enough!" he said, his voice low and harsh. "I will not be dictated to by some whelp. May I remind you that if your words or actions are in any way inappropriate or you think to rain down chaos upon me and mine, I will ruin you. Entirely destroy you."

Shock filled Selkirk's face.

"I advise you to take the very generous legacy your father thought to leave you. Retire to the country—and stay there, Selkirk."

He watched his half-brother walk away, the spring in his step no longer present. Selkirk had been warned.

And Pierce would do anything to protect the women he loved.

Chapter Eleven

NALYSSA WATCHED CAREFULLY as the duke returned to the drawing room. She had focused on him instead of Mr. Selkirk as the reading of the will occurred. She thought Stoneham was handling himself well, especially considering the circumstances. But as he took a seat, she knew he was upset, despite the smile he gave them.

"Is everything all right?" she asked.

"Perfectly so," he replied. "Selkirk simply has much thinking to do. I wanted to thank him for being so gracious to Mama and Pen. He is young, not even finished with university, and needs time to think through his situation. I know Potter's visit to us came out of the blue. Finding out I was now a duke and us having to leave our home and places of business to journey here had the three of us a bit numb. It is the same with Selkirk. He only learned of his father's death today and at the same time, he learned he will never be a duke. Or a part of the London social scene."

"You were a man at Selkirk's age," Amanda said to her son. "You would never have retreated to your room to sulk or pout."

"I was raised differently, Mama," the duke pointed out. "I learned to fend for myself at an early age. Yes, I had already completed my schooling by the time I was Selkirk's age and held three or four jobs. His view of the world is limited, though, by his experiences. In the *ton*, he is still almost a boy. Perhaps when he graduates from university and assumes the reins at his new estate, he will begin to grow up a bit."

Nalyssa thought Stoneham was being quite generous in his assessment of Selkirk. Though the young man had not attended any *ton* events, she had heard stories of how wild he was. She had also captured him glancing at the duke and been astonished to see the amount of hatred glittering in Selkirk's eyes.

Stoneham turned to her. "I believe you had scheduled a dance lesson for us, my lady. Followed by a riding lesson."

"So much in one day?" Amanda asked.

"I only have a limited amount of time and need to make the most of it," she said lightly. "Although His Grace is soaking up everything I say, dancing requires quite a bit of practice. Riding is a sport that takes time to be mastered. We will need to devote time to both these activities each day."

"Then please go ahead," Amanda said. "I want my son comfortable when he participates in both these tasks." She looked to the duke. "What of the funeral?"

"Potter and Pugh, along with Mrs. Pugh, are handling the details, Mama."

Nalyssa spoke up, telling the duchess, "I suggest that you and Penelope meet with Mrs. Pugh and Cook to discuss what will be served after the service. I expect a good number of people will come to the house after the burial." She paused. "By now, word will have leaked about the new duke and his family who have taken up residence at Stonecrest. Others will want to come meet you and see how Hardwell—that is, Selkirk—is handling the situation."

"More eyes upon us. I hope we will be ready," Amanda said wearily. "Come, Penelope. We need to meet with Mrs. Pugh and also see about what we will wear tomorrow."

"Jenny can help you in making any adjustments," Nalyssa reminded. "Please ring for her and take her advice."

"We will," Penelope promised. "She already has talked with me about ideas for my new wardrobe."

Thinking it a good time to broach the matter, Nalyssa said, "I know we discussed hiring two lady's maids when we went to town. I think, though, that only one will need to be provided by the employment agency. I suggest that you employ Jenny as one of your maids."

"Oh, we cannot take your maid away from you, Nalyssa," Amanda said.

"No, I think it would be a good idea," she countered. "Jenny is wise beyond her years and is ready to move on. That is, if either of you might be interested in her services."

Penelope looked to her mother. "Oh, Mama, I would truly enjoy having Jenny as my maid. Would you mind?"

The duchess smiled at her daughter. "As long as you will share her with me for the next several days, I think it would be acceptable. She is close to your age and has the necessary skills and experience." Turning to Nalyssa, Amanda asked, "Would Jenny be disappointed if she served Penelope and not me? If rank is so important to those in the *ton*, I feel certain that servants might also think the same."

"Jenny is not most servants," she assured the pair. "I think she and Penelope would do quite well together. I hope you would even take Jenny with you when you wed."

"Of course, I would," Penelope promised.

"Then why don't you tell her now?" Nalyssa suggested.

"We will do so," Amanda assured. "Now, go off and teach my son how to be a proper gentleman on the dance floor."

The four exited the drawing room, with the women going one way and Nalyssa leading Stoneham to the empty ballroom. She had him help her in drawing back some of the curtains so that enough light shone into the space.

"I can see it now, all lit and filled with dancers," he said. "I am eager to host this country ball which you mentioned. The one to celebrate the autumn harvest."

"It could also be one in which you introduced your bride to the neighborhood," she said. "If you wed at the end of the Season while in town, a ball would be a delightful way to allow your new duchess to meet her neighbors."

"That's a splendid idea," he praised.

"Then to get a bride, you must learn to dance, Your Grace. Before we begin, I must ask you something."

His eyes twinkled. "Go ahead. I am an open book to you, my lady. You already seem to know me, flaws and all."

"Did Selkirk say something to upset you in the corridor?"

The duke stiffened. "Why would you ask that?"

"Because you are right, Your Grace. I am getting to know you and I sensed something amiss upon your return."

"It is nothing," he said dismissively.

"It *is* something," she pushed back. "What?"

His lips thinned. "Selkirk is most unhappy with his situation. With his father. With losing the dukedom. I feared he might spread ugly rumors about Pen and Mama, and told him that he is to walk a straight and narrow path."

"You threatened him?"

"Only if he threatened my loved ones. I thought all was well because he was most polite to Mama and Pen." Stoneham paused. "But in the hallway, he did not insinuate but rather boldly proclaimed his hatred for me and mine, telling me that he would have his revenge."

Nalyssa shuddered. "That is awful."

"That is a man cornered," the duke corrected. "One who foolishly threatened another man who doesn't take kindly to threats against himself or his loved ones. Selkirk may foolishly try to strike out. If he does, I will destroy him."

"Could it possibly be bluster on his part?" she asked. "As you have noted, Your Grace, Selkirk is in a world of hurt. Confused. Lost. Hopeless."

He looked at her, his ice-blue eyes volatile as he said, "It is the only reason I have not taken his head from his body, my lady. Selkirk is immature. Rash, as some young men can be. My mother was correct in saying I was already a man by the time I was Selkirk's age. It may take him years to become one."

The duke's eyes narrowed. "I hope that he is only speaking out of anger and off the top of his head. That he doesn't mean to seek revenge. But know this, my lady—I will not allow Selkirk or any other man to idly issue threats. What is mine is *mine*. I would die protecting it."

A shiver ran through her. For a moment, Nalyssa wished to be loved so fiercely and passionately that a man would lay down his life for her. It could not be this man, though. He was the Duke of Stoneham, and she was on the lowest rung of the members belonging to the *ton*.

"Then let us hope Selkirk blurted out things he did not mean and will come to his senses once a little time has passed," she said. "It must be hard for him, losing the life he had always assumed to be his, as well as feeling the betrayal of a father he may very well have loved. Enough talk of Selkirk, Your Grace. We do not want to put off your first dance lesson any longer."

Nalyssa began explaining different dances to the duke, showing him a few steps and having them repeat those steps together, side-by-side. He picked them up very quickly, moving with natural grace and ease. Put this man in black evening clothes and out on a ballroom floor, and he would steal the hearts of even the oldest matrons who sat and watched the dancers.

She explained to him how sets were formed and some dances done in fours, sixes, or eights. They spent over an hour practicing these dances, sometimes taking one another's hands as they did. Each time they did so, a fresh thrill ran through her. She would have to harden her heart in order for it to remain in her possession and not be stolen by this handsome duke.

"I think what we will do tomorrow is pull a few of the servants to dance with us," she told him. Then shaking her head, Nalyssa corrected herself. "No, the funeral is tomorrow. Perhaps the day after, then. As I mentioned before, country balls are popular and many of the servants will know these dances and their steps. It would be good for you to practice within a group."

She paused and then added, "I will even see if I can find one of them to fiddle for us as we dance. It is so much easier to move to music than it is me counting the beat to you." Nalyssa smiled and said, "I believe we are done for our dance lesson today. I do not want you to become bored or restless."

"We learned several group dances today. I know there is a time, however, when couples dance solely together. I overheard two of my customers discussing this. What is the name of that dance?"

"The waltz," she told him, her heart beating fast at the thought of being in this man's arms.

"Then we should also practice the waltz, my lady. I want to have a full complement of dances in my repertoire."

"You are right, Your Grace. I will tell you that dancing the waltz is very special. It allows a couple to be in close proximity to one another. They can actually converse as they dance. Other dances, such as the reels and quadrilles, are far too active for a decent conversation to take place. You must learn when you arrive at a ball which dances that evening will be waltzes. Reserve those for the women you wish to get to know better. Are you still considering making one of the new debutantes your bride?"

"I may have had a change of heart as far as that goes," he said, his gaze boring into her, causing a shiver to ripple along her spine. "I am already thirty myself and believe that I would be bored with a woman a dozen years my junior. No, I need a fully mature woman. One who fits into Polite Society with ease and can run my household without a second thought. You asked me what I wanted before, my lady, and I am ready now to tell you."

Nalyssa's mouth grew dry as she wondered exactly what this man did want.

"Not only do I want a woman of some maturity, but I also desire her to be intelligent. I know you have lectured us already on the types of conversations to hold in social situations. Frankly, those topics bore me. I need a woman of substance. A woman who can keep up the pace and be my equal. A woman of beauty, compassion, and understanding. One who values the hard work that will go into making Stonecrest and my other estates not only profitable, but also places tenants want to live and work upon.

"Moreover, I must wed a woman who is fond of children and wants to give me several of them. I long for daughters I can rock in my arms, as well as sons I can teach all manner of things. I know only my eldest will be able to inherit Stonecrest. I want to make certain that the other boys know how to run a business, as well as an estate. I might choose to do what my father did for Edwin Selkirk and buy properties for each boy to manage and live upon. I am comfortable teaching them about business. My haberdashery was quite successful and I had planned to open other branches of it across England. Perhaps I will have a son or two who wish to follow in those footsteps."

"I see," Nalyssa said, surprised at the vehemence and thoughtfulness in the duke's words and how he'd already thought of providing for all his children and not simply his heir.

"I want to wed a woman who, like Pen, wishes to spend time in the nursery. I understand that we must hire nannies to care for them while they are young, but I am not going to miss out on the various phases my children go through. I want to see them take their first steps and hear them utter their first words." He grinned. "Perhaps one of those words might be "Papa," aggravating my duchess the slightest bit."

Nalyssa chuckled. "You have quite a list, Your Grace. I will begin thinking of women in society who are eligible and might have as many of the qualities that you believe are necessary on this rather lengthy list."

"You do that, my lady. And now, I want to learn more about this dance called the waltz. If it is truly that important in my search for a bride, then I must be able to dance it with perfection."

"I am glad you are up to the challenge, Your Grace. As long as you can count to three and follow me, I think the waltz might become your favorite dance."

Since he had caught on so quickly to previous dance steps, Nalyssa took the gentleman's role, holding her hands in the correct position and moving her feet in the simple steps as she stood next to Stoneham. She demonstrated twice and then the duke imitated her actions as they moved along the ballroom floor, dancing beside one another, partnerless.

"This is quite simple," he remarked. "The easiest of anything you have shown me."

"Let's try a few turns," she suggested, showing him how to make small turns and then grander ones.

"I am ready to have a partner, my lady."

He turned and faced her and bowed as she curtseyed to him. Her pulse quickened as he placed one hand on her back and took her hand in his free one. Her mouth grew dry, and she wet her lips nervously, even as she watched his eyes distracted by her movement. His hand tightened imperceptibly on hers, making the place between her legs tighten again.

Clearing her throat, she said, "I will count for us. Start on the third count of three if you would, Your Grace."

He nodded and she said, "One, two, three. One, two three," her body humming as she reached the start, and he moved her backward.

Nalyssa continued counting for a full minute, letting him get the feel of the floor, and then stopped counting. They continued moving as one, the count in their heads, their feet gliding effortlessly across the floor of the empty room. Then she began humming a waltz. The duke pulled her closer, the intimacy between them causing her pulse to pound. Nalyssa's head grew light, and she lost herself in the music she created, allowing Stoneham to lead her across the floor. His turns grew wider. Her gown began flowing. She worried her pins might come out and her hair fall down her back, their movement was so fast.

Her song came to an end, the last note dying in her throat. The duke stopped moving, but his gaze remained on her, his arms still about her. Her breath came in rapid spurts as her body tingled from head to toe.

Then he lowered his mouth to hers.

Fire shot through her body, a blaze that instantly raged out of control. Need filled her. Their bodies suddenly pressed against one another, and she could feel his heart as it raced within his chest. She brought her hand up and stroked his cheek before sliding it to his nape, pulling him closer. She felt his smile against her mouth and did the same.

Suddenly, his tongue ran along the seam of her mouth, startling her. She wasn't certain what was happening because these sensations were so new to her—but knew she wasn't ready to stop.

He eased her mouth open and his tongue swept inside, brushing against hers, sending shivers dancing along every limb. His tongue began leisurely exploring her, making her heart gallop within her chest. Her breasts ached, the nipples becoming sensitive as they pressed against his massive chest.

His hand on her back began moving up and down in sensual strokes, matching those of his tongue. Nalyssa thought she might go mad because her core began to throb, wanting—needing—his touch there. She tried to pull away then, wanting to tell him what she needed, but he held her fast to him, his kiss leaving her weak and breathless.

Her fingers played with the hair at his nape and then pushed up, feeling the soft, dark blond waves. She heard a growl and realized it came from him. That he must like her touch.

She began imitating everything his tongue did, stroking his as he had hers, hearing the noise of raw need coming from him. It finally made sense to her, those women who had been ruined. Nalyssa understood now how a man's touch could be addictive. How a woman could crave it—and do anything to receive it.

But she was not any woman. And she certainly was not the woman for this man.

Once more she broke the kiss, turning her head away. His mouth grazed her cheek, traveling to her ear, his tongue outlining the shell of it, even plunging inside it, giving her delicious chills. She wanted this to go on forever. She knew it must end, though. He still had hold of one of her hands from the dance, but she used her other one to nudge him away. The contact between them was broken though he was still so close that she could feel the heat radiating from his magnificent body.

Before she could speak, he raised their joined hands and tenderly kissed her fingers.

"I will never forget my first waltz, Nalyssa," he said, his voice low and rough.

Then he released her hand and took a few steps away. She almost cried out for him to come back and bit her lip to prevent from doing so.

"I will meet you at the stables in half an hour," he told her, striding from the room, leaving her shaken. Weak. Confused.

No, not confused. She had been aware from the time they met that he desired her.

Now, she understood that she wanted him, too.

CHAPTER TWELVE

NALYSSA LEFT THE house and headed toward the stables, knowing she was about to lie to the Duke of Stoneham. She didn't think she could be around the man without wanting to throw her arms about him and kiss him again. The urge to do so consumed her—and Nalyssa knew she was toying with fire. Her head told her she could in no way become involved with the duke because he was meant for another. It would be paramount for him to wed a woman embraced by the *ton*.

Lady Nalyssa Shelbourne was definitely not that woman.

She arrived at the stables and was met by Pinchel, the head groom at Stonecrest. She had spoken to him the day she had arrived, assuming she would do some riding with the new duke, although she had not known that she would teach him to ride. She had let Pinchel know her preference in horses during their meeting.

The groom now beamed at her. "Good afternoon, my lady. Are you riding with His Grace or by yourself today?"

"His Grace does not know how to ride, Pinchel," she revealed. "I am afraid we must start from scratch with him. Would you be willing to take His Grace in hand and teach him the basics over the next several days?"

The groom frowned. "I could certainly do that, my lady, but wouldn't he prefer learning from you?"

"His Grace, I fear, needs a break from me. I am talking in his ear at every turn and I believe—and I am sharing this in confidence, Pinchel—that he might take better instruction from a man than a woman," she fibbed.

The groom nodded in understanding. "I will teach His Grace myself, my lady. Once he is fit to ride, will you be escorting him across Stonecrest?"

"I will be happy to do so at that time. Thank you, Pinchel. This will free me up to spend more time with Her Grace and Lady Penelope, teaching them all they need to know before they enter Polite Society."

The groom cleared his throat, and Nalyssa glanced over her shoulder, seeing the duke striding toward them. Just the sight of him made her heart turn somersaults. She had never experienced such feelings, much less the physical attraction. They made her giddy and vulnerable at the same time.

"Good afternoon," the duke said as he reached them.

"Your Grace, this is Pinchel, your head groom. He is going to take you through the stables and show you the horseflesh you possess at Stonecrest. He is also a master at teaching others to ride and so I am going to have him take charge of your lessons."

She saw his brow crease and added her white lie. "I neglected to bring my riding habit with me and will retrieve it when we go to town. By the time we return, you will have learned the basics from Pinchel and I will take you out on your estate myself. This will allow me to spend time with Her Grace and Lady Penelope. I do not wish to neglect them and their lessons."

Nalyssa knew by bringing up his mother and sister that the duke would not protest. If she had learned one thing about this man, it was how fiercely he loved his family and how he would go to any lengths to protect them.

"Will you at least go through the stables with us?" he asked.

"I would be happy to do so."

For the next half-hour, she accompanied the duke and Pinchel as they went through the stables, the groom stopping at each stall and naming each horse, sharing with the duke about the animal's lineage.

"Why do I have so many horses?" he asked, perplexed.

She nodded, deferring to Pinchel, who said, "Horses are an investment, Your Grace. Even if a nobleman does not ride or does so infrequently, his stables are usually full. The horses we have seen so far are those to be ridden. The ones in the next section are carriage horses."

"I think I will leave you at this point and return to the house," Nalyssa said. "Remember, Pinchel, His Grace has never been around horses. He will need the basics, starting with the saddle itself."

The groom smiled. "I will take care of His Grace, my lady. Go and do as you must."

She left the pair, guilt washing through her at abandoning the duke to another. She needed time away from him, though. On their tour of the stables, she had been all too aware of his every movement. Of his scent. Of his size. She must rein in the wild feelings within her.

And never kiss Stoneham again.

Nalyssa went into the house and came across Mrs. Pugh, asking the housekeeper where the duchess might be. Learning that she was in her rooms, Nalyssa went upstairs and knocked at the door.

Lady Penelope answered the knock. "Oh, come in, Nalyssa. Mama and I have already met with Mrs. Pugh. Everything is set for the mourners who will visit Stonecrest tomorrow after the funeral. Jenny is with us now and has been telling us about the latest fashions. You were correct. She is a fount of knowledge as far as clothing goes."

The two women joined the duchess and Jenny, who said, "My lady, I have been offered a position in His Grace's household. Lady Penelope wishes for me to become her lady's maid."

"That is wonderful news," Nalyssa said, embracing her now-former servant. "You will do well with Lady Penelope."

"Jenny has promised that she will go with me when I marry. It means a lot of change for her, but for me, too. It will be wonderful to have a friendly face when I do leave my brother's household for another."

"Have you decided what to wear to the funeral tomorrow?" she asked. "And how long your mourning period will be? I had not thought about that when we discussed your wardrobes."

"Jenny has taken two of our dresses and already dyed them black," the duchess informed Nalyssa. "Tomorrow will be the only mourning we do. At least publicly," she amended. Looking to her daughter, Amanda added, "I cannot ask Penelope to mourn a man she never laid eyes upon. Even though she is not making her come-out this year, I still want her to meet people who come to the house and allow her to see a bit of London, as well. The same goes for me. I plan to accompany Stoneham to the events we are invited to."

A tear rolled down the duchess' cheek, and she brushed it away. "I will forever mourn in my heart for my husband, but it will be a private matter."

"I believe you are making a wise decision, Your Grace," Nalyssa said. "I was hoping you had time now, though, to meet with Mrs. Pugh and Cook regarding the household and meals. You, as well, Lady Penelope."

"We can do so," the duchess said. "Jenny has everything in hand and ready for tomorrow."

"You do not have to attend the funeral service and burial," she explained. "In fact, it is rare for women to do so."

Determination filled the duchess' face. "No, I will be in the church tomorrow and accompany my husband's body to the gravesite. I will see him buried."

"Then we should go downstairs," she suggested, leading the two women to the drawing room and ringing for Mrs. Pugh, explaining that they would like to meet with Cook regarding the upcoming menus and determine a time when the duchess would confer with Cook each week.

Soon, Cook arrived and the five women talked about how meals were prepared at Stonecrest and local specialties of the area. The duchess shared her son's favorite dishes, as well as the ones she and her daughter preferred.

"Annie cooked and cleaned for us for years," the duchess explained. "She will be arriving soon. I don't know what capacity she should have within the household, though. She is used to doing everything for us."

"Leave it to Annie and me, Your Grace," Mrs. Pugh said. "We will be able to work out what her role in the household should be."

"Although my son doesn't want me to do so, I believe I will move to the dower house once he takes a wife. We might have Annie be in charge of the staff there," the duchess suggested. "I realize that might not be for several months, though. Please do your best to make Annie feel welcomed when she arrives, Mrs. Pugh."

"I understand how important Annie is to you, Your Grace," the housekeeper said. "She will be treated with all due respect."

They got down to the planning of menus then, with Cook and Mrs. Pugh contributing to the conversation. Nalyssa reminded the others that they would be traveling to town soon, so some of the meals planned might be put off until they return to the country.

The housekeeper and the cook left just as the duke entered the drawing room, his hair looking slightly windblown, making him all the more appealing.

"Have tea brought now if you would, Mrs. Pugh," he told the housekeeper. "I know it is a tad early, but I am famished."

He came and joined them, sitting in a chair, much to Nalyssa's relief. Of course, Penelope sat beside her and there would have been no room for him to squeeze between them. Still, she was grateful for the distance between them until she realized they sat directly across from one other, and she would face him throughout tea.

"Tell us about your riding lesson, Stoneham," Penelope said.

"I believe I am going to enjoy riding quite a bit," he shared. "My stables are full of beautiful creatures waiting to be ridden. Pinchel, my head groom, took me in hand and is quite the teacher."

The duke went on to explain how he learned about each part on a horse and how to prepare to ride one.

"Pinchel taught me the names of everything involved with the saddle and bridle. I even know now how to prepare my own horse to ride." His gaze met Nalyssa's, and he added, "Of course, I know that is always done for me, but you never know when an emergency might arise."

"Did you actually mount a horse?" his mother asked.

"I did, Mama," he said enthusiastically, looking almost boyish. "I was put on a horse with a sweet nature and a tough mouth and led about an enclosed pen on what is called a leading rein. Pinchel seemed quite pleased and promised to take me off this rein at tomorrow's lesson."

He looked again to Nalyssa. "I scheduled it for mid-afternoon, my lady, knowing we had the funeral at ten o'clock and mourners who would return to the house with us. Were you speaking to Cook and Mrs. Pugh about what to serve?"

"We did discuss it, Stoneham, as well as planning meals for the week to come," Amanda said. "Nalyssa reminded us that we will be leaving for London soon, however."

"Call it town, Mama," the duke said, winking at Nalyssa. "I have learned that is how we should refer to it. Though I still have much to see of Stonecrest, I am looking forward to the great city and seeing my townhouse and other sights. When are we leaving, my lady?"

"I should receive word tomorrow from the shop owners and the employment agency. They will let us know when our appointments have been set."

The teacart arrived, and Nalyssa told Amanda that she was to pour out for them.

"There is nothing to be nervous about," she reassured the older woman. "In fact, I will talk you through everything." She chuckled. "I have talked so much already, I am certain you are hearing me in your head day and night."

"I like hearing your voice, Nalyssa," Amanda said. "It is comforting to me. When I am in doubt, I will simply close my eyes and hear you with me, whispering in my ear what I am to do."

Tea went well, with Nalyssa telling the trio what the Season was like. She explained when it began and the various events to which they would be invited. When she revealed the number of ballgowns Amanda would need, her new friend gasped in shock.

"So many?"

"Yes, there are fifty to sixty balls each Season. You are to wear a different gown to each one held."

"This seems so wasteful," Amanda complained.

"You may think so, but think of the business you are bringing to those who prepare you for these affairs. The modiste who creates your gowns. Her workers who cut and sew them. And it is not just gowns," she added. "You will need hats and bonnets. Gloves. Stockings and slippers. Undergarments. You are sending quite a bit of business to others. Some shop owners make the majority of their funds for the year in the weeks leading up to and during the Season."

"You have told us of evening events—balls, routs, musicales. What of the day?"

"There will be a few affairs held during the afternoon. Mostly garden and tea parties. You will also hold visiting hours when guests might call upon you. Don't ask me to explain why, but they are called morning hours—even though they are usually held between one and three in the afternoon. Most likely, you will not have many call upon you until you make friends with others. Who *will* be visiting others during that time of day will be His Grace."

The duke's brows shot up. "Why?"

Nalyssa chuckled. "Because you will be calling upon ladies, Your Grace. You will go to various ladies' homes and spend fifteen to twenty minutes at each. That is considered the proper amount of time for a call. A gentleman must spend time at the residence of a lady he is interested in—or one he is pursuing. I have already begun a list in my head of eligible ladies. You will meet them at various *ton* events and then call upon them in their drawing rooms the next day. More importantly, you must send them flowers if you decide to visit them. I will work with you on the size and type of arrangement to send."

"It all sounds rather tedious to me," Stoneham said.

"You mustn't think of it that way, Your Grace. After all, you are choosing a wife for life. You will attend these events and seek eligible women. You will then call upon them and get to know them a bit better."

"Who will even invite me to these affairs? I don't know anyone in Polite Society beyond you, Lady Nalyssa."

She giggled, finding his naivety charming. "Everyone already knows *you*, Your Grace. They may not know what you look like, but they know you now bear the ducal title. There are few dukes in England, and they are all always invited to every single event held during the Season, whether they know the host and hostess or not. It is a true coup when a duke does arrive at someone's home. Your mere presence will make your host and hostess popular."

"It is hard for me to understand that people who would not have spoken to me if we passed one another on the street when I was a lowly shopkeeper, will now grovel at my feet because I bear a title."

She shrugged. "That is the way of Polite Society."

He gazed at her intently. "I will be glad to have you by my side, my lady."

Nalyssa did not correct him, but she would never appear next to him in public. They might travel to events together but would enter the ballrooms separately. She wanted this man to succeed in every way.

And that meant breaking ties with her.

Chapter Thirteen

Nalyssa awoke to thunderstorms and went to the window, seeing the ground drenched. She wondered if the duke would insist upon holding the funeral in such terrible weather. If he did, she would insist that Amanda and Penelope remain at Stonecrest.

Crossing the room, she pushed aside the curtain and curled up in the chair beside the window, watching the rain fall at a steady pace, knowing further sleep would be impossible. As she sat staring out across the lawn, she brooded over the last few days and came to a decision.

She would leave Stonecrest.

It would mean returning a good portion of what the previous Duke of Stoneham had given her since she would not be completing her assignment, but Nalyssa realized she wasn't needed all that much. The new duchess, though a lowly clergyman's daughter, was quite refined. Nalyssa could write out a few instructions to help Amanda manage the household. They had a gem in Mrs. Pugh, who was competent and efficient. The housekeeper would make certain the duchess would not go astray.

As for the duke, he didn't truly need lessons from her. Generations of nobility had been bred within him. It was obvious because he had risen to the top of his former class without help from anyone else. He had an excellent steward here at Stonecrest and would learn what he needed to of estate management from Mr. Dixon. Once the duke toured his various estates throughout England, he could decide whether to retain or hire new stewards for each of them as he saw fit.

For the rest of it? The duke would cut a swath through Polite Society in his own fashion. He might not always toe the line as to what the *ton* expected because even with her sharing the rules he should follow, Stoneham would always be his own man. He did not really need her help to launch himself into society, confident as he was. He would easily land a bride on the Marriage Mart since he would have his choice of any single woman within the *ton*. Since she would be a lady of excellent breeding, his new duchess could put the final finishes upon him.

Pinchel would continue the riding lessons and since the duke had picked up dance steps so easily, Nalyssa would merely have a dance master come in for a few sessions while they were in town seeing to the wardrobes. Although she knew the duke had impeccable taste, she did want to be there to guide his choices and that of his mother and sister. Once the wardrobes were completed, they could return to Stonecrest.

Without her.

It would mean tightening bootstraps on her part since she had no other clients this Season. Once word leaked out that she'd had a hand in preparing the Duke of Stoneham and his family for taking their places among the *ton*, however, she hoped it would bring a future client or two for next Season. She would spend conservatively. Already, Jenny had made over many of Nalyssa's gowns from previous Seasons. It was not as if someone in her position would be expected to have an entire new wardrobe each Season, much less be taken of notice. She would, however, need to replace Jenny at some point. Her other maid could help her dress for the Season, and Nalyssa would do her own hair, which she had a talent for. She could possibly hold off hiring a new maid until next year or see how it went this Season. She might be able to get away with having someone come in a day or two a week to help with things such as laundry and heavy cleaning.

Nalyssa felt good with the decision she had reached. It would be the right thing to leave Stonecrest and this family. Already, she was becoming far too attached to Amanda and Penelope, which would serve them ill since they were both sweet, loyal women. They did not need to be associated with her.

As for the duke, she needed to keep her distance from him during the next week. There could be no more shared kisses between them because she would succumb to temptation, possibly demanding even more of him than he wished to give her.

Then a thought came to her.

What if she did give in to those heady desires?

It wasn't as if she would ever have an opportunity again to see what it was like to couple with a man. She would never receive any more offers of marriage as she had a decade ago. This might be her only opportunity to experience what lovemaking could be like. Nalyssa shook her head, thinking of the naïve young woman she had been when she made her come-out, one who was full of joy and laughter and had absolute certainty that she would find love with a dashing young man and marry him. Well, it certainly wasn't love with the duke. It would be nothing but acting upon pure lust.

It surprised her—but she was ready to explore that for one night only. One glorious night.

It would be easier to do so here at Stonecrest. The house was vast and though servants seemed to linger at every keyhole, it would be easier to accomplish this coupling in the country rather than when they went into town. She might even use their encounter as the excuse to break away from him.

Nalyssa knew there was always the possibility a child might be made during the time a man and woman came together. Surely, Stoneham would know how to prevent something of that nature. A sudden longing filled her, thinking of holding her babe—his babe—in her arms. Nalyssa had never had such thoughts or maternal feelings. It would be impossible for her to have a child and survive, though. She pushed those thoughts away. She had to prepare for her future, especially now that she had decided to leave Stonecrest. If no other clients came to her, she would be forced to sell her small home in town, which Lord Starling had bought for her all those years ago. She could live on those funds for quite a while. Not a lifetime. Since she had been gently bred and raised, she could always seek employment as a governess or companion. Her looks, though, might be too tempting for the master of the house and cause trouble for her.

Perhaps she could use the funds to open a small shop herself. What she would sell, she had no idea, but it was a thought. If not, she could rent rooms and seek employment, working for a modiste, possibly, or in a bookshop. She would need to explore these various possibilities and reminded herself it would be only if new clients did not appear. She might be worrying for nothing. Her nature had changed, though, from that idealistic young girl, one who was optimistic and romantic. She had to harden herself, knowing she must be all business. There was no room for love in her life. She never let others get close to her. She remained focused at all times. It was the only way she could survive after the mess her father had left, gambling away his fortune and her dowry.

Fortunately, as she watched from her window during the next hour, the rain slowed and then came to a halt. The skies were still gray and gloomy as dawn broke, wind sweeping away the dark storm clouds until the sky no longer threatened today's funeral.

Nalyssa rang for Jenny, wondering if the former Earl of Hardwell would attend his father's funeral. The young man had retreated to his bedchamber and had not been seen since. They had dined without him last night and retired to the parlor, where Stoneham had asked her to play the pianoforte for them. She had done so, conscious of his gaze upon her the entire time. Once again, that reaffirmed the decision she had reached.

Leaving Stonecrest was the only solution.

Jenny appeared, and Nalyssa congratulated the servant once more on her new position.

"I hope you do not mind helping me dress as long as I am here at Stonecrest."

"Of course not, my lady," Jenny said. "You took a chance on me long ago. I may have a new employer but my loyalties will always lie first and foremost with you."

"That is most kind of you to say, Jenny, but Lady Penelope and her mother must come first from now on. I am now an afterthought. I am very happy for you, though. Lady Penelope has a sweet nature and I think the two of you will suit well together."

"It will be fun to take care of her and introduce her to life in the *ton*," Jenny agreed. "She has already been so kind to me. Since we are of a similar size, Lady Penelope has offered to give me some of her gowns once she gets a new wardrobe."

"I am glad to hear that."

Once she was dressed, Nalyssa dismissed the servant, telling her that she would be doing her own hair from now on. Jenny did not question her in this matter and left.

After she had arranged her hair, Nalyssa decided since it was still early, she would go to the library and read for a bit until breakfast was served. She took a lighted candle with her and entered the large room. Once, she had been a great reader, her head filled with the dreams of what she had read. Thanks to her father, though, reality had given her a swift kick, and she had put aside books for good. She went to a shelf, holding her candle high in order to read the titles on the spines.

Then a voice spoke from behind her. "If it isn't the infamous Lady Nalyssa Shelbourne."

Wheeling, she held the candle high and caught sight of a silhouette sitting in a chair. Nalyssa moved toward it, seeing it was Edwin Selkirk, an empty brandy snifter in one hand and a bottle in the other. He was quite disheveled, as if he had slept in his clothes.

"A gentleman would never have spoken those words," she chided, moving toward him and setting down the candle nearby.

"I am no gentleman, am I, my lady? I am but a well-dressed, well-educated bastard. I will soon be the laughingstock of the *ton*."

"True, you will be the subject of much gossip, but your father loved you enough to provide handsomely for you upon his death. You only have a few weeks left until graduation, and he provided funds to see you through until the end of the term. Not many noblemen would think to buy an entire estate for their bastard sons—but yours did. You will not be a penniless young man with no opportunities, Mr. Selkirk. You will have a home to go to and tenants to help generate an income for you. Why, the details of the duke's will even mentioned providing the salaries of your servants for the first three years. So, do not act as if you have nothing. You have more than most."

Selkirk threw the glass against the wall, and it shattered. He slammed the bottle in his hand onto the table.

"You talk of opportunities and income," he hissed. "*I* was meant to be the Duke of Stoneham. I was raised to have everything at my fingertips. Now, I see it all slipping through my grasp and I am powerless to do anything. Yes, I will have an estate but not half a dozen. I will be plain Mr. Selkirk, always an object of pity and gossip." He snorted. "For a short time, at least. Then the *ton* will forget me and move on. There will be other people and events to gossip about. I will no longer exist for them."

"You can make a new life for yourself in Somerset," she insisted. "You may not possess a title, but you will own Bigby Hall. Knowing the duke, it is a large, profitable estate or he never would have invested in it for you. You will be a gentleman, Mr. Selkirk. You will be able to wed and enjoy the company of others of your rank in your neighborhood. Your father could have left you destitute. He did not, however."

"He was a fool," Selkirk said harshly. "He wrote me of how he loved his sweet Amanda and how his terrible father kept them apart. That he was forced to wed *my* mother. He claimed he loved my sister and me, but I know that to be a falsehood. It was guilt—not love—that had Stoneham buy me an estate. He bought my sister a husband. He dangled a hefty dowry in front of the man she fell in love with. Stoneham encouraged the match, knowing Eliza would most likely go to Scotland and never return to England. She has a titled husband and an easy life now. Gossip in England won't matter to her. The Scots don't care a fig about London's *ton*. I am the one who suffers by not becoming the duke."

Anger flared within her. "Quit feeling so sorry for yourself. Whether you received what you did from the duke out of guilt or love, the fact is you *did* receive it. You will never have to struggle as others do."

"Ah, that is right," he said, an understanding light entering his eyes. "You had a father who left you with nothing except a reputation in tatters. No gentleman of good breeding wishes to wed a woman with no dowry and a scandalous suicide in her past. You have had to work for what you have gained, haven't you, my lady?"

His gaze slid up and down her lasciviously, causing her to blush.

"There won't always be clients like my half-brother who come knocking at your door seeking your guidance in entering Polite Society. You must be a good decade older than I, yet you are still a beautiful woman. Perhaps it would be wise on your part to guarantee your future."

Selkirk stood and moved toward her, standing so close that she could smell the brandy on his breath and see the stubble on his face. He gripped her shoulders so tightly that she knew bruises would appear.

Smiling evilly, he said, "I could use someone of your looks and charm by my side to ease my transition, my lady. What do you say?"

"Say?" she sputtered, struggling to escape.

He only strengthened his grip. "To my offer of marriage, Lady Nalyssa."

Shock filled her, but somehow she found her voice. "I would rather be a charwoman and scrub floors than take your name and go to your bed."

She slammed her palms against his chest, knocking him loose. The drunken Selkirk stumbled back, falling to the ground. He gazed up at her, snarling.

"You will regret that, bitch. You all will regret what you have done to me."

Nalyssa fled the library, running from the room.

And smack into the Duke of Stoneham.

Chapter Fourteen

Pierce decided to rise after a night with little sleep. Doubts plagued him at every turn.

Today he would be on full display to all as the new Duke of Stoneham. He would be meeting his tenants, as well as residents of the neighborhood and nearby village, as all would attend the funeral service for his father.

His father . . .

Conflicting feelings filled him. He thought back to his youth, to the man who had come to visit him and Mama at their isolated cottage. He recalled how Mama's eyes would light up each time the earl arrived and how he always was friendly and interested in everything Pierce did and said. He still believed the earl weak, not standing up to his own father, but as Pierce learned all of the little rules and idiosyncrasies regarding Polite Society, he almost sympathized with his father's dilemma. His father had been trapped and, having been raised in the world of the *ton*, did not know how to escape it. He could have struck out on his own until his own father's death and assumed the dukedom, but he hadn't. Instead, Mama had been the strong one, forging a new life for herself and her children, while freeing her husband to remain in the world familiar to him.

Now, though, Pierce and his family were a part of this world.

He would be able to survive the gossip because he wouldn't listen to it. He doubted anyone would dare say anything to his face and if they did, he would call them out and make mincemeat of them. His priority now was to protect Mama and Pen. At least Pen would not have to go into the fire this Season as he did. Pierce would swim those shark-infested waters, along with his mother.

And Lady Nalyssa.

He felt good about his decision to make her his duchess. She would resist, of course, which is why he would go through the motions and pretend to search for a bride on the Marriage Mart. In the end, though, Pierce knew she was an uncommon woman and would do a fine job helping him and his loved ones transition into Polite Society.

He also couldn't wait to kiss her again.

Pierce doubted she had been kissed in a good long while. According to her, she skated the periphery of the *ton*. Nalyssa deserved much better, however, and he would see her restored to the pinnacle of Polite Society. From what he gathered, no one crossed a duke, much less his duchess. The *ton* would accept her because of the title she held. She would no longer remain in the shadows but be free to blossom and come into her own, with him by her side.

He wouldn't be getting anymore sleep and decided to go ahead and rise. Pierce went to the window and saw how wet the ground was. He had listened to the thunderstorms throughout the night. It looked as if the worst was over now.

Ringing for Wattleby, the valet appeared, looking sleepy.

"I am sorry to call for you so early," Pierce apologized.

The servant's jaw dropped. He recovered quickly, though, and said, "There is never a need for you to apologize to me, Your Grace. I am here to assist you whenever you desire."

He hated the class distinction that stood between them and said, "It wasn't that long ago when I, myself, was earning a living, Wattleby. I hope simply by acquiring a title that I did not lose common courtesy.

If I wish to apologize to you, you are to accept my apology graciously."

A smile tugged at his valet's lips. "Of course, Your Grace. Thank you for getting me out of bed so early so that I might assist you."

Pierce grinned in return and knew in that moment that his relationship with the valet had changed for the better.

Wattleby shaved Pierce and then helped him to dress. He wished he already had his new wardrobe as he met all the strangers who would become known to him. Wardrobe could be like a suit of armor. He believed he was going into battle today at a disadvantage, dressed as mere Pierce Selkirk, and not the Duke of Stoneham. He noted Wattleby had chosen the finest coat Pierce owned, however, and that his shirt was ironed and starched to perfection. A new cravat awaited him, however, and he asked about it.

"I know Your Grace is waiting to go to London to be fitted for your new wardrobe. Though the previous duke was not of your size, he possessed numerous cravats. I thought this one especially fine and suited for today's occasion." Wattleby paused and then added, "I also thought it might make you feel closer to His Grace today."

"You knew the previous duke, Wattleby. What was he like? I met him when I was a child but did not see him over the last two decades."

The valet grew thoughtful. "I believe His Grace was an unhappy man and tried his best to hide his unhappiness from the world. He was always kind to his servants, though, and me, in particular. His Grace spent much of his time alone in his study." Wattleby met Pierce's gaze. "I think he was unhappy because he lived a life without his duchess and their children."

Curiosity filled Pierce, and he asked, "What of his other children?"

Wattleby smiled. "Everyone loved Lady Eliza. She was a good baby and grew into a kind girl and woman. She was most unassuming and the staff at Stonecrest were happy when we received word of her marriage in London at the end of last Season."

"She married a Scotsman?"

"Yes, Your Grace. From my understanding, it was a love match. I doubt Lady Eliza will be returning to England. With her mother and father gone, she has a new life with her husband in Scotland."

"You don't think she would return to visit her brother?"

A shadow crossed the valet's face. "No, Your Grace, the two were never close. Lord Hardwell—that is, Mr. Selkirk—was what we refer to as too big for his britches, if I'm not speaking out of turn. Where Lady Eliza was all kindness and warmth, Mr. Selkirk was a spiteful child. As he grew older, he was definitely aware that he would become the duke one day."

"He was not easy to be around then, I suppose."

"It is not for me to say, Your Grace." Wattleby paused. "Although I will say the staff will be glad to see him gone after today's funeral." Then the valet said, "I apologize, Your Grace. Mr. Selkirk is your half-brother. I should not have spoken ill of him to you."

"Mr. Selkirk wants nothing to do with me," Pierce said flatly. "I told him this was his childhood home, and he would be welcomed always. He has indicated to me that he will not return."

The valet let out a sigh of relief. "That will be for the best, Your Grace. Mr. Selkirk can be demanding and hateful. I am sure he is not taking to his new circumstances with grace." Wattleby paused and then added, "Watch yourself when it comes to Mr. Selkirk."

Pierce would take this servant's warning with more than a grain of salt. After what his half-brother had said yesterday, he'd decided that Edwin Selkirk should be banned from Stonecrest.

"I believe that to be sound advice," he told the valet. "After today's service for the duke, Mr. Selkirk will not be allowed to set foot at Stonecrest again."

Pierce knew it was still too early for breakfast. He had yet to meet with Dixon, his steward, and so had no business to look over. He decided to go to the library that Pen had raved about and read for an hour until the breakfast buffet would be set up. He was still a few steps from the library door when it flew open and Lady Nalyssa came hurrying out, running smack into him. He grabbed her elbows to steady her.

"What is wrong, Nalyssa?"

It was the first time he had used her Christian name and he saw she recognized that.

"Nothing, Your Grace. If you will excuse me."

She pulled away from him and hurried down the corridor. Pierce followed her, needing to know what had upset her. He caught up to her and passed her, wheeling to face her, her path now blocked.

"We are both up rather early, my lady," he noted. "Would you care to come to my study and talk for a while?"

"The drawing room," she countered, and he realized the drawing room was a more appropriate place for the two of them to be alone together and converse.

Pierce offered her his arm, a small gesture she had taught him to do, and he had practiced by escorting his mother and Pen to the dining room for meals and the drawing room afterward. This was the first time Lady Nalyssa placed her hand on his arm since she usually trailed after them. The moment her fingers touched his sleeve, he felt the jolt run through him. Pierce smiled to himself, knowing they would be well suited both in and out of bed.

They reached the drawing room, and he led her to a settee. She took a seat, and he sat beside her.

"Do you wish to discuss what upset you?" he asked.

"Only if you promise to stay here with me," she told him.

"All right. I agree. Go on."

"I came downstairs to fetch a book and found Mr. Selkirk in the library. Foxed. He said a few unkind things to me."

Pierce tensed. "What things?" he demanded.

"There is no need to go into our conversation, Your Grace. I fear, however, that Mr. Selkirk will not be in any condition to attend his father's funeral. You might want to place a footman or two near him and prevent him from doing so. I fear he might embarrass you and your family and your name if he did attempt to attend."

"I hate to keep him from his own father's funeral."

She gazed at him steadily. "I am not asking you to do so, Your Grace. I am telling you. You do not want the scene this man might create. There will already be gossip enough regarding how you came into the title. In time, others will see the good man that you are and how well you care for your estate and its tenants. Do not borrow trouble today, of all days."

"I thank you for your sound advice, Nalyssa."

"You mustn't address me in this manner," she said quietly. "It is different among women. The best I can do is refer to you as Stoneham. Even then, I will not do so if I run into you at different gatherings in town."

"I thought we were to travel to these events together," he said. "You had mentioned in the carriage that we would talk about things. People we would meet."

She shook her head. "You are your own man, Stoneham. I have been teaching you some of the rules to follow in Polite Society. Truth be told, dukes usually make their own rules. I do not believe you and your family are going to need me nearly as long as I had first anticipated. I should hear today or tomorrow regarding our appointments in town. When we go there, I will help you familiarize yourself with your home and staff and help you and your family in selecting your new wardrobes. At that point, I believe my task will be done."

Panic filled him. He thought he was going to have several more weeks before the Season began, weeks in which he could win her over. How could he do so if she remained in London, while he journeyed back to Stonecrest?

"I believe that is for me to decide, my lady. I know you were compensated handsomely to do a job. I expect you to live up to the bargain you made with my father."

She smiled wistfully. "His Grace would have been so proud of the man you have become." She hesitated. "If you wish for me to return the bulk of the funds given to me, I will—"

"This isn't about the money, Nalyssa. It is about seeing that I am fully prepared for society."

Pierce felt a sudden gulf widening between them and knew he was losing her before he had ever started to have her.

She rose, her hands clasped in front of her. "Let us get through this day, Your Grace. It will be a trying one for you. We will continue our lessons in the country and do the same when we arrive in town."

Lady Nalyssa bobbed a curtsy and then quickly left the room.

Pierce wasn't certain what had just happened.

All he knew was that in order for him to succeed in this life—in this world he had been forced into—he would need Lady Nalyssa Shelbourne by his side.

Chapter Fifteen

THEY GATHERED IN the foyer, ready to leave for the church. Potter had told Pierce that the family should arrive half an hour early in order to meet with the Reverend Clayton and discuss the service.

Pugh said, "The carriage is ready, Your Grace."

"Shall we?" he said, indicating for them to leave.

They entered the carriage, and Mama said, "Shouldn't we wait for Mr. Selkirk?"

He tapped on the roof and the vehicle took off. Pierce had never kept any secrets from his family and would not begin to do so now.

"Mr. Selkirk will not be attending the service. He drank himself into oblivion. I found him passed out on the floor in the library before breakfast, an empty bottle of brandy beside him."

His mother gasped. "Oh, no!"

Continuing, he said, "I had Charles and Peter carry Mr. Selkirk to his room and put him to bed. They were charged to watch over him."

His gaze met that of Nalyssa, who sat opposite him, and she gave a slight nod of approval.

"Apparently, Mr. Selkirk has a bit of a drinking problem. Potter told me as much, as did my valet. It's for the best that he remain at the house, lest he cause a scene at the funeral."

Actually, Selkirk would have no chance to attend. If he did awaken and try to leave his room, smelling like a distillery and looking disheveled and unshaven, Pierce had charged the two footmen on duty to bar the former heir apparent from leaving his room, much less the house. He doubted that would be necessary, though, having observed the drunken stupor Selkirk had been in when Pierce had gone to the library after speaking with Nalyssa. At some point, though, his half-brother would rouse himself. Pierce only hoped Selkirk's head would ache enough to prevent him from coming downstairs while the mourners were still present.

They arrived at the church, the day still gray and cloudy. At least the rain had subsided. Mr. Clayton met them when they alighted from the carriage.

"Ah, Your Graces, it is so good to see you. I am just sorry it is under these circumstances."

Introductions were made and the clergyman invited them into the parsonage, which stood adjacent to the village church. There, Mrs. Clayton had a pot of tea waiting, telling them a cup would take the chill from them.

His sister and Lady Nalyssa engaged Mrs. Clayton in conversation, allowing Pierce and Mama to speak with the clergyman.

"Is there anything special you wish said during the eulogy, Your Grace?" Clayton asked Mama, sympathy in his eyes.

"No. Do as you see fit," she replied, her eyes misty with tears.

Clayton told her, "His Grace spoke to me once about you."

"He did?" Mama's shock was obvious.

"Yes, he did. His Grace was a good man in an impossible situation."

Mama dabbed at her eyes with a handkerchief. "You are kinder than most, Mr. Clayton."

"I do not condone what the duke did," the clergyman said. "He put aside his true family for another one. His guilt over doing so was great, Your Grace. He made it abundantly clear to me that he loved you and your children very much."

"Thank you for sharing that," Mama said quietly.

After they finished their tea, Mr. Clayton said it was time for them to go to the church, explaining the family had a designated pew in which to sit.

"I suspect by now the building is filled to the brim. Everyone is waiting to get their first glimpse of the new duke," Mrs. Clayton remarked.

Her words irritated Pierce, but he kept silent. He would not create trouble on this day, one in which his mother mourned for the husband she had loved from her youth.

Turning to Nalyssa, he said, "You must sit with us, my lady, in the family pew."

"I am not family," she protested.

Pen took Nalyssa's hand. "Please. We all need you today."

"If you insist," Nalyssa said, following them from the parsonage as Pierce escorted his mother and sister inside the church.

It was as Mrs. Clayton said, filled to capacity, with some even standing in the back and along the sides of the room. He spied the empty pew at the front and to the side and guided his party that way, his head held high as they went up the center aisle. Pierce had his mother sit in the middle, with Pen and him on each side of her. Nalyssa took a seat beside him.

He gazed out at the congregation, seeing curiosity on the faces of many. Soon, he would know most of the people present. His tenants. His neighbors. The people of the village. For now, though, he would concentrate on seeing his mother get through this funeral service.

As Mr. Clayton spoke, grief washed over Pierce, overwhelming him, even surprising him. He thought back to the earl and his visits to them over the first ten years of Pierce's life. How impressive he had been, arriving on the large black, bearing gifts for both Mama and him. Pierce had received books. Puzzles. Tins of sweets. Even little toy soldiers. He remembered throwing out all those gifts when he was older, not wanting anything associated with the man who had sired him out of wedlock. Little did he know that he had been the firstborn and legitimate heir to the earl.

Suddenly, Nalyssa's hand covered his. The gesture was hidden from view since Pierce's hand rested on the seat beside him. But he felt warmth and comfort flow from her into him. He turned his hand, lacing his fingers through hers. They remained that way until Clayton finished his eulogy.

The service ended in a prayer, with the clergyman inviting all present to the burial and, at Pierce's request, back to Stonecrest for a reception. Clayton indicated the family was to leave first with a nod of his head. Reluctantly, Pierce released Nalyssa's hand.

But not before leaning and whispering, "Thank you," into her ear.

He stood and helped his mother to her feet. She had wept silently throughout the service and now dabbed her eyes again before they moved down the aisle. Pierce felt all eyes on them, knowing how curious everyone present must be about the situation. They must also wonder where the former heir apparent was, missing his own father's funeral.

The graveyard was on the far side of the church, and they followed Reverend Clayton to the section where countless Selkirks had been buried over the years. A few more words were spoken once all had arrived, with a last prayer being said. Then a weight seemed lifted from him. His father was gone. The dukedom was now his to do with as he saw fit.

In that moment, Pierce vowed to be a better man than his father had been—and a better caretaker as the Duke of Stoneham.

NALYSSA JOINED THE family in the ducal carriage as they traveled the short distance back to Stonecrest. Once more, she sat across from

Stoneham. This time, she would not look at him. How virile and muscular he was. How his sensual lips called out to her. Instead, she turned her gaze out the window and watched the passing countryside.

She had always enjoyed life in the country more than the city and had hoped she would marry a man who felt the same as she did. Nalyssa enjoyed country pursuits. Riding. Fishing. Walking. Gardening. She had yearned to find love and raise a family. Instead, she spent a majority of her time in town, the only escapes to the country rare instances such as this one. Her sojourn at Stonecrest would soon end, though. She was determined to remain in town after Stoneham and his family returned to Sussex—and just as determined to couple with the duke before she severed their connection.

Turning her head from the window, she found him watching her, those ice-blue eyes burning with desire. She wondered if her own reflected the same.

They arrived at Stonecrest and went inside, being met by the butler and housekeeper. Quickly, Nalyssa ran through a list with the pair, making certain all was prepared for the mourners who would soon follow.

"How do you do that?" Penelope asked as the Pughs hurried off.

"Do what?"

"You have so much in your head," her friend said. "How do you recall everything that should be done?"

"Part of it is experience," she explained. "The rest is hiring competent staff and clearly communicating with them." She looked to Amanda. "You have true gems in the Pughs. They will be able to guide you long after I am gone." Nalyssa took the duchess' hand. "You have soldiered on today. I know it has been difficult. These next few hours with many strangers may also prove trying."

"I will be ready to retire to my rooms when our guests leave," Amanda admitted. "I will need some quiet time to myself."

"You should go freshen up," she suggested. "People will be here soon."

Amanda and Penelope went up the staircase, leaving her with the duke.

"Thank you," he said quietly. "For your support today."

"I know you had not seen your father since your youth. That did not make attending his funeral any easier. I'm sure you have some regrets as to how your relationship played out."

Stoneham nodded. "You guessed correctly. A part of me wishes I could go back, knowing what I know now. I always looked forward to his visits, but I would have appreciated them and the gifts he brought more. I also would have wanted to spend more time with him." He paused. "Though I understand now that he wanted a majority of his visits to be spent with Mama. It is still something I will never understand. How he could keep her at arm's length. How he allowed her to walk away from him."

Nalyssa placed a hand on his arm. "She did so in order to give you a life. You and Penelope. She was thinking of her children and put your happiness and well-being above hers."

The duke sighed. "As always, you are right about that. If we would have stayed in the cottage he'd bought for us, tucked away and hidden, our lives would have been quite different. By leaving Cambridge and moving far away, Pen and I got to experience school. We made friends. We started our family businesses. Mama is the one who suffered in silence. She loved him to the end, you know."

"I do," she said softly. "Love can be a powerful thing."

He snorted. "Love is the last thing that I would want in my life. I have seen up close how hurtful it can be."

His words assured Nalyssa that once she asked him to couple with her, he would not read anything more into the situation. As a man, he was no doubt used to having affairs, keeping his personal feelings from his physical desires.

"I have something to ask of you," she began.

Before she could elaborate, the first of their visitors arrived. Soon, the house was filled with people from the nearby village, as well as neighbors and tenants from Stonecrest. Nalyssa circulated about the drawing room, making certain everyone had what they needed, even as she watched Stoneham and his family in action.

Penelope stuck close to her mother's side but seemed to relax as time went on. Amanda was warm and gracious, acknowledging each visitor and thanking them for their attendance. The duke, while not as open as his mother, did a good job circulating about the room, meeting others. It reaffirmed that he no longer needed her guidance.

Only a handful of mourners remained in the drawing room two hours later when she heard a commotion. Suddenly, Edwin Selkirk bounded into the room, his hair and clothing askew. He still wore what he had on when she had encountered him early this morning, and she supposed he had finally awakened from a drunken sleep.

The two footmen appeared, both a bit disheveled, and Nalyssa assumed there had been a scuffle before Selkirk's arrival in the drawing room.

"Ah, the last of the mourners coming to call at Stonecrest," Selkirk said, striding toward the center of the room as he looked about him, holding his arms wide as he turned in a circle. "Those who thought the duke was so wonderful and kind. The same people who believed—as I did—that I would be hosting today's little reception upon my father's death. Instead, I am suddenly considered unacceptable, unwelcomed in my own home."

The new duke stepped forward. "I have made it abundantly clear that you are welcome at Stonecrest, Selkirk. You are the one who believes otherwise."

"Why would I care to be here? In the place that was supposed to be *mine*?" the young man raged. "The man who sired the both of us betrayed me. I was meant to have it all. Now, I have nothing."

Stoneham shook his head vigorously and told those present, "Our father's will generously provides Mr. Selkirk with the means to finish his university education, as well as gifts him Bigby Hall, an estate near

Taunton in Somerset. I will not have you disparage His Grace's name to his neighbors, friends, and tenants, Selkirk."

Selkirk laughed harshly. "Say what you will—but know this. None of these people will ever truly accept you. You may hold the title, Stoneham, but no one, not even Lady Nalyssa Shelbourne, can turn you into a diamond. You will forever be a piece of stinking coal, duke or not."

Nalyssa saw the cold anger on the duke's face as he ordered, "Get out. Now. Potter was to accompany you back to university since you still seemed like such a lost boy. You are a man, however, Selkirk. Pull yourself together. You have been given a livelihood by your father. Make the most of it and your life."

Stoneham turned to the two footmen. "See this man taken into Brighton and put on the first mail coach heading north."

Charles and Peter rushed toward Selkirk, grabbing him by the arms as he cursed away. They dragged him from the room as a hush descended over the drawing room.

Stepping forward, Mr. Clayton said, "Well done, Your Grace. Mr. Selkirk has been given his education and a home. You have no further obligation to him. What you do now with your title and power is up to you."

"Hear, hear," several echoed, moving to the duke and offering their hands, clapping him on the back.

Nalyssa breathed a sigh of relief. Selkirk had been dealt with, and it seemed as if Stoneham's neighbors would be supportive of the new duke, especially since he wasn't a spoiled, immature, drunken brat as his half-brother was.

A quarter-hour later, the last of the mourners departed as the clock chimed a quarter to two o'clock.

"That was draining," Penelope said. "All I want is a hot bath and a good book to read."

"I second that," Amanda said. "I will retire to my rooms for the rest of the day, Pugh," she said to the hovering butler.

"I will do the same," Penelope echoed.

"I shall have hot water prepared, Your Grace, my lady. Mrs. Pugh will send up tea to you. And Cook can prepare trays for your dinner."

The butler departed, and Amanda said, "I hope you don't mind our absence, Nalyssa. Perhaps you can take my son in hand and further his instruction regarding the ways of the *ton*." She looked to Stoneham, touching her palm to his cheek. "I do think, other than Mr. Selkirk's untimely diatribe, that today went well."

He took his mother's hand. "I agree, Mama. Everyone seemed quite friendly. I agreed to receiving invitations from our neighbors to dine, as we are not a true house of mourning, due to the unusual circumstances. Be expecting to receive several in the next few days."

"It will be good to get to know our neighbors," Amanda agreed. "Penelope also will need a bit of a social life. Come along, my darling," she said to her daughter, linking their arms. "We will see you tomorrow, Nalyssa."

"Good day to you both," she replied, now finding herself alone with the duke.

"I feel the need to get out," he said. "I canceled my riding lesson with Pinchel, not knowing how long the mourners would stay. Being among so much company has left me feeling a bit restless. Would you care to walk with me, my lady?"

"I would be happy to do so, Your Grace."

She rang for Jenny and instructed the maid to bring her bonnet and spencer, along with her boots, not wanting to ruin the slippers she currently wore. The maid promptly retrieved the items. Nalyssa then accompanied the duke out the front doors.

"Where to?" she asked, inhaling the fresh, cool air of the afternoon.

"I have a place in mind," he said, slipping her hand through the crook of his arm and leading her away from the house.

CHAPTER SIXTEEN

A SHOT OF lust raced through Pierce as he took Nalyssa's hand and tucked it securely against his arm. Then in a display of further protectiveness, he placed his free hand atop it. He wanted to make certain that she wasn't going anywhere.

Except straight to the rendezvous he had in mind for the two of them.

The air was cold and crisp, no rain clouds in sight. Neither was anyone stirring about. Pierce supposed after the funeral that others had returned to their homes and were keeping warm inside them. It would make it all the easier to make their way to the dower house and what he had in mind.

Since he no longer had two months of her company before the Season began, he would have to act more quickly than he first believed. He had decided that Nalyssa would refuse any marriage offer from him, believing herself not worthy of him. That was why he needed to make sure she was thoroughly compromised.

Something he would enjoy doing—and hoped she would, as well. Instinct told him that Nalyssa had a sensual nature.

And that he was the one ready to help her discover it.

Guiding them away from the house, he asked, "Do you think Selkirk's outburst was met with any sympathy? At least there weren't many left to view it."

"I think Mr. Selkirk's reputation preceded him. It is not a good one. The young man drinks and thinks far too much of himself. I believe everyone is relieved that he did not become the new duke." She paused. "You, however, made a very favorable impression upon everyone today, as did your mother and sister. I hope that you will make good friends with those in the neighborhood and patronize the shops in the local village."

"I did speak to a few fellows that weren't half-bad," he admitted. "I also met several people from the nearby village, as well as some of my tenants. I cornered Dixon and told him we were overdue for a long meeting. I scheduled that for tomorrow morning. I want to hear about the workings of the estate." He paused. "You admitted you know much about an estate. Perhaps you might care to sit in on our meeting."

"No, I will leave estate business to you and Mr. Dixon. I can easily spend that time with your mother and sister. I want to make certain they both know the ins and outs of running a large household, both in the country and town. Mr. Dixon will guide you in learning about Stonecrest. Oh! I thought you were going to have another riding lesson today."

The only riding in his near future was this woman sitting atop him.

Pierce smiled at that thought. "You forget . . . I thought it too muddy to ride today and had no idea how long our guests would remain so I canceled my lesson. I will meet with Pinchel tomorrow. After all, my expert in all matters has informed me it is the best way to get about the country and see my tenants and others."

"I wouldn't necessarily call me an expert, Your Grace."

"Can't you call me Pierce?" he asked.

She frowned. "We have discussed this and the answer is a firm no. In all honesty, your own wife will most likely call you Stoneham and nothing else."

"My wife? You mean we would not be on a first-name basis even after marriage?"

Nalyssa shrugged. "Many married ladies in the *ton* refer to their husbands by their titles."

"Another of those unwritten rules?" he said teasingly.

She laughed. "I am not saying that I agree with all of the rules. I am merely making you aware of them."

"Well, when I wed, my wife will call me Pierce. Except in public, of course. I know enough to know that would be a terrible mistake."

"Who knows? You might allow her to call you Pierce and start a trend among the *ton*, with wives calling their husbands by their Christian names." She chuckled.

He liked the sound of that. He liked her and everything about her.

The dower house came into view, and Pierce said, "Why don't we stop here? I never did see any of the upstairs rooms when we visited."

Her cheeks reddened, and he recalled why he hadn't been upstairs.

Because they had been kissing.

"If you wish, Your Grace."

As they moved to the front door, she squeaked. "Oh, dear. I have stepped in mud. I will stay outside and not traipse any inside."

"You'll do nothing of the kind," he said, quickly scooping her into his arms, relishing the feel of her warmth against him.

"Your Grace! Put me down at once!" she commanded.

"Ah, but I am a duke, my lady," he told her. "I believe dukes make up their own rules."

He carried her to the front door and wiped his own boots thoroughly on the mat before entering the house, closing the door behind him.

"Careful. You'll get mud on you," she warned.

He shrugged. "You tell me I'll be shedding these clothes anyway for a new wardrobe. Besides, a little mud never hurt anyone."

Pierce carried Nalyssa to the kitchen and sat her atop a large, square work table. He bent, unlacing her muddied boot and removing it from her foot. Her ankle was trim, and her stockinged foot long and elegant.

Slipping his hands under her skirts, he unfastened her stocking and pulled it from her incredibly shapely calf.

"What do you think you are doing?" she demanded, one foot and leg now bare.

"I took off your muddy boot and stocking," he said matter-of-factly. "So that when we walk the house, you won't get mud anywhere. You are a thoughtful woman. Surely, you don't want to create extra work for my servants, do you?"

"Of course not," she said, a hot blush spilling over her cheeks and rising to her roots.

A blushing Nalyssa Shelbourne was a thing of beauty. It took every bit of willpower he possessed not to kiss her senseless.

"Let me see to the other foot so you aren't walking lopsided," he declared, making quick work of the boot and stocking, though he allowed his fingers to linger a little longer than he should have this time.

Pierce decided willpower was far overrated. He rose and stepped close to her, his body between her legs.

"Your Grace?" she said, her breath hitching as she gazed up at him.

"I am going to kiss you, Nalyssa. It will be a kiss of great length. It will start with your mouth and go places you have never dreamed a kiss might land. But I promise you will enjoy it."

He paused, waiting for her reaction, ready to counter any argument she gave him.

Instead, she grabbed the lapels of his coat and yanked his mouth to hers.

The movement was unexpected—and thrilling. She must want him as much as he wanted her. Which was a very, very good thing.

His arms went about her, his mouth easing hers open. His tongue slipped inside, stroking hers. He caught the scent of roses coming off her skin, the smell subtle but growing in strength as her skin heated. He leisurely explored every crevice of her mouth, even tickling the roof, causing laughter to bubble up from her. His hands began stroking the length of her back, ready to help her shed the layers of clothing.

Without breaking the kiss, he untied the bonnet strings beneath her chin and pulled it from her head. Growing bolder, his fingers found the buttons on her spencer and undid them. Pierce pulled the spencer from her, sliding it from her shoulders and down her arms, discarding it.

Nalyssa broke the kiss. "You have quite a talent, Your Grace, kissing and removing pieces of a woman's clothing. Must I remind you that this house is unoccupied? It is simply freezing in here. Why, I am shivering."

He looked at her lazily. "I think you are protesting to try and delay me further." Pierce grinned at her. "I have far better talents, Nalyssa, than undressing you. I plan to show them to you—and I guarantee that I will keep you warm while doing so."

She looked shocked at his comment.

"I do have one request, though." His gaze pinned hers. "Call me Pierce."

"Pierce," she echoed breathily, causing desire to flare within him, hearing his name come from her lips, her perfect, rosy, full lips.

He moved back to her mouth, nipping at her bottom lip, surprising her from the sound she made. Then she imitated the gesture, causing fire to flood his limbs.

"You are learning," he praised, his lips trailing to her throat, his fingers clasping her shoulders as he nibbled delicately where her pulse throbbed.

"Oh!" she exclaimed, gripping his coat.

He lifted his head. "We can do better than an *oh*."

She studied him, her sapphire eyes large. "What is better?"

His hand covered her breast and squeezed it, causing her eyes to widen further. He slipped a hand into her bodice, pulling the material down, exposing her breast. His mouth went to it and began sucking, hard, hearing her gasp. He continued sucking and then laving her nipple, causing her to squirm. Lightly, he grazed his teeth across the nipple.

"Oh! Pierce!" she proclaimed.

He stopped and looked at her. "That's a start."

He spent long minutes on one breast and then the other, feeling her fingers move to his hair, pushing through it, tightening her grip on his locks. He feasted until he heard how she gasped for a breath, knowing he had more to show her.

Moving his mouth away, he hiked up her skirts with both hands, bringing them above her knees. He still stood between her legs and slipped his hands under those skirts, kneading her smooth thighs.

"I would keep kissing your breasts—but I want to see you when you come," he said, his voice husky.

"Come?" she asked, confused. "Where might I be coming?"

He laughed softly. "To a place you have never been before, Nalyssa. To the heights of pleasure."

Still, she frowned. "I am not certain you—"

She stopped, mid-sentence, because his hand had moved to her core. His middle finger stroked it. He watched her face and heard the small whimpers begin. Slowly, he pushed the finger into her, watching her eyes widen.

"Did you just do what I think you did?" she asked, her voice high.

"I did." He smiled playfully. "Let's see what I can do while I am there."

Pierce began caressing her, yearning to kiss her more, but wanting to see her face the first time an orgasm struck her. He added a second finger, his strokes deeper, longer. Nalyssa began panting, her fingers clutching his shoulders.

"It's . . . there's something . . . building. Some anticipation. Something . . ." Her voice trailed off.

"Something wonderful is about to happen. You will thank me later," he said smugly.

"Oh! Oh! Oh . . ."

"Yes. Feel it. It's a wave of pure pleasure. Ride it, Nalyssa. Ride it into oblivion."

Her moans became louder and then a sound emerged from her that let him know she had reached her peak. She began writhing, moving to meet his hand, calling his name. In that moment, Pierce felt needed. Wanted.

By this woman. By this magnificent, beautiful woman.

Her body went limp, her head dropping to the shoulder he put in front of it.

"I am . . . so weak. And yet I feel . . . powerful," she mused.

Pierce chuckled. "You are feeling your feminine power, Nalyssa. It has always been within you. I merely have helped you unleash it."

She lifted her head and their gazes met. "Show me more."

"With pleasure."

Moving back, he again lifted her into his arms and headed from the kitchen to the staircase.

"We shall investigate the bedchambers and choose the one which best suits us." He paused. "Or I can be greedy and make love to you in every one of them."

Her mouth formed a perfect *O*, no sound coming out. Then she found her voice. "I think that is a wonderful idea, Pierce."

He reached the next floor and paused. "Should I question why you are being so cooperative? Even daring?"

"You could," she said primly. "Or you could continue your lessons. I have been doing all the instructing, Pierce. It is time you showed me things *I* need to know. I will pause giving lessons and allow you to start yours."

"You little minx," he teased. "Who knew such a hot-blooded

woman lay beneath Lady Nalyssa Shelbourne's cool exterior?"

Striding down the hall, he entered the first door that appeared on their left.

"Thank God it's a bedchamber," he murmured, pausing to give her a deep, lingering kiss.

Pierce placed Nalyssa on the bed and then went and opened the curtains, returning to her.

"What if someone sees us?"

He sniffed. "We are well above the ground. No one will be passing by with a ladder and think to use it to look in this window. Besides, I need the light. To watch your face again as I make love to you."

"Then I suppose I will also need it to see your face, as well," she responded saucily.

"Who *are* you?" he asked. "Where is the practical, rigid tutor I have come to know?"

She bit her lip, causing desire to ripple through him. "Perhaps she has taken the day off, Your Grace," Nalyssa said huskily. "I am here now, ready to explore with you. Teach me what you think I need to know."

"With the greatest of pleasure."

Pierce fell onto the bed, rolling with Nalyssa in his arms. A small part of him warned that he should question why she was suddenly behaving in such a manner, but his base instincts won out. He wanted this woman. Here. Now.

And nothing would stop him from having her. Not only now.

But always.

Chapter Seventeen

Nalyssa knew there would be no going back the moment she and the duke entered the dower house. She wondered if on their first visit he had decided it would be the place to seduce her. A quiet place to entice her into a physical relationship.

She had needed no coaxing, however. She had decided she wanted to explore what happened between a man and a woman. Stoneham was her first and only choice. No man had ever tempted her to stray from the strict moral code placed upon unwed women of Polite Society, a group which ironically was known for its loveless marriages and extramarital affairs. Nalyssa had lived in limbo, though, too old and tainted to wed, sitting high on her shelf as she watched the nefarious doings of those around her.

The time was right to taste the pleasures of the flesh. This physical, sensual man whom she was wildly attracted to had offered her a glimpse into the forbidden. And what he had already shown her was nothing short of eye-opening.

He kissed her now, and she returned those hot kisses, her body coming to life in a way it never had before. Heat rose from her and ran through her blood. She needed more of him.

"I want to touch your bare skin," she murmured against his lips.

Breaking the kiss, she saw a knowing look in his eyes. "Then you shall. But I must have the same from you."

Pierce—for he was now Pierce to her and always would be when she thought of him—released her and pushed from the bed. He reached for her, his hands encircling her waist, and lifted her from the bed.

"We shall help one another to undress. You may have the honors of starting with me."

Her cheeks burned as she began her task, her fingers fumbling at first. He captured her hands and pressed hot kisses to them.

"Take your time. We are in no rush, Nalyssa."

Nodding, she returned to his knotted cravat and a calm descended upon her. She would remember each moment. Each touch. Each kiss and caress. They would be the treasures she would store and take out and remember as the years rolled by.

It took a good five minutes to remove everything from him and when she finished, she gazed openly in admiration at his hard, muscular body. The impossibly broad shoulders and flat belly. The sprinkling of hair covering his chest, tapering down. And his member, jutting out from a nest of dark curls, proud and demanding even as he was.

"Do you approve of what you see?" he asked.

"Since it's my first time to see a naked man, other than a sculpture in a museum, I have nothing to compare you to," she teased, biting back a smile. "I would say you are most attractively made, Your Grace."

He growled, seizing her, his naked body pressed to hers as he kissed her. Hard. Demanding.

When he finally allowed them to both come up for air, he told her, "I am not a duke in this bedchamber, Nalyssa. I am merely a man. One who wants to be with you in the worst way."

"Then I suppose you should remove my clothes, Pierce," she said lightly, her heart drumming wildly.

One corner of his mouth turned up. "You are full of good ideas."

Slowly, he removed every piece of her clothing. Her gown. Her shift. Her corset and petticoat. He had already rid her of her stockings and boots downstairs. With a last gesture, he pulled the pins from her hair, letting it spill about her, falling to her waist. She now stood before him, self-conscious of her nakedness, bringing her crossed arms in front of her.

"No," he said gently, lacing his fingers through hers and opening her arms wide. "Let me see your beauty. All of it."

His gaze roamed over her body and then met hers. "Perfection."

"I am old," she told him. "The girls you will consider to be your duchess will be a good ten years younger than I am."

Pierce placed a finger against her lips. "No talk of others. We are here now. Together. Let's make the most of it."

Taking her hand, he led her back to the bed. Her body began humming again as he lay next to her, his heat immense. His mouth moved to her breast again, and he cupped both breasts with his hands as his lips and tongue and teeth did the most marvelous things to her.

Tentatively, she began touching his bare flesh as he did so, reveling in the feel of him. He was hard to her soft, his scent tantalizing and so masculine.

His mouth moved to the valley between her breasts and then lower, kissing his way down her body. The lower he went, the more she tensed, realizing where his final destination would be.

Pierce raised his head. "Relax," he ordered.

She sniffed. "That is easy for you to say. I have never done this before. And you were correct—I did not think you would kiss certain . . . places."

He laughed softly, one hand stroking her belly. "You will be pleased. I guarantee it." He took her hips firmly in his hands.

"You are awfully sure of yourself."

He grinned. "I am, aren't I? But you will have to see for yourself."

His lips returned to her belly and descended from there. Nalyssa did her best to relax but was still shocked when they pressed against her core. Then his tongue licked the seam of her sex, and she nearly bolted from the bed. If not for his steady hold on her hips, she would have fled the bed.

He continued toying with her, pushing her legs up and apart to give him better access to her. When his tongue plunged inside her, Nalyssa gasped. He nipped and sucked and licked and drove her to beyond the point of madness. Once again, that pressure built inside her until she exploded, crying his name.

"Pierce! Pierce!"

She moved, letting the waves of pleasure wash over her, a pleasure so great she might never recover.

Then he loomed over her, kissing her again, the taste of her on him. His cock pressed against her core and suddenly pushed inside. Nalyssa dug her nails into his shoulders.

Slowly, he began to move, in and out of her, bringing delicious feelings. He had her lock her legs about him, and she felt him slip more deeply into her. They began a rocking motion, a dance of sorts, a dance unlike any she had ever known. It went on and on until the both of them cried out. She felt a flood inside her, knowing his seed now lay within her, hoping no child would result.

Pierce collapsed atop her, driving her into the mattress, covering every inch of her. He kissed her neck, nuzzling it, making her feel wanted. Then he rolled so that they faced one another.

"What do you think of making love?" he asked, tracing lazy circles on her back.

"I can see now why some women lose themselves and succumb to being ruined," she said honestly. "It is a most magnificent feeling and you are an expert at lovemaking. I am certain you have been told so before."

"Are you jealous?" he asked, a smile tugging at the corners of his mouth.

She placed a fingertip in the small cleft of his chin, smoothing it. "No. You are a man thirty years of age. It is only natural that you would have coupled with a woman before now. I have no hold on you, Pierce."

He frowned. "What we have done means that you are ruined for another man."

She shook her head sadly. "There are no other men. I have told you as much. The gentlemen of the *ton* look upon me as undesirable."

He kissed her. "They are very much wrong. You are the most desirable woman I have ever seen. Beautiful. Accomplished. I will admit that I wanted you from the moment I laid eyes upon you."

She sensed the blush tinge her cheeks. "That is very sweet, Pierce, but I am an outcast. No man would offer marriage to me because I have no dowry and sport a scandalous past, which ruined me long ago." She hesitated and then revealed, "My father was a gambler. He lost everything and when nothing was left, he killed himself. His suicide will always haunt me. Not that we were close, but his actions made me an anathema to others in Polite Society."

He smoothed her hair. "They are fools if they do not recognize your value. I don't need a dowry. And I have a scandalous past of my own. We have that in common. Our fathers' actions have led others to judge us harshly."

Nalyssa feared he was about to offer for her. Marriage with him would be a dream—but she could never wed him. She was ruined in the eyes of Polite Society, not only by what her father had done, but by the fact she had worked all these years to support herself. She wanted everything for Pierce. For him to be a leader of his class. To take his place in the House of Lords. To marry a beautiful, charming wife.

"We do," she agreed. "My job is to make you fit into the *ton*. They will soon forget that your father was a bigamist. You are his legitimate heir. Polite Society can be very forgiving to dukes."

She pulled away from him. "We should dress and return to the house."

"Why?" he asked. "Mama and Pen have retired to their rooms." He took her wrist and pulled her back. "We have all the time in the world."

He was right. There was no need to rush back, not when they could remain here and make memories for her to live on the rest of her life.

Placing her palm against his cheek, she kissed him. "Then teach me more, Pierce."

He made love to her again, taking his time, allowing Nalyssa to ask questions as they went. She touched him more this time than she had the first, asking what pleased him. When they came together again, a joy and lightness filled her. This experience was definitely the pinnacle of her existence.

When they finished, they lay entwined in one another's arms and talked for a while. Pierce asked about her childhood, and she told him the things she enjoyed doing. In return, he shared about growing up near Bristol and some of the jobs he had held before opening his own haberdashery.

"I told you previously that I had in mind to open branches of it all across England," he confided. "It was called The Crafty Gentleman."

"A clever name. I like it. Who runs it now for you?"

"I promoted Wilson, my head clerk, to store manager the same day that I learned I had become a duke. Actually, just prior to learning so. Mama convinced me to break ties with my business since I had a title and tenants to care for. I gifted the store to Wilson." He chuckled. "I suppose I could buy it back from him and have him continue to manage it in order to have the rights to the name once more."

He hesitated. "For now, it is only a dream to think of once more becoming involved in a business. My priority is to get to know more about Stonecrest and my other estates. I plan to visit them in person. I would rather do that sooner than later."

"No, the Season is more important, Pierce," she insisted. "You must get to know your fellow peers and take your seat in the House of Lords. It is imperative that you make a good marriage because this will also help Penelope when she makes her own come-out next Season."

He looked at her quizzically. "I have no need to make a marriage with someone else, Nalyssa. I thought you understood that."

"Understood what?" she asked, pretending to be puzzled yet dreading his next words.

"After what we have done this afternoon? You know what lies in our future."

"Do not say it," she warned.

"I will say it, by God." His eyes darkened, whether in anger or desire, she did not know. "We will marry."

"No, we will not," she told him firmly.

His brows shot up. "You are telling me that you are turning down an offer of marriage from a *duke*?"

She sat up, glaring at him. "First of all, I heard no offer from you, so there is no need to believe that I turned you down. Second, you will wed someone appropriate to your station. I will not see you embroiled in further scandal and have that affect Penelope. She is my friend and I have grown fond of her. I would not see her hurt. You must think not only of your future, but hers, too, Pierce. I can never be a part of that future. I have made that abundantly clear. Accept it—and move on."

Nalyssa scrambled from the bed and began dressing. Pierce rolled from the other side and began doing the same.

The silence between them was deafening.

When she slipped into her corset, she was forced to ask, "Would you please help me tighten the strings? I cannot do this alone."

He came to her and did so without a word, so expertly that she knew he had done so on many previous occasions. Jealousy flared within her, and she tamped it down. She had no hold on this man. He was merely being a gentleman in wishing for them to wed. But he was a duke—and had a great future ahead of him. She would be an albatross about his neck if she allowed them to speak their vows to one another.

Nalyssa finished dressing, kneeling to collect the pins which he had pulled from her hair. She smoothed it into place as best she could without the aid of a comb and twisted it into a chignon, securing it in place with the pins.

By now, Pierce was almost dressed. He tied his cravat, one she supposed had belonged to the previous duke, thinking it clever of his valet to add it to the new duke's wardrobe.

She moved to make the bed.

He stepped to the opposite side and said, "No one comes here. I will make sure this is taken care of."

Turning abruptly, he left the bedchamber. She gazed upon the bed, thinking of the memories she now held.

And how the Duke of Stoneham had claimed her heart.

She joined him downstairs and headed to the kitchen, where she collected her stockings and slipped into them, followed by her boots. Mud was still clinging to the one boot, and she looked about the kitchen for something to clean it with.

Pierce had followed her and saw her dilemma. "Here, I will carry you again."

Though reluctant to be in his arms, Nalyssa allowed herself to be picked up. She told herself it was because she did not want to leave a muddy mess on the floor for servants. The truth was that she enjoyed this last bit of closeness with him, the feel of his powerful arms enfolded about her.

They left the dower house and walked the short distance to Stonecrest, where they were greeted by Pugh.

"We were a bit worried about you, Your Grace," the butler revealed. "You and Lady Nalyssa missed teatime. It is almost six o'clock."

When Pierce remained silent, she said, "I fear I am weary to the bone, Pugh. His Grace and I have walked several miles of the estate. I know we missed teatime. I hope that didn't inconvenience Cook. Since Her Grace and Lady Penelope are having trays sent to their rooms, might I do the same?"

She turned to Pierce. "After such strenuous exercise, Your Grace, I do not believe I would be a worthy dinner companion."

He nodded curtly and strode from the foyer.

"Is His Grace all right?" Pugh asked.

"It has been a difficult day for him," she replied truthfully. "He has conflicting feelings about his father. The scene Mr. Selkirk caused was also troubling and painful to His Grace. I believe the long walk did him some good, however. We talked a bit of today and his future, which I believe to be quite bright."

"Before you go upstairs, my lady, a few letters arrived for you," Pugh informed her.

"Good. They most likely are from people in town, ones I had asked to schedule appointments with."

Nalyssa took the time to open and read them before the butler, nodding in confirmation.

"Yes, we will need to leave Stonecrest sometime tomorrow for town, Pugh. In the next few days, we have appointments with a tailor, bootmaker, modiste, and milliner. We also will stop by an employment agency and hire a lady's maid for Her Grace. Would you please let Wattleby know? I am certain he will accompany us to town. The same goes for Jenny."

"I will inform the stables and both servants, my lady," the butler told her. "I will also tell His Grace. Might you need anything else?"

"No, thank you, Pugh. I will retire to my room now."

Nalyssa sat in the chair in her bedchamber, her mind drifting, until her dinner tray arrived. She picked at it, setting it outside her door and ringing for Jenny.

When the maid arrived, Nalyssa said, "We will leave for town in the morning after breakfast. You and Wattleby will accompany us. Would you pack my things now?"

"Of course, my lady. How long will we be in London?"

"Probably three or four days, but you are to pack all my belongings. I am not returning to Stonecrest."

Nalyssa saw the questions in Jenny's eyes and added, "I believe by the time the Selkirks are ready to return to Sussex, my task will be complete. There will be no need for me to return. If they have need of me once they return for the Season, I will be happy to accommodate any requests they have."

"The duke is a strong-willed man, isn't he, my lady?"

"He is," she agreed. "I believe he knows enough now and can enter Polite Society on his own terms."

As Jenny bustled about the room, she said, "Well, my lady, we know dukes pretty much do as they please. At least you had His Grace for a client. If he makes a good impression upon the *ton*, I hope that it will bring new clients to you."

"I hope so."

Nalyssa retreated to her chair, watching Jenny pack. When the maid finished, the servants helped Nalyssa undress for the evening.

"Please tell Her Grace and Lady Penelope that we will be leaving tomorrow when you go to them."

"I shall do so, my lady. Goodnight."

She climbed into bed, thinking of how she had lain in Pierce's arms only a few hours ago. He had been gentleman enough to propose the idea of marriage. She smiled. Or in a very Pierce-like way, he had merely informed her they were to wed. She couldn't help but chuckle. Bringing her fingertips to her lips, she touched them gingerly, saddened that she would never taste his kiss nor feel his touch ever again. Still, it had been worth it to see what the world of lovemaking was like.

It was all for the best, however, because Nalyssa now had a monumental task ahead of her. She must do everything in her power to forget Pierce Selkirk and what had passed between them. It would be difficult, however.

Because she had fallen in love with him.

Chapter Eighteen

Pierce had been disappointed that his meeting with Dixon, his steward, had to be put off, even if they were going to the great city of London. He had decided to ask Dixon to ride to town with them, however, so they could speak of the estate's business on the way.

As they rode, he'd assumed the ladies would have their separate conversation, but he was proven wrong. Nalyssa seemed quite interested in what Dixon had to say regarding Stonecrest and asked far more questions of the estate manager than Pierce did himself. He could tell how much she knew about the running of a large estate from her thoughtful questions and worried once more that he had ruined his chances with her.

And didn't even know how or why.

He didn't think their lovemaking had put her off yet something had. Even though she obviously had been a virgin, he had never felt the physical and emotional intimacy with any other woman as he had with her—and he knew he had pleased her greatly. He wondered if she might be experiencing guilt for having coupled outside of marriage. Still, she had refused him.

He would have to use the time they were together in London to his advantage and press his suit with her again, despite being turned down. He understood, in a fashion, why she had refused to marry him.

She had emphasized how he needed to wed a woman of his own rank, one without a spot of scandal attached to her name. It would help him assume his position in Polite Society. Moreover, it would help Pen when she made her come-out next year. If Pierce had learned anything from Nalyssa's tutelage, it was that a duke was in a lofty position of society. With so few of them, he could make his own rules. He was determined to make Nalyssa his wife.

Polite Society be damned.

Once they wed, the *ton* would come around. Pierce was certain of this. He didn't think marrying Nalyssa would hurt Pen's chances of making a good match if Nalyssa were her sister-in-law.

It certainly would make marriage more palatable to him.

He liked Nalyssa a great deal. She was warm and clever and very kind to all, be they servant or duke. He knew he would be rescuing her from a pit she had been tossed into, with no way out, a situation not of her own making, but one she had been blamed for a good decade now. He still had yet to figure out how to persuade her to agree to be his wife. That would be what this next week in London would consist of, finding a way to convince her to be his.

They arrived at the outskirts of London, and Pierce told Dixon they would pick up on their conversation once they reached the townhouse. For now, he wanted to take in the sights of this legendary city. The number and size of the various buildings amazed him. The streets teemed with people and carriages, with vendors selling all kinds of wares. Pierce couldn't wait to get out of the confines of his carriage and actually walk these streets and browse the many shops.

His carriage pulled into a huge square and stopped at the largest house on it. A thrill ran through him. It was still hard to believe the changes in his life and that this glorious townhouse belonged to him.

The party descended from the carriage and was met by Hassell and Mrs. Hassell, his town butler and housekeeper. Nalyssa had insisted that Pierce send word ahead that he would be arriving soon and he had done so, explaining he and his family would come to town for a brief visit in order to have clothes made up for the upcoming Season. Now, he introduced himself and the others as footmen scrambled to bring in luggage from the second carriage which had followed them, bringing Wattleby and Jenny along with them.

The Hassells led them inside. The foyer was grand and the chandelier hanging there probably cost more than Pierce would have earned in a lifetime at his haberdashery. He met the entire staff, making a point to stop the footmen carrying in the luggage so that he could also learn their names, as well.

Mrs. Hassell showed everyone to their rooms, and Pierce was astounded at the opulence of the townhouse. While Stonecrest was large and richly furnished, his London residence resembled a palace.

They agreed to meet in the foyer in half an hour so that Mrs. Hassell could take them on a tour of the place. When she did, Pierce lost count of the number of rooms but knew it had to equal that of Stonecrest. He supposed the townhouse was more sumptuous because more guests visited it than his country estate. With so much entertaining done in town, he assumed most townhouses were built and furnished to impress the members of the *ton* who came calling.

They had tea in the drawing room, inviting Dixon to join them, and Mama and Pen asked the steward a few questions of their own. Dixon was a friendly sort, knowledgeable and able to answer everything asked of him with ease.

Nalyssa suggested the gentlemen adjourn to the duke's study and continue their conversation once tea ended. He figured she had other tidbits to impart to Mama and Pen and so he took Dixon with him. By the end of the day, Pierce felt he had a solid grasp on the workings of Stonecrest and was eager to return and see more of the estate and its people.

He slept soundly and was the first at the breakfast table. The women followed shortly, along with Dixon, who would return to

Stonecrest today.

"What is scheduled for today, Lady Nalyssa?" Pierce asked.

"I will be accompanying Her Grace and Lady Penelope to the modiste. We will be at the shop several hours, choosing fabrics and discussing wardrobe needs. Both ladies will need to be measured. They should have several day gowns in their possession by the time we leave in a week."

"So, we will be in town a week?"

"Yes, Your Grace. As for you, the two of us will head to one of the most reputable tailors in town this afternoon."

Nalyssa provided him with the name of the shop and shared that their appointment began at one o'clock.

"Then I will meet you there, my lady," he informed her. "While you are at the modiste's, I plan to get out and see a bit of London on my own. What street is this tailor located on?"

She told him, and he said the ducal carriage would be at their disposal, ready to take them to their appointment and back and then deliver Nalyssa to the tailor's shop.

Breakfast ended, and Pierce set out. If he knew how to ride, he would have taken a horse so that he might cover more distance and see more of the city. For now, however, he was content to walk and decided the choice a better one than a carriage.

By walking, he was able to take in his surroundings better. The immense size of the townhouses overwhelmed him. He knew, of course, that he was in the poshest part of town and that not all of London would look like this, so clean and neat. Nalyssa had called this area of town Mayfair in the carriage, and Pierce left the residential part of it. The streets were clogged with vehicles. Carriages and carts, along with riders, came to and fro. Vendors and their carts lined the streets. He came across a row of exclusive shops, judging by the goods in their windows. Entering a bookshop, he was astounded by its size and the number of books on countless shelves. He would have to bring Pen here and let her shop to her heart's content. He thought to buy a book for Nalyssa but was afraid she wouldn't accept a gift from him. He left and entered several more shops, including leather goods, a chandler's, and a tobacconist.

He did pass the tailor's shop they would visit later today and did not go inside, instead continuing on until he reached a haberdashery. Going inside, Pierce walked it with interest, assessing the merchandise it carried and believing his The Crafty Gentleman goods to be equal to what he now saw.

Hearing his belly growl, he stopped and bought a meat pie from a street vendor, walking slowly as he savored each bite.

When it grew close to his appointment time, he made his way back to the tailor's, seeing his ducal carriage in front of it when he arrived. It was just like Nalyssa to be early for the appointment, and he entered the store with a smile.

Immediately, he was greeted by a gentleman with puffs of snowy-white hair on each side of his head, the top being bald.

"Ah, Your Grace. I am Mr. Tibbets. Lady Nalyssa has told me you are in need of an entire wardrobe. Shall we start?"

Pierce glanced to his left, seeing Nalyssa talking with a clerk as she thumbed through fabric samples.

"We better have my expert by my side, Mr. Tibbets."

"I have heard Your Grace is an expert when it comes to clothing," the tailor said. "Lady Nalyssa shared that you previously owned your own haberdashery before you came into your title." The older gentleman smiled. "On my travels, I have been into The Crafty Gentleman, Your Grace. I found it to be a fine establishment and was treated well by your staff. In fact, I bought my favorite cravat from the place and wear it on special occasions."

"I am sorry I do not remember you, Mr. Tibbets," Pierce apologized. "I usually have a good eye for a face, if not the name."

"You were buried in your ledgers. A Mr. Wilson assisted me. That is why you do not recall my visit, Your Grace. Come, let's consult with Lady Nalyssa. She has already given me quite a lengthy list as to your needs."

They joined Nalyssa and she said, "Oh, Mr. Tibbets, I am finding some wonderful selections. Good afternoon, Your Grace," she added, acknowledging Pierce.

"I hear you and Mr. Tibbets have already discussed my wardrobe. Other than being measured, I am not quite certain *I* am needed here," he said teasingly.

"You have a fine eye for fashion and quality goods," she told him. "You must be included in this entire process."

"Shall we sit?" Tibbets suggested, leading them to a set of chairs. He motioned to his clerks, one bringing fabric samples and the other a pad and pencil to take notes as they spoke.

"Walk me through this list of yours, my lady," Pierce said. "I would like an idea of not only what I need but *why* I need it."

For the next ten minutes, Nalyssa elaborated on the various requirements a duke would have and what would be worn to each event. She also described what he would wear every day, not only in town, but in the country. As she spoke, she suggested various materials, flipping through samples and showing what she meant.

"Thank you for sharing," he told her. "I like to be informed."

Then he took the samples from her and began making suggestions for which materials he would like to be made up for him. Mr. Tibbets nodded in agreement and occasionally made a suggestion, which Pierce always approved of. He knew between this tailor and Nalyssa that he might very well become the best dressed gentleman in London.

"It is time to see you measured, Your Grace," Tibbets said. "We shall go to a separate room for that. May I offer you a cup of tea, my lady, while we are gone?"

"Thank you, Mr. Tibbets. I believe I will wait for tea until we return to His Grace's townhouse."

Pierce accompanied the tailor to the back and was measured from head to toe.

"I will send your measurements to the shirtmaker Lady Nalyssa has selected. That way, you won't have to endure this process twice."

"Thank you for your thoughtfulness. May I see your cutting and sewing rooms?"

Surprise filled the tailor's face. "Of course, Your Grace, though no one has ever asked to do so in all the years I have been working here. My grandfather started this shop. I toiled under him and then my own father before I inherited the place."

"Lady Nalyssa might find this interesting, as well." He turned to a clerk. "Have her summoned if you would."

Nalyssa joined them. "I am eager to see your other rooms, Mr. Tibbets. No client has ever asked to do so before." She gave Pierce a smile, one which made him grow weak in the knees. "Then again, I have a most unusual client this year."

They went first to the cutting room, a large, airy place with numerous tables. He watched a few of the men at work and then went to one.

"No, it is much easier another way—and it is more efficient. May I show you?"

The tailor looked confused and turned to Tibbets, who nodded and said, "His Grace knows about tailoring. Step aside and allow him to demonstrate."

Pierce asked the tailor a few questions and then turned to the fabric. He began to cut and explained what he was doing as he worked. Soon, the other three tailors in the room, along with Nalyssa and Mr. Tibbets, had gathered around him, listening to his lesson.

"I have never seen cloth cut with that method, Your Grace," Tibbets said, his eyes twinkling. "Thank you for showing it to us. It will certainly save time. Would you mind allowing all my tailors to cut in this manner as you walk them through it?"

"I would be happy to do so."

Quickly, Tibbets had each man return to his station and then had a clerk list the duke's measurements on a large slate at the front of the room. The tailor and his clerks brought bolts of material which had been selected for Pierce's new coats, and these were given to each tailor.

Pierce said, "Instead of speaking to the group as a whole, I would prefer going to each station and watching each man cut."

For the next twenty minutes he did so, walking the staff through the measuring and cutting before returning to Tibbets and Nalyssa.

"You were taught well, Your Grace. This will save my staff considerable time. Thank you for sharing your knowledge with us."

"When I bought my haberdashery, I wanted to learn every step of a process. One of the two tailors I hired taught me how to sew." He chuckled. "I do so better than my sister."

"You better not let your valet know what you can do or he will be out of a job," Mr. Tibbets said, laughing. "I will have my staff begin on your wardrobe at once, Your Grace. As you see, they are already making headway on it as we speak. Return in two days' time for a first fitting."

The shop owner turned to Nalyssa. "How long are you in town, my lady?"

"A week, Mr. Tibbets, then His Grace will return to Stonecrest."

Pierce noted she did not include herself.

"After the fitting two days from now, we can finish up quite a few pieces for you, Your Grace. I will make certain we work exclusively for you this week. After your lesson, my tailors will be more than happy to focus on your wardrobe. Once you've come for that fitting, we can schedule another, final fitting three days later. You may take everything completed at that point. We will continue to build upon your wardrobe while you are in the country." Tibbets smiled. "If you weren't a duke, Your Grace, you would be hired upon the spot for my shop."

"That is quite the compliment since Lady Nalyssa tells me you are the best tailor in London, Mr. Tibbets."

"Lady Nalyssa has brought me many customers over the years, helping my reputation to grow. None as unique as you have ever walked through my doors, however. It will be a pleasure making up your wardrobe this Season—and I hope for many more to come."

Pierce thanked the man, and he and Nalyssa left the tailor's shop. As they approached his carriage he asked, "Do you have a maid waiting in the carriage? You have mentioned how young, single women must be chaperoned wherever they go."

"I may be unwed, but I am not young, Your Grace. At least by Polite Society's standards. I am now of an age when I can serve as a chaperone to younger women since I am on the shelf."

She turned and allowed the footman to hand her into the carriage. Pierce followed, sitting not across from her but beside her. She didn't speak and turned her gaze out the window as the horses started up.

"You earned every penny you were paid by my father today," he told her. "Although I do know about clothing, you brought insight and experience into the choices. If I have not told you before, I appreciate the services you have provided to my family and me."

She turned from the window, their gazes meeting. "Your father desperately wanted you to fit into the *ton*, Your Grace. He knew I could help make that a reality."

"Do you reject me because I wasn't raised in his household? Do you believe, as others will, that I shouldn't be a duke?"

She frowned. "You *are* the Duke of Stoneham. Your background and upbringing do not matter. As it is, your mother did a wonderful job raising you and your sister. Your transition into Polite Society will be a smooth one, Your Grace. You already have impeccable manners. Soon, you will have the wardrobe and look the part. You will also be armed with the knowledge of the rules and idiosyncrasies which the *ton* adheres to. No one would ever guess you were not born and bred for the role."

Nalyssa paused. "You will make an excellent duke."

"Then why won't you marry me?" he asked softly.

She shook her head stubbornly. "You must respect my wishes. I am doing what is best for you."

Pierce cupped her cheek. "I know what is best for me—and that is you."

He lowered his head and kissed her, sensing the spark that flickered to life between them. His gut told him that he might never get enough of this woman.

She did not protest. Nor did she push him away. Instead, Nalyssa kissed him back, and Pierce felt the magic in that kiss. They continued their heated kisses the entire way to the townhouse. When the carriage began to slow, however, she pulled away. He saw regret—and tears—in her eyes.

Reaching up, she brushed a lock of hair from his brow. "I cannot wed you. Please get this foolish notion out of your head, Pierce. And I beg you not to kiss me ever again. Be the gentleman I know you to be and please honor my wishes."

The door opened, and Nalyssa quickly moved to it, exiting the carriage. Pierce followed, the fear of losing her engulfing him. And it wasn't only being afraid of not having her in his life. It was much more.

For Pierce knew in that moment—despite everything—that he had fallen in love with Nalyssa Shelbourne.

Chapter Nineteen

PIERCE SAT AT his desk, frustration filling him. His feelings toward Nalyssa had not changed—or lessened—in the seven weeks since his family had left London and returned to Stonecrest. Nalyssa had remained behind, telling Mama and Pen that she would correspond with them weekly and see them once they returned to town.

She had been as good as her word, sending lengthy letters two to three times a week to all three of them. He never asked Mama or Pen what their letters contained. His were full of information that Nalyssa deemed necessary for him to know. She wrote of a place called Tattersall's, which sold the best horses, even telling him what to look for when he eventually purchased some on his own. She had told him of White's, a club for gentlemen, explaining the layout of the building and the activities within. Not only did she tell him how to claim his membership at White's, but she also explained the process of how he was to take his seat in the House of Lords.

She even told him how to go about having an affair after he wed.

Nalyssa explained that most *ton* marriages were ones of conveniences. Although she hoped he would find a woman he might love, she understood that might not be the case, going into great detail that oftentimes marriages were made for political alliances. If that were the case and he found he did not love the woman he took as his duchess, it was perfectly permissible for him to have an affair. She cautioned him, though, telling Pierce that it would be wiser to get his heir and spare off his wife before he pursued such an avenue. Her explanation included writing that affairs were a practice deeply ensconced within the *ton*, and as long as he practiced discretion and did not publicly embarrass his duchess, he would be well within his rights to conduct one—or multiple—affairs.

She even gave him pointers on how to keep things clandestine, detailing places and ways he might meet his lover. If he decided it would be more practical to keep a mistress, Nalyssa explained where to find one and how to set up a residence for her, recommending a specific neighborhood and even appropriate gifts for him to give this mistress.

Pierce had been shocked but realized Nalyssa was merely being thorough in her preparation. After all, he had openly spoken to her of his disdain toward love and not wanting to suffer as his mother had.

But suffer now, he did.

They had returned to town a week ago, and Nalyssa became a regular visitor to his household, coming daily for various reasons. She had hired a dance master for him in order for him to review what she had taught him and allow him to get in some practice before the night of the opening ball. She even had Pen attend these lessons, as well, having the siblings partner together while she observed. Pierce had thought he might get her to dance at least once with him, but that had not come to pass.

They had gone riding together once, accompanied by his head groom in town. Pierce had ridden daily at Stonecrest, taking all of Pinchel's lessons to heart. He now felt at home in the saddle, and Nalyssa even praised his riding form. She had directed them to Rotten Row and watched as he and the groom raced up and down it.

Nalyssa had looked over the wardrobes created for the three of them, suggesting what they should wear at tonight's opening ball at Lord and Lady Capwell's residence. She was coming this afternoon for tea in order to impart last bits of wisdom before he and Mama made their debut into Polite Society.

A knock sounded at the door, and Pierce called, "Come."

When the door swung open, he saw Annie enter his study. She closed the door and came to sit in the chair in front of his desk.

Smiling, he told her, "I am so glad you decided to come to town with us, Annie. We would not know what to do without you."

"You have a fine staff at both your houses, Mr. Pierce."

Annie did address him correctly when in front of others, but Pierce was glad she remained familiar to him behind closed doors. The woman had been almost a mother to him and Pen and a good friend to Mama, as well as their loyal servant.

"I wanted to see how you are doing," Annie continued. "I know your mother is both excited and nervous for tonight. How are you?"

"I find it hard to say, Annie," Pierce admitted. "I know Mama and I will be talked about by everyone who attends tonight's opening ball. Somehow, I will be universally accepted by a large body of strangers simply because I hold a title I never knew I would. Lady Nalyssa has warned me that gentlemen will fawn over me, trying to gain my friendship, while ladies seeking to wed will throw themselves at my feet. I may need to talk over what occurs tonight with you, Annie. You have always had a good head on your shoulders and been a good judge of character. Your advice to me has always been sound."

"None of that matters, Mr. Pierce." Annie paused and added, "Especially since you are in love with Lady Nalyssa. I expect you will make her your bride."

Pierce's jaw dropped. "What are you talking about?"

Annie gave him a knowing look. "I was clear in what I said to you, Mr. Pierce. I suppose you haven't worked out your feelings yet for the young lady. Are you going to make her your wife or not?"

Bitterness filled him. "I have already tried and failed to do so, Annie." He raked a hand through his hair. "I didn't ask her to marry me as much as assume she would."

Annie clucked her tongue. "That wasn't smart on your part, Mr. Pierce. Lady Nalyssa is a strong woman, one of good character, but she still is a woman. She would not want to be told what to do. Instead, she will need to be courted by you."

"You aren't hearing what I said. She refused me, Annie," Pierce said, not mincing words. "It goes back a good decade, to when her father killed himself. He left her destitute. No dowry. No prospects."

"Why would that matter?" Annie asked, round-eyed. "Lady Nalyssa is a beautiful, charming woman. Frankly, I'm surprised she isn't already married."

"According to her, men look for two things in a wife. First and foremost, a large dowry. The other? Social connections. She has neither. She taught her country bumpkin cousin how to be an earl and has earned her living in that manner ever since then. No gentleman will consider her as his wife because of the horrible gossip her father's suicide caused, along with the fact she brings no dowry and actually works for a living."

Annie snorted. "Well, I like her even more for knowing all of this. I suppose you do, too."

"How did you know I have feelings for her?"

"Because when you think no one is looking, you can't help but stare at her. You need to let your feelings be known, Mr. Pierce. If you being a duke has such an impact, then Lady Nalyssa can regain her respectability if she simply marries you."

"As much as I wish for that, I can tell you that she won't do it. She's stubborn as hell. She believes I need to make a brilliant marriage and that will lead to Pen making one, as well."

"She is close with Miss Penelope and would want the best for her," Annie agreed. "I still think you being a duke outweighs everything."

Annie's gaze bored into him. "You must make things right, Mr. Pierce. You need to love this woman, but good. If she has been an object of gossip for ten years, it will take a miracle to restore her reputation—and marrying a duke could do just that. I'm afraid if you don't, both you and she will be unhappy for the rest of your lives."

"I plan to keep trying, Annie. I just hope I can meet with success."

She rose. "I have faith in you, Mr. Pierce. You were the most determined child I'd ever seen when I came to you and your mother. Harness that determination and make things right for both you and Lady Nalyssa."

"I better head to the drawing room," he told her. "Tea will begin soon and Lady Nalyssa is our only guest."

Pierce went upstairs and found Mama and Pen already in the drawing room with Nalyssa. She had her back to him as he approached, but he could hear the animation in her voice. Mama and Pen already adored Nalyssa. Pierce had to find a way to make her his.

As a last resort, he could ruin her. She had explained very carefully to him in a lengthy letter how a woman might be publicly ruined, voicing her fears that some young lady might try to trap him into marriage. Although he knew it might be a way to force to wed him if he compromised her, it would be done under a cloud. Pierce did not want that. Not only did he want her to accept his offer willingly, but he also wanted no scandal associated with their marriage. He wanted the *ton* to know he held the utmost respect for his duchess and not have them believe he was forced to wed her.

"Ah, Stoneham," Mama said. "Come and join us. We are talking of Lord and Lady Capwell's ball this evening. Nalyssa has agreed to ride to the ball with us. She will take us around the ballroom before the dancing begins, introducing us to others."

Pierce thought it ridiculous that people could not even speak to one another unless they had been introduced by a third party, familiar to both, prior to their meeting. He was used to approaching strangers who came into his store and speaking to them, learning about them, and helping them make their selections. The fact that he could not approach someone at a *ton* event and greet them without a previous introduction was one of the ridiculous rules of the *ton*.

He took a seat in a chair since Nalyssa sat beside Pen and there was no room for him on the settee. The teacart arrived, and they had a lively teatime, with Nalyssa entertaining them with stories about various members of Polite Society.

"You will have to make special note of all the gowns the girls making their come-outs wear this evening," Pen said. "I cannot wait to do so myself next Season."

Pierce smiled to himself, glad to hear his sister's enthusiasm. Pen could be a bit shy at times. Hearing that she eagerly awaited her own come-out was good news.

"Nalyssa, you must help us with Penelope's come-out next year," Mama insisted.

"I don't believe I will be needed, Amanda. After all, Penelope has sat in on almost every lesson I have given you. I have written her at length and discussed what her come-out will entail. I have even arranged for the dance master who has come to your townhouse this week to return next year to work with her." She paused. "Besides, His Grace will have wed. I am certain his duchess will guide Penelope."

"I may or may not wed by Season's end," Pierce declared, seeing Nalyssa's brow furrow.

"I have made this clear to you, Your Grace," she said sternly. "You will be accepted more quickly into Polite Society if you marry by Season's end—and marry well. It will make Penelope's come-out go more smoothly if you do so. Her chances of making a more suitable match are much greater." She tilted her head, a teasing light coming into her eyes. "Besides, you are thirty and growing long in the tooth. You need to wed and secure your ducal line."

"I agree with Nalyssa, Stoneham," Mama said. "You must wed, not only for yourself—but for your sister."

Nalyssa opened her reticule and withdrew a folded page. Handing it to Pierce, she said, "This is the list of candidates which I would like you to consider. You may eliminate women from it as the Season progresses. You may also wish to add a few names if a certain lady attracts your attention favorably. Do you still have the name of the florist I recommended? It is imperative that you send bouquets to those ladies you are interested in and will call upon. I expect you to start making your calls on women of good character tomorrow afternoon."

Oh, she was as organized and obstinate as any army officer. "Yes, my lady, I know the florist's name and have given it to my secretary."

Pierce opened the paper and glanced at the list, seeing over a dozen names upon it.

"I would like to go over this list now with you, Your Grace, and tell you a little about each name upon it," Nalyssa said. "I have created this list carefully. As you can see, it is broken down by girls making their come-outs this Season, ones who have a Season or two behind them, and a couple of young widows returning to social occasions after their mourning period. There are fifteen names in all. I hope you will find this list useful and that your future duchess is among these names."

He glanced at the names on the list again, knowing not one of them would hold a candle to the woman who had composed the list.

Passing the sheet to his mother, he said, "Tell us about each lady you have placed here, my lady. If I am going into battle tonight, I must know my enemy."

Mama clucked her tongue. In a rare breach of etiquette, she hissed, "Pierce! These women are not your enemies. One of them, most likely, will become your wife. I am sure that Nalyssa took time and care to compose this list for you. You are to be respectful to her and the ladies who appear upon it."

Mama turned to Nalyssa. "Tell us something about each candidate for Stoneham. The first name is Lady Martha Milton."

Nalyssa launched into an explanation of each name on the list. Pierce sat, pretending to listen, but did not hear a word she spoke. All he could do was study her and think of how she would make for an excellent marriage partner and a formidable Duchess of Stoneham.

Nalyssa finished speaking. "Do you have any questions for me, Your Grace?"

He smiled. "Only what time you wish for my carriage to call upon you tonight, my lady."

Chapter Twenty

NALYSSA TRIED TO calm her racing heart. She sat at her dressing table, gazing at her reflection. She was already dressed for the ball in a gown from four Seasons ago, one which Jenny had dyed from pale blue to a shade of deep midnight, bringing out the blue in Nalyssa's eyes. Her former maid had already redone the sleeves and placed trim around the edge of the gown before she had left Nalyssa's household. No one looking at her would realize the gown was years old.

Then again, no one truly saw her at these balls.

She knew she continued to be invited for several reasons, one of them being pity. Another was so members of the *ton* could watch her as her latest protégé make his entrance into Polite Society. It was no secret that she had been working with the Duke of Stoneham prior to this Season. She had already seen references to it in the gossip columns of the newspapers. While she had not had anyone ask her if Stoneham might be her client, various clerks in London shops had seen her with the duke, duchess, and Lady Penelope.

More items had appeared in the newspapers regarding the passing of the Duke of Stoneham and the title shifting to the new Stoneham, Pierce Selkirk. Much was made of the fact that his father had wed a Cambridge clergyman's daughter, who bore him two children, and how these children and the duke's wife lived apart from him while he took on another as his wife.

Nalyssa actually agreed with the former Lord Hardwell, believing his sister, Lady Eliza, would not suffer much from learning she was a bastard. The few Scots who came to London looking for a bride rarely returned to socialize once they claimed one. Nalyssa recalled Lady Eliza being extremely in love by the end of last Season, marrying a Highlander laird and leaving England shortly after the Season ended. It was less than two weeks later that the Duchess of Stoneham had died and talk began of the duke's poor health.

The gossip columnists had been especially cruel to Edwin Selkirk, mocking him and his resemblance to his father and delighting that he'd had his title of Earl of Hardwell stripped from him. That title would be reserved for the eldest son of the current duke. Nalyssa hoped Edwin Selkirk would learn to be happy as a country gentleman and not stir up trouble for Pierce.

She placed her palm against her heart, still feeling it beat in double-time at the mere thought of the duke. How many times had she lain in bed, reliving every moment as he had touched her, bringing her to the heights of ecstasy? It was foolish to continue to do so, but she couldn't help herself. She was madly in love with Pierce. At the same time, she was encouraging him to wed anyone *but* her. Nalyssa doubted even marrying a duke could restore her tattered reputation. It would be selfish to do so and keep him and his family from the company they should keep.

Tonight, she would do her best to introduce him to those who mattered most to the *ton*. She had no doubt Pierce could handle himself in any situation. Amanda, too, would win over most of the doubters with her sweet nature and gracious manner though Nalyssa would keep her eyes out for any man who might try to cozy up to her because of her son's title. Hopefully, Pierce would work his way through the list Nalyssa had provided to him and find not only a suitable duchess but a woman who would suit him, as well. After all, what woman wouldn't be attracted to the new Duke Stoneham? He was sinfully handsome, with his impressive frame and mesmerizing eyes. The small cleft in his chin, the only thing he seemed to have inherited from his father, other than his title, only added to his good looks.

The only thing she truly worried about was some young lady and her enterprising mother backing Pierce into a corner and having it look as if the duke had compromised the young woman. While she had warned him of this very thing, Nalyssa believed Pierce thought himself invulnerable to such a ruse. Little did he know how scheming women of the *ton* could be. She would watch him like a hawk tonight. Not because she wanted to—but because it would be for his own good.

At least that's what she told herself.

She raised her wrist and sniffed, smelling the rose scent that clung to her. Perfume was something that she never indulged in. Usually, she used an unscented soap and added no oils to her bathwater. Those could prove to be expensive, and she made economies when and where she could. Her practical, frugal nature never allowed her to spend money on herself, knowing how tight her budget was and if she didn't pull in new clients, it would be easy to lose everything she had.

At Stonecrest, however, Mrs. Pugh had provided her with not only scented soap but the most expensive of bath oils, both a rose scent. Nalyssa had wrapped what remained of the bar of soap and brought it home with her, as well as a small vial of the rose oil. She had used both in her bath a short while ago, feeling she smelled like a princess now. It would be nice if she had a necklace or earrings to wear, but those items had been taken from her and sold long ago when her father was trying to make a dent in his debts. Nalyssa told herself it didn't matter. That no eyes would truly be upon her, assessing her appearance. She would merely receive the occasional glance as others followed Stoneham's every move, as well as that of his mother, and then look to her to see her reactions. She had no fear with these clients. Of all those she had worked with, Pierce and Amanda were the easiest to prepare for their entrance into Polite Society.

Wrapping a shawl about her because the early April night was cool, Nalyssa left her bedchamber and went downstairs to wait for the arrival of the duke and duchess. She stood next to the window in the parlor. When she saw the ducal carriage pull up, she went to the front door and let herself out, having no butler or housekeeper to do so. Her cook and maid had already gone to bed. Usually, Jenny had let Nalyssa out and then slept until her mistress came home. Now, however, Jenny was happily employed elsewhere, no doubt paid far more than what she had earned at Nalyssa's house.

The footman opened the carriage door. Before he could hand her up, Pierce bounded from the vehicle and down the stairs.

He paused, taking in her appearance. "You look breathtaking, Nalyssa."

She did not bother to correct him, enjoying the compliment while she could, knowing that most likely after tonight, she would not be riding to a *ton* event with this pair.

"Thank you, Your Grace," she said, giving him her gloved hand and allowing him to help her into the carriage as a shiver ran through her at the touch.

He followed behind her, choosing to sit next to her and not his mother. Nalyssa felt his body heat and caught a whiff of sandalwood.

"Don't you look lovely, my dear," Amanda praised.

"Thank you, Your Grace," she said, choosing to set the tone in the carriage for tonight. "I hope you are pleased with what the modiste did. I have never seen you look more beautiful."

"Thank you," her friend said. "I don't believe there's a single gown I am displeased with. The same is true for Penelope. It has been exciting for the three of us to all have new clothing to wear."

"I have visited a few other tailors and haberdasheries," Pierce shared. "None reflect the quality of Mr. Tibbets' shop."

"I assured you that you would be pleased with Mr. Tibbets' work," she reminded. "His reputation has grown the last several years. In fact, he moved into the space he now occupies over three years ago because he needed more room with his client list growing."

"He told me if I weren't a duke that he would hire me as a tailor. I took that as the highest of compliments." The duke's satisfied smile let her know just how pleased he had been, and she did not remind him that she had been standing beside him when Tibbets awarded the compliment. "Any last words of advice?"

"Only that you should dance every dance possible," she said. "No ducking into the card room tonight. I want you to speak with as many of the names on your list as possible. I also want you to go to White's as soon as you can. You will meet gentlemen tonight and can follow up on forming friendships with them at White's."

"Do you also have a list of appropriate men I should become friends with?"

She heard the teasing in his tone. "No, but I could draw one up if you wish," she said saucily.

Pierce laughed, and Nalyssa and the duchess joined in the laughter. She was glad the pair was in such high spirits.

The carriage began to slow, and she glanced out the window. "Oh, dear. It is as I feared. The opening ball is always one of the best-attended ones of the Season. Your coachman may have to park farther away than you would like."

"I have never minded walking," Amanda said. "The pavement is dry after this morning's brief storm. It is not as if my son will have to carry us to the Capwells' front door."

She glanced to Pierce and saw his eyes darken, knowing he recalled their walk after his father's funeral and how he carried her into the dower house after her boots became muddied.

And of what they had done once inside.

Gathering her shawl more tightly about her, she said, "I believe your coachman has gotten us as close as he can. Before we disembark, though, I want to remind you that there will be some gossip about you—though none will reach your ears. Have confidence in who you both are and simply be yourselves. That will do nicely."

The door opened, and she gave her hand to the footman, who saw her safely to the ground.

After the other two descended from the carriage, she said, "Go ahead if you will. You will join the receiving line once you enter the townhouse. I am afraid it can be dreadfully long this first night. I will meet you once you enter the ballroom and take you about, introducing you to as many people as I can before the dancing begins."

"You aren't joining us?" Amanda asked.

"No, Your Grace. I never take part in receiving lines."

Nalyssa hurried off, worried that Pierce would demand that she stay with them and go through the line together. She had nothing to say to her hosts, however, and no one would have talked to her while they were in line. It was better for Pierce and Amanda to do these things on their own. As they did, she would take note of everyone already gathered inside the ballroom and watch for the new arrivals. She would then take her clients on a turn about the room, introducing them to the right people and making certain Pierce signed programmes along the way.

Entering the townhouse, she avoided the receiving line and took a moment to locate the retiring room so that she could share that information with Amanda. Then Nalyssa entered the ballroom and quickly turned to her left. She moved to a large potted plant and stood beside it, her eyes skimming the room. Carefully, she made mental notes of those who Pierce and Amanda should meet as she watched the doorway for others. So far, she had spotted seven ladies on her list and had seen an eighth exiting the retiring room. All fifteen were bound to be at this opening ball. She did have preferences on the list but had not wanted to sway Pierce in any way. She hoped he would be attracted to one of those fifteen women and that he might actually fall in love with his wife, despite him lecturing her on how he never wanted to be in love.

If she could see him happy and wed, maybe her heart would stop hurting so much. Right now, he was still available, tempting her to consider another tryst with him. It was important that he find an appropriate lady and become quickly betrothed, if only to signal to her that he was now forbidden fruit. Once Pierce became engaged, Nalyssa would stop attending events for the rest of the Season. She had no other clients to look after. Better to lick her wounds in private than allow anyone to learn she had foolishly fallen in love with the Duke of Stoneham.

Her eyes passed the orchestra and then doubled back. Curiously, a woman was seated among the musicians, one she had never seen play before at a *ton* event. Nalyssa didn't even know women might be allowed within an orchestra. The woman was petite, with golden blond hair and a delicate bone structure. She almost looked as if she could be a member of the *ton*. It would be interesting to keep an eye on the gossip columns and see if any of them bothered to follow up with a story about a female musician entertaining at a *ton* event.

After several minutes, she saw Pierce crossing the threshold, Amanda on his arm. Even though this was his first ball and he was a stranger to this crowd, Pierce looked as if he owned this place. His elegant evening clothes and their cut only accentuated his fine looks and muscular frame. Amanda, though she must be in her late forties by now, looked regal and as attractive as much younger women.

Quickly, she made her way toward her clients and joined them, facing them and keeping her back to the room.

"Try not to be too obvious," she began, telling them where various people from the list stood and what those ladies wore. "If you are unsure about whether you are to sign a dance card or not, Your Grace, merely look at me. I will indicate yes with a nod. If my head does not move, you are under no obligation to sign. Unless it is someone not on the list that you find interesting."

She turned then, facing the room, knowing many curious glances had come their way.

"Shall we?" she said, smiling.

Sometimes, a nobleman and his wife might turn away as she approached with a client in a subtle snub. Tonight, however, no such actions occurred. Everyone wanted to meet the new Duke of Stoneham and his mother, the duchess, who was hidden away for years and only now stepped out into Polite Society as a widow. While Nalyssa knew some within this room hoped the pair failed miserably, she believed a majority would be won over by the two.

They circulated about the room, with Nalyssa making the appropriate introductions and then stepping aside so the duke and duchess could converse briefly. A few times, Pierce looked to her, and she signaled him to sign the programme of the lady he had just met. Of all the women on the list, Lady Martha Milton seemed to have the most genuine smile and true interest in Pierce. Most of the others saw him as nothing more than a duke. Not a person—but a title. Lady Martha seemed different, and Nalyssa hoped that Pierce noticed that difference.

As they had made a full circle of the ballroom, a trio stepped from the entryway, and she recognized the former Viscount North, now the Duke of Linberry. North's father and grandfather had both died a year or so ago, with the viscount leaping from earl to duke in less than a day. She liked North very much and thought Pierce would, too.

In Linberry's company were the Duke and Duchess of Westfield. Westfield had made quite a stir last Season with a very public proposal. Even the musicians had stopped playing as the duke dropped to one knee, asking Lady Margaret Townsend for her hand in marriage. The moment had been breathtaking to watch. Nalyssa could still hear

Westfield say how he loved Lady Margaret more than life itself.

Then when his proposal had been accepted, Westfield gave his new fiancée the most passionate kiss witnessed by Polite Society, a kiss which Nalyssa believed would be talked about for years to come.

She smiled to herself. *These* were definitely two men Pierce would get along with.

"I spy two dukes I think may become close friends of yours," she told Pierce, leading them in the direction of the three.

As they approached, she saw Linberry gazing about the ballroom, distracted, and wondered whom he searched for. His time of mourning was up, and she supposed now he held the ducal title that Linberry would be searching for his duchess.

"Your Grace?" she asked, gaining his attention for a moment. "May I present to you His Grace, the Duke of Stoneham, and his mother, the Duchess of Stoneham?"

Linberry greeted them absentmindedly and then excused himself, heading straight for the orchestra. Nalyssa had no time to waste, fearing the Westfields might turn away.

Stepping up again, she said, "Your Graces, I am honored to introduce you to the Duke of Stoneham and his mother, the Duchess of Stoneham."

Fortunately, the couple greeted her clients with warmth, and they stood chatting a moment.

"Lady Nalyssa, please come join us," Westfield said, taking a step back to make room for her within their circle. "I hear you are new to your title, Stoneham," Westfield continued.

"New to everything," Pierce said cheerfully. "The money. The title. The houses. The clothes."

The Duchess of Westfield laughed. "It is refreshing to hear one speak in such a manner, Your Grace. And you look lovely tonight, Your Grace. Might I ask who your modiste is?"

The two duchesses began conversing. Nalyssa had not met the

duchess before this evening but certainly knew of her. As Lady Margaret Townsend, she had been a portrait artist, something the *ton* disapproved of. Her husband had encouraged her to keep painting, though, and Lady Margaret had done so, even as she had given birth to a child a couple of months ago. Yes, this unconventional pair would be good for Pierce to know and possibly even show him what he could do as a duke. The Westfields, being a love match, would also be a shining example to Pierce and show him love and marriage could go hand in hand.

"Forgive Linberry," Westfield said. "He normally possesses the best of manners. His head has been turned by love, however. I am hoping he will succeed in making a match with Lady Fia Sawyer."

The duke glanced across the ballroom, and Nalyssa saw Linberry conversing with the female member of the orchestra.

Linberry was interested in *her*?

"Have you been in town long?" Westfield asked.

"Not long enough to cause any trouble," Pierce replied.

Westfield laughed. "Perhaps you'd like to meet at White's."

"I am told that I am a member. I suppose I should see the place at some point," Pierce said.

"Linberry and I have an appointment in the morning. Perhaps we could meet up the day after tomorrow?"

"I would like that, Westfield."

"The dancing is about to start," the Duchess of Westfield said. "Would you care to sup with us this evening, Your Graces? And you, as well, my lady."

"We would be delighted to," Pierce answered for the three of them. "We will see you then."

The Westfields moved away, and Nalyssa said, "Westfield is well thought of, Your Graces. I would encourage a friendship between you."

"The duchess is charming," Amanda said. "She told me she paints portraits. I told her she simply must paint my son."

"I will have to think about that," Pierce grumbled. "It doesn't sound like much fun."

"But your portrait could hang in the picture gallery at Stonecrest," Amanda said. "We will talk about this with Her Grace at supper."

"Do you know your first dance partner?" Nalyssa asked. "You should go to her now. Your mother and I will join the matrons."

Pierce frowned. "You are not a matron."

"Neither am I someone who is ever asked to dance," she said lightly. "It is where I always sit. Go, Your Grace," she urged, leading Amanda away.

They reached the section of chairs and Lady Rawlins waved them over. Ignoring Nalyssa, she said, "Oh, you must sit with us, Your Grace. We are so eager to talk with you."

"Thank you, my lady." Amanda turned toward Nalyssa.

"Go ahead. I always sit in the corner. I must watch Stoneham. If I am talking, I might miss something. Please, make friends, Your Grace."

Reluctantly, she saw Amanda join Lady Rawlins and her friends. Nalyssa slipped away and sat at the end of the chairs, her usual spot. Rarely did anyone ever address her. They knew enough not to be seen speaking with her, especially when she was working, as she was now. She would observe her client and share with him those observations on the carriage ride home.

Pierce danced with Lady Martha Milton in the opening set. It was a country dance, lively in pace. She saw that he never missed a step and seemed to be having the time of his life. Tamping down the jealousy that threatened to eat her alive, Nalyssa watched in silence as he went from partner to partner as the evening progressed. She had neglected to ask him which young lady he would partner with for the supper dance. He knew enough not to ask anyone to dance twice this first evening. She had been strict on that account, wanting him to meet as many eligible women as possible. It was too bad that Lady Martha had not been his choice for the supper dance. Still, Pierce would be able to call upon her tomorrow afternoon.

The orchestra finished their tune and couples left the dance floor, searching for their new partners for the supper dance. She lost track of Pierce in the crowd and sat tall, leaning to see if she could spot him.

"Looking for someone in particular?"

Nalyssa shot to her feet, finding the subject of her search before her. "You need to find your partner, Your Grace. The dance is about to start."

His eyes gleamed at her. "I have found my partner, my lady. It is you."

CHAPTER TWENTY-ONE

"NO," NALYSSA HISSED.

Just as Pierce had expected she would.

He merely smiled at her, seeing her irritation grow.

"Your Grace, I do not dance. Ever."

"Why, I know that to be a bald-faced lie, my lady. You *do* dance, exceedingly well. I know so because you are the one who first taught me how to dance."

"Let me clarify for you. I do not dance in public."

She seated herself, and he did not move.

"Go on," she encouraged. "It is not too late to find another partner."

"I have found the partner I wish to dance my first waltz with," he insisted genially. "Now stand up and take my arm, or you will bring unwanted attention to me. To us."

Nalyssa rose. "You are committing social suicide by being so disagreeable and insisting we dance together." She placed her hand on his sleeve. "Don't say I didn't warn you."

This battle over, Pierce began leading her onto the dance floor. Her fingers tightened on his forearm, and she brought them to a halt.

"Here is fine," she said quietly.

"Nonsense. This is the edge of the dance floor. I have taken quite a liking to the center of the ballroom floor. After all, I have been the center of attention tonight. Why stop now?"

They started up again, her fingers digging into his arm, indicating her displeasure with him. It did not matter. He was about to waltz with the woman he loved in front of all Polite Society.

Let the gossip begin.

Pierce assumed his position, slipping one arm about her and taking her gloved hand in his as the music began. He had only waltzed with Nalyssa back at Stonecrest. He had practiced with Pen, however, and felt confident of the steps. The music seemed to fill his soul as they moved as one. Nalyssa had an innate grace, and he believed her to be the most beautiful woman on this dance floor. Yes, he knew they would attract attention by dancing together, but it was all a part of his master plan to help ease her back into the good graces of Polite Society.

"I hope you are happy," she snapped.

"Incredibly so," he told her, twirling her about the floor with ease, caught up in the music and the fact that she was finally in his arms again. He would not let this night pass without kissing her once again. He had been silent long enough and must make his feelings known to her.

"I won't sup with you," Nalyssa said brusquely.

"You must, my lady. Partners for the supper dance always dine together."

She looked at him and sadly shook her head. "I heard the Duke of Westfield invite you to sit at his table. He is a good man, Your Grace, and would make a fine friend to you. He has been a respected member of the *ton* for many years. Even though his marriage is a bit unconventional, Polite Society has put their stamp of approval upon it. Go and sit with him and his duchess—but leave me out of it."

Pierce tightened his grasp on her, pulling her closer to him as they turned again. "I believe that I am the duke here. Your client. You have no say-so in this matter, Lady Nalyssa."

"Do you realize how the gossips will skewer you for this?"

He grinned shamelessly. "I am a duke," he reminded her. "A single, eligible duke. One looking for a wife. You think one dance with you will change that? There are plenty of women in this ballroom who will still be interested in setting their sights upon me after this one dance."

The defiance in her face wilted. Pierce did not want to hurt Nalyssa, but he must have her sup with him this evening. It was important for the *ton* to see that he was the one pursuing her and not the other way around.

They finished their waltz in silence, and he reluctantly released her when the music ended.

"Come to the supper room," he said. "It is expected that we should be together now."

Pierce led her into the room and spied the Duke and Duchess of Westfield. He guided Nalyssa toward them and the duchess greeted them.

"I am so glad that you were able to join us, Your Grace, Lady Nalyssa. Linberry will also sup with us and my friend, Lady Fia Sawyer, is also expected to join us."

They sat, and he saw the surreptitious glances tossed their way as the Duke of Linberry joined them.

He collapsed into his seat, anguish on his face. "Even though I arranged things with Lady Capwell, Fia denied me. She says she has to play throughout supper."

The duchess looked sympathetic. "I am sorry, Linberry. I know you were looking forward to spending time with Fia. There will be another chance. I promise you." She glanced up and waved.

Pierce turned and saw his mother approaching with an elderly woman, one who was still regal and beautiful at her advanced age. He felt guilty because he had forgotten about Mama, only concentrating upon Nalyssa. Springing to his feet, he greeted them.

Mama said, "Stoneham, I would like you to meet my new friend, the Dowager Duchess of Westfield."

He took the old woman's hand and bowed. "It is a pleasure to meet you, Your Grace."

"Likewise. Your mother is a very interesting woman, Stoneham. I have enjoyed speaking with her this evening."

Pierce turned and presented Nalyssa to the dowager duchess.

"Ah, Lady Nalyssa. We finally meet in person."

Nalyssa curtsied to the woman. "It is a great honor to make your acquaintance, Your Grace."

They seated themselves and the dowager duchess said, "Why don't you gentlemen make yourselves useful and bring back something to eat for us?"

"An excellent idea, Gran," the Duke of Westfield said, rising.

Pierce and Linberry did the same.

He said to Nalyssa, "I know what Mama would like to eat. Do you have any particular favorites?"

"I am not that hungry, Your Grace."

"Then I will select a few items for you, my lady."

He followed the two dukes to the buffet and Westfield told Linberry to stop sulking. Pierce saw Linberry gazing upon the woman who now seated herself at a harp. He had noticed this woman playing in the orchestra, finding it interesting that a woman was allowed to do so.

"First, she won't dance with me. Now, she won't dine with me," Linberry complained.

"You knew it would be an uphill battle with Fia," Westfield told his friend. "I have faith in you. You will think of something to let her know how you feel."

They went through the buffet's line, and Pierce was astounded at the lavish spread. He balanced plates for Mama, Nalyssa, and himself, bringing them back to the table and distributing them. Linberry brought a single plate to the table and placed it before the Dowager Duchess of Westfield, having gotten nothing for himself.

As they conversed, Pierce found himself liking the Westfields quite a bit. He would definitely take up the duke's offer to meet at White's and get to know the man better. As for the Duke of Linberry, he contributed nothing to the conversation, staring morosely at the harpist throughout the meal. She was excellent, and Pierce commented on her talent.

The Duchess of Westfield smiled. "Lady Fia is a new friend of mine and most talented. She has given music lessons to children of the *ton* for several years."

"Has she never made her come-out?" Nalyssa asked, speaking for the first time since they had seated themselves. "I have never seen her at any gatherings."

The duchess frowned. "No, she has been living under the roof of her cousin, a man who assumed her father's title. Lord Parkhurst."

"Oh!" Nalyssa said, sounding startled. "I did not realize the previous earl even had a child."

Linberry's brow furrowed. "Lady Fia has been kept away from Polite Society by her odious cousin."

"We are trying to help her break free of the man," Westfield added. "Lady Fia is a talented musician in her own right."

"Has she ever played at a ball before?" Pierce asked.

Linberry said, "No. Never. It is her goal, however, to be a musician and to write music, as well. If you will excuse me."

After Linberry left, the dowager duchess told them, "Linberry is in love with Lady Fia. They will have to work out a few details, but I believe the course of true love will prevail."

They finished their meal and spoke a few minutes longer, listening to Lady Fia play her harp. The Duchess of Westfield then asked, "Would you like to come to the retiring room with me, Lady Nalyssa? I feel the need to freshen up."

"Certainly, Your Grace," Nalyssa said, rising and joining the duchess.

Mama looked to Pierce. "It was a bold move, asking Lady Nalyssa to dance with you."

The dowager duchess smiled sweetly at him. "Bold—and wise. That girl has suffered for many years. Especially after the scandal her father caused. Lady Nalyssa is the epitome of grace and charm."

"I have found her to be quite charming, Your Grace," he replied.

"I am an old woman now, Your Grace," the dowager continued. "I used to resent old people who tried to meddle in the affairs of younger ones." She paused. "But let me say this—it is about time someone came along and saw Lady Nalyssa's worth and helped her understand it, as well. As a duke, your actions hold sway over many in Polite Society. Know that if you wish to pursue this match, Stoneham, I will do all in *my* power to make known that I am for it."

Her words touched him. "It is good to hear that I have your approval, Your Grace," Pierce said, liking the old woman very much. He glanced to Mama. "Do you feel the same?"

His mother said, "I think the world of Nalyssa. You know that. It would make me very happy if the two of you wed. I have only one question for you, Stoneham. Do you love her? She deserves to be loved."

"I do, Mama," he told her, aware that the others were listening.

She and the dowager duchess smiled in approval.

"Has it been an uphill battle?" asked Westfield. "It certainly was between Margaret and me. Love can prevail, Stoneham. I am a living example of that."

The dowager duchess chuckled. "My grandson was the talk of the *ton* last Season, Stoneham. He danced a waltz with Margaret and then proposed to her in front of everyone."

"How romantic," Mama said, her eyes misting with tears.

"They are still discussing the kiss between those two," the old woman added. Then her gaze met Pierce's. "It may take a grand gesture on your part, as well, Stoneham. I do not know Lady Nalyssa, but I have watched her over the years. It is obvious she feels that she is not worthy to return to her former place in Polite Society, much less be at the top echelon of it. I wish you all the best in your pursuit of her."

"Thank you, Your Grace. I thought I was a man who would never bend to love and have found that love can change a man's mind." He paused. "Nalyssa is very strong-willed, possibly more obstinate than even I am. We will butt heads over this issue, but in the long run, I plan to make her my duchess."

He turned to Westfield. "Might I ask a favor of you? Would it be possible for you to see my mother home this evening?"

The duke nodded. "We would be happy to escort Her Grace home."

Then he caught a glimpse of Nalyssa as she and the Duchess of Westfield entered the supper room again. His heart swelled. With pride. With love.

With need.

The ladies joined them, but Nalyssa did not take a seat. Instead, she said, "Your Grace, we must discuss a few things before the dancing begins again." She turned to the Westfields. "Thank you for allowing me at your table, Your Graces. It is a kind gesture that I will never forget."

Curtsying to them, Nalyssa turned and moved away.

"Good luck, Stoneham," Westfield called as Pierce hurried after her.

He caught up to her just outside the supper room. "What do you wish to chastise me about, my lady? At least I assume this will be a private scolding."

"This is no joke, Stoneham. Yes, you deserve a severe tongue-lashing."

A slow smile spread across his face at her choice of words. She realized what she had said and a blush stained her cheeks.

"A reprimand," she corrected.

"You are beautiful when you blush," he said, taking her elbow.

She pulled away. "Do not touch me in public," she chastised, her voice low. "I beg you. I already teeter on the edge of society as it is. If even one person believes I am your paramour and speaks it aloud, I will be ruined. I will never gain a single client again."

"Would that be so terrible?" he asked softly.

Color now flooded her face. "I had thought you—above any other client I have ever worked with—would understand because you yourself worked for a living. Well, so do I, Your Grace, and a woman who must support herself dances a fine line, no matter what level of society she inhabits."

Nalyssa took a step back, putting distance between them. "Go and fulfill your dance commitments for the rest of the evening, Your Grace. I will refuse you if you ask me to dance again."

Pierce knew he had pushed her enough. "I will do as you advise, my lady. I hope you will still allow me to escort you home this evening."

She seemed to waver, and he added, "I know Mama and I will appreciate your observations from tonight."

Her mouth set in stubbornness, and it took every bit of willpower he possessed not to kiss her in public.

"I will see you after the ball ends," Nalyssa said curtly and wheeled, marching away from him.

He watched her go, his blood heating. He looked forward to the carriage ride home.

And the challenge of convincing this woman that they belonged together.

CHAPTER TWENTY-TWO

NALYSSA DIDN'T TRUST Pierce. Not after he had almost ruined all the hard work she had put into launching him into the *ton*. She watched now from the sidelines, back in her usual spot, where she could observe the dancers and not have to speak to anyone else.

Pierce had been right. It seemed as if it hadn't mattered that he'd partnered with her earlier. Every woman that he took out onto the ballroom floor gazed at him in adoration, as did their approving mamas. Those women sat in the rows designated for matrons and gossiped as fishwives about the new Duke of Stoneham. She caught comments on how handsome he was. What an elegant figure he cut on the dance floor. How charming he had been when being introduced.

Tearing her eyes from the dancers, Nalyssa glanced to see that Amanda was chatting happily with a group of ladies. It pleased her to no end to see her friend making new ones. It was a shame that the previous duke had thought Amanda, being a lowly clergyman's daughter, would have been a detriment to the Selkirk family. Instead, she was now its chief asset. She would help propel both her son and daughter into Polite Society.

It struck Nalyssa that she was no longer needed. She had come to that conclusion when she had not returned to Stonecrest, believing the duke and his family to be in good hands with those at his country seat.

She had only spent time with them this past week because it led up to the Season and wanted to assure them that they were totally prepared for it. But there was nothing for her to do anymore. Pierce and Amanda were assimilating nicely this evening. Yes, most likely some gossip had occurred regarding them. That was only natural anytime a new duke took his place. Their circumstances were more unusual than others who ascended to their titles. In the grand scheme of things, however, Pierce and Amanda were already being accepted into the fold. They both possessed a presence about them which drew others in. They each displayed impeccable manners.

They no longer needed Lady Nalyssa Shelbourne to pave the way for them.

She sighed, knowing she had done her best with the Selkirks. She had introduced Pierce and Amanda to a good number of people this evening. Those people, in turn, would help open more doors for the pair. Their titles would do the rest.

It was time for her to go.

Perhaps she would forgo attending any more *ton* affairs this Season. Usually, she waited until much deeper into the Season before she stepped back, wanting to observe her clients at different events and advise them accordingly. Her latest clients had proven they were worth their salt. By removing herself from the equation, she would save the dresses Jenny had made over for next Season. It would give her time to herself—and possibly lend an air of mystery about her by vanishing from the public eye for a while. The Duke and Duchess of Stoneham would be her greatest successes. Hopefully, that would bring others to her doorstep, hoping they could achieve the same results.

It was easy to slip from the ballroom because no one watched her. She moved past the group Amanda sat with, noting the Duchess of Westfield was among them, grateful for the woman taking Amanda under her wing. As she reached the entrance to the ballroom, Nalyssa gazed across the dancers for a final time, seeing Pierce laughing as he danced a longways set, moving down the line of dancers with his partner. He seemed in his element, no longer the haberdashery owner from the west, but a true leader of Polite Society.

Her heart twisted a moment, the pain almost physical, as she saw the happiness on his face, contrasting to the gloom within her. Yet she loved him enough to wish him well in his new life. Nalyssa left the ballroom. She would retreat to her quiet life, carefully managing her finances until the next Season appeared on the horizon.

A lone footman was on duty and stood when she appeared in the foyer.

"Are you leaving, my lady?" he inquired, a puzzled look on his face.

"Yes, I am."

"Shall I escort you to your carriage?"

She could not return to Pierce's ducal carriage and ask the coachman for a ride. It would be asking too much.

"No, thank you, but I appreciate your kindness."

Exiting the townhouse, she walked a few blocks, knowing once she got past the maze of waiting carriages that there would be a few hansom cabs waiting, hoping to earn a fare. Though she hated to spend the coin on a ride home, it would be much safer than walking the entire distance. London's streets, while safe for the most part during daylight hours, could be dangerous at night.

Especially for a woman alone.

She wound her way through the maze of vehicles and came out a few blocks later, hailing a hansom cab and giving her address to the driver. When they arrived at her home, he handed her down, and she gave him a coin. He insisted upon walking her to the door, and she thanked him for the escort.

Going inside, a lone candle burned by the door. Nalyssa took it and headed to her bedchamber. She undressed without the help of her maid, taking a few minutes before she struggled from her corset. She paused, thinking of how Pierce had helped her in and out of it, imagining his fingers skimming her body. At least no child had resulted from their time together, for which she was grateful, even if it did sadden her a bit.

Slipping into her nightgown, she then pulled the pins from her hair, setting them in their case, and brushing her locks. She was about to braid her hair before going to bed when she heard something. Pausing, she cocked her head and listened.

It was . . . knocking.

A thought began to take shape in her head, filling her with dread. Quickly, she hurried to the window and opened it. Yes, the knocking was coming from downstairs. On her door. It could only be one person in the world.

Pierce . . .

Nalyssa grabbed her dressing gown and shrugged into it as she left her bedchamber and hurried downstairs. Betsy, her maid stood there, a candle in hand, looking scared.

"Go back to bed," she told the servant as she knotted the belt on her dressing gown. "I will take care of this."

"Yes, my lady," the girl said, rushing off.

Moving to the door, the pounding—which had ceased for a moment—started up again.

"I know you are in there," Pierce shouted over his banging fist. "Open this door now."

She took a deep breath. "No," she said, loudly enough so he could hear her through the door.

"No?"

"No," she echoed, instead cracking open a tall, narrow window on one side of the door. "I will not open it to you, Your Grace. Go back to your ball. You will have missed too many dances as it is."

He moved to the window, and she could see a sliver of him now.

"Why did you leave?"

Nalyssa heard the anguish in his voice. "Because it is *your* world, Pierce," she said softly. "Not mine."

"It wasn't mine until a short time ago," he countered. "I need you, Nalyssa." His voice broke as he said her name, twisting her insides painfully.

She mustered her courage. "You only think you do. You have a strength within you that will see you through anything, Pierce. You can do anything and everything you choose. You will mark your mark upon the *ton*." She paused. "But you must do it without me."

"I love you," he said, his voice low and tender. "I want to make things right between us. I need you, Nalyssa."

How she had longed to hear those words from him and tell him the same. Still, she wanted the best for him.

And that meant letting him go.

"You don't, Pierce. You are still trying to play the gentleman. Forget we ever met. Forget our short time together. You have the world to claim and the rest of your life to do so. Now, go. Please do not come back. My door will be forever closed to you."

A long silence dragged on. She did not hear his footsteps leave and as tears streamed down her cheeks, prayed he would do as she asked. Already, her willpower was waning. If he did not go soon, she feared she might open the door and fall into his arms.

"I will wait for you. Until my last breath, Nalyssa."

Then she heard his heels clicking on the pavement, moving away. Slowly, she closed and locked the window. She placed her palms and forehead against the door, knowing he had stood on the other side of it moments ago. Saying he loved her.

Nalyssa told herself that she had been right to send him away. He would make a brilliant marriage. Become a leader among his peers. Pierce would be a good husband and father.

Slowly, she made her way up the stairs and to her room. Locking the door, she climbed into bed, pulling the bedclothes over her head.

And wept until dawn.

PIERCE RETURNED TO the hansom cab he had taken to Nalyssa's house, his shoulders weighted down in defeat. Nalyssa had prepared him for every part of Polite Society, drilling him about proper etiquette. Rotten Row. House parties. Gentlemen's clubs. Gaming hells. Marriage laws and settlements.

But she had not schooled him on what to do with a broken heart.

Frustration filled him as he instructed the driver to return to Mayfair. Pierce climbed into the vehicle and brooded. Short of kidnapping her and forcing her to wed him, he had no idea how to resolve things. He realized that he would give up everything he had gained with his father's death—the ducal title, the vast wealth, the numerous estates—if he could return to his former life. If he were a haberdashery owner, he believed Nalyssa would have married him. It was the *ton* she was afraid of. The vicious vipers who had rejected her, an innocent young woman, all because of her father's weakness. Lord Starling's suicide killed not only the earl. It also, in effect, killed Lady Nalyssa Shelbourne's future. Her hopes and dreams. Not quickly, as the earl went with his bullet, but Nalyssa died a slow death each day.

Pierce had always despised bullies. That was what the *ton* was.

How could he get such a large group of people to recognize how their error in judgment had emotionally harmed a young lady of their own? Polite Society no longer saw the innocent Nalyssa had been. They barely saw her at all now and when they did, they judged her harshly because of the actions of her father years ago and the fact that she had to support herself in order to survive.

He knew that if she married him, she would once more become a darling of society. The gossips loved nothing more than to wag their tongues about some new scandal. One involving a new duke and his bride would give them plenty to talk about since they would be the first engagement of the Season. Then he believed she would be accepted.

Now all he had to do was make it known that he and Nalyssa were to wed.

The Dowager Duchess of Westfield had said he needed to perform a grand gesture. Her grandson had asked for a woman's hand on the dance floor with all of Polite Society as witness to it. He couldn't repeat the same action. He would need to do something else, just as public, something Nalyssa could not refute.

Then it came to him.

The cabby pulled up to the spot where he had first picked up Pierce. Climbing from the seat, he paid the man and asked, "Would you wait for me? I need to go inside and ask a question of someone, then I will have a new destination to go to."

"Sure thing, my lord," the driver said. "I'll be waiting right here for you."

Pierce entered the Capwell townhouse again and mounted the stairs, went inside the ballroom once more. He heard a buzz as he moved through the crowd, as the orchestra was not playing and preparing for their next number.

Going to the section of matrons, he spied Mama and the Dowager Duchess of Westfield and headed toward them.

When he reached them, Mama frowned. "Where have you been, Stoneham? You have missed several dances." Disappointment shone on her face.

"I am sorry for that, Mama. You will have to take the carriage home yourself. I have an important errand to run." He looked to the dowager duchess. "Your Grace, I will need your help in this matter."

The old woman's satisfied smile made Pierce smile. She looked to the Duchess of Westfield. "His Grace will see me home, Margaret."

She held out a hand, and Pierce helped her to her feet. He escorted her from the ballroom.

"Are we going on an adventure, young man?" she asked.

"We are, Your Grace. You seem to be a woman who knows quite a bit. I am most thankful for your help."

As he led the dowager duchess from the house, Pierce told her what he wanted done and asked if they had time in which to complete their mission.

She pondered his question. "It will take a good deal of footmen. And possibly a promise of coin to follow. I do believe, however, that you can make it happen."

"*We* will make it happen, Your Grace."

CHAPTER TWENTY-THREE

NALYSSA FINALLY ROSE, her head aching from lack of sleep. She opened the curtains and sunshine streamed through the window, causing her to squint. She turned, only to see last night's ballgown lying across the back of a chair. Seeing it caused a lump to swell in her throat. Tears sprang to her eyes, which she knew had to be puffy from all the crying she had done.

That was over now. Her association with Pierce and his family had concluded. She suspected Amanda would invite her for tea in the next day or so. Nalyssa would send a brief, polite note, explaining that she was engaged. She would continue to send the same response until Amanda ceased issuing invitations. Although she longed to see her friend—and Penelope—one last time, she could not afford to run into Pierce when she visited.

She hoped that he hadn't alienated too many people by leaving last night's ball. Even if he had, Polite Society could be very forgiving of a duke simply because he was a duke. After all, they forgave rakes left and right for ruining women and sporting bad behavior. A duke who missed a handful of dances would only raise a few eyebrows. If Pierce could behave himself and keep to the list of eligible, suggested women which she had prepared for him, he could find himself engaged by the end of the Season.

If not sooner.

Sighing, she performed her ablutions and then rang for her only maid, beginning to dress before Betsy showed up. When she did, Nalyssa said, "Good morning," turning her back so the servant could lace the corset. Betsy then helped lift the day gown over her mistress' head.

"Thank you, Betsy. That will be all for now."

"Yes, my lady," said the maid, exiting the room.

Though Nalyssa missed Jenny, she was grateful the maid had gained her new position in a duke's household. Penelope would be good to Jenny. The pair would probably be together for the next three or four decades. She only hoped she and Betsy could form a close bond in the years to come and thought she would make a point of conversing with the maid more, even bring Betsy into her confidence to make her more comfortable. It had taken time for her and Jenny to grow close. Hopefully, she and Betsy would form a lasting relationship.

Going to her dressing table, Nalyssa sat and absently brushed her hair. She wound the locks and secured them with several pins, looking at her reflection. Yes, her eyes were slightly swollen. It wouldn't matter. No one would call upon her today or any other day. Unless Pierce tried to do so. She decided to have a talk with Betsy and Cook and make certain they understood never to admit the Duke of Stoneham. She was never to be at home to him, no matter what the hour or day or how insistent he was upon entering the household.

Nalyssa left her bedchamber, her stomach rumbling. She hadn't touched anything Pierce had brought back from the buffet last night, too self-conscious to be sitting at a table with three dukes and three duchesses. She would go to the kitchen and have Cook make her a cup of tea and some toast points.

She went down the staircase and heard knocking at the door. Her heart beat wildly as her maid opened the door, worried that Pierce was on her doorstep again.

"Thank you," the servant said as Nalyssa rounded the corner and stopped on the landing as the girl shut the door, balancing a large flower arrangement composed of red and white roses.

"What's this?" she asked, hurrying down the rest of the way.

"They've been coming for the last hour, my lady," the maid informed her. "I've been putting them in the parlor. Shall I put this one in there as well?"

Snagging the card from it, she nodded her head, indicating for the servant to take the flowers to the parlor. Following behind her, Nalyssa looked at the card.

Congratulations on your engagement! We look forward to seeing you tonight at Lord and Lady Danby's ball.

The Duke and Duchess of Westfield

"What?" she cried, confused by the message she had just read.

Then Nalyssa entered the parlor and saw a good dozen more arrangements scattered about the small room.

"Would you like something to eat, my lady?" the maid asked.

"These all came this morning?" she asked, ignoring the servant's question.

"Yes, my lady."

Knocking sounded again. "Excuse me," the maid said, bobbing a curtsy and hurrying away.

She moved from one arrangement to the next, pulling the cards and reading the messages. They all wished her best wishes and congratulated her on her engagement. Somehow, a florist had made a terrible mistake.

Or had he?

An inkling of fear rippled through her. What had Pierce done?

She fell into a chair, the cards spilling to the floor. Her maid entered with yet another bouquet and placed it down before scooping up the cards and setting them on a nearby table.

"A cup of tea will do you a world of good, my lady. I'll bring one straight away, along with the morning post and the newspapers."

Nalyssa sat in a daze, afraid that Pierce had returned to the Capwells' ball and announced their engagement. It was the only thing she could think of. Not one card had mentioned the Duke of Stoneham by name, but she suspected Pierce had acted rashly. Why would he do such a thing? Ruin all his chances?

The maid returned with a tray, which bore a cup and saucer and a few letters, as well as the morning newspapers. Waiting until the servant left, Nalyssa opened the first paper to the gossip columns.

Not a single mention about any engagements.

Still, these floral arrangements had arrived for a reason. She looked over the other newspapers and saw not a single word in the gossip columns mentioning her name. Now, the Duke of Stoneham was mentioned numerous times, all flattering tributes to the new duke.

She had to make sense of this. Picking up her tea, she sipped at it, returning to the first newspaper, her favorite, and skimming the news. Then she spied it. Her heart stopped. Her breath hitched. It was a betrothal announcement.

For the Duke of Stoneham and Lady Nalyssa Shelbourne.

This made no sense to her. How could the gossip columns not hold any mention of this news—and yet a betrothal announcement appeared in all the morning newspapers?

Nalyssa would have to put an end to this nonsense. She must go see Pierce in person. No, Stoneham. She must keep her distance from him emotionally, if not physically. She set the newspapers aside and left the parlor. As she crossed the foyer, another knock sounded, most likely a new floral arrangement arriving. She would put an end to this, as well. Waving off Betsy, Nalyssa answered the door herself. She could not even see the messenger because the flowers were the largest grouping she had ever viewed.

"Take it back," she ordered sternly. "I am accepting no more flowers."

She started to close the door, but the deliveryman stuck out a foot and blocked her from closing it all the way. His audacity riled her temper.

"I said—"

"I heard what you said, Nalyssa," a familiar voice said. "However, this bouquet is from me and I will see it delivered to you."

He moved forward, and she had no choice but to get out of his way. Pierce marched into the foyer and glanced about, turning to his left to enter her parlor. Nalyssa closed the front door and followed him inside, watching him set down the arrangement. She shut the parlor doors, wanting privacy as she dressed him down.

"I do not know why—or how—you did it. Yet it must be undone, Stoneham," she told him sternly, upset that her voice shook.

He stood his ground. "You told me if I was interested in a woman, I should send her a floral arrangement. I chose the largest one available. It has tulips and roses. I hope you like them. Nothing is too good for my future duchess."

She stomped her foot in anger. "I am *not* going to be your duchess, Stoneham. You have made a horrible mess of everything. I wanted you to be accepted by the *ton*."

He waved a hand, indicating all the bouquets in the room. "It seems the *ton* is congratulating you on our engagement."

She shook her head, bitterness filling her. "You fool. Every single arrangement—but one—has come from a former client of mine. The only one which did not was from the Duke and Duchess of Westfield. No one else in Polite Society is eagerly sending me best wishes. They all probably believe that you and I were caught in a compromising position by someone who is keeping quiet for the moment. Someone who is insisting that we wed."

"I don't care," he boldly told her. "You are my choice. You are the one I want to spend the rest of my life with, Nalyssa. I told you before—and I will tell you every day until the last breath finally passes from my lips—I love you and I will make you mine."

"This cannot be," she declared, her heart breaking in two as she spoke. "I have told you that you are destined for great things and you need an appropriate woman by your side. Polite Society wrote me off years ago. I am not and can never be that woman for you."

She paused, swallowing her hurt. "This can be undone. I will simply make it known that I have broken the engagement. I did not go into this with you, but I will explain it clearly now. If a woman ends an engagement, it reflects solely on her. She could be innocent of any wrongdoing and her fiancé a cad, known to the public to be unfaithful, but blame is always assigned to the woman. Rarely will she be welcomed back into Polite Society. That means I am the one who will break this false engagement. True, gossip will follow you for a bit, but once it is known that you are available again, the line of women will form once more, just as they did last night at the Capwell ball."

He came toward her and took her hands in his. "I refuse to break this engagement, Nalyssa, nor will I allow you to do so. It is what I want. *You* are the woman I want."

She tried to pull away, but he held fast to her hands. His mouth descended and met hers. Her resistance fled. His kiss was loving but insistent. It tasted of promise. Of what their future could be together. Nalyssa kissed Pierce back with everything she had, hope growing within her.

When he broke the kiss, he smiled down at her in triumph. "I will do whatever it takes to make you mine, Nalyssa. I cannot be happy in this new world I inhabit unless you are by my side. I know there will be talk—but I also know that I am a duke. I will strike down anyone who even looks at you the wrong way."

He dropped to one knee. "Let's make this official. Will you, Nalyssa Shelbourne, agree to marry me?"

Her last bit of resistance melted away as she saw his love for her shining in his eyes. "Yes. A thousand times yes."

He sprang to his feet and embraced her, holding her so close that she felt the pounding beat of his heart. Then he kissed her deeply and for the first time in years, Nalyssa relaxed. She was loved. This man would protect her. Care for her. Give her children.

"I do love you," she admitted to him. "I have for the longest time."

Joy filled his face, and Pierce kissed her over and over again enthusiastically.

"I thought I would have to work hard to win you over. To win your love." He smiled at her. "Knowing that you love me as I love you makes me feel as if I could conquer the world."

He kissed her again soundly.

Then a knock sounded at the parlor door, and he released her. Nalyssa went to answer it, finding Betsy standing there.

"My lady, there is a modiste here to see you."

"A modiste? I did not send for one."

Pierce moved to the door. "I did. Send in Madame Planche."

She shook her head. "Were you so sure of my answer?"

He captured her hands in his and lightly pressed his lips against hers.

"I am confident in all I do, especially having you by my side. I went to Madame Planche's shop early this morning after asking Pen and Mama which one they had used. Madame said she was only too happy to come to you."

The modiste and two assistants entered the room. Pierce told them, "My fiancée will need an entire new wardrobe. Everything. Spare no expense, Madame."

He turned back to Nalyssa. "I will return for you tonight and escort you to Lord and Lady Danby's ball. I want us—and Mama—to arrive together."

"All right," she agreed, her heart swelling with happiness.

Her fiancé leaned down and brushed his lips against her cheek. "I will see you tonight." Then Pierce glanced at Madame. "Remember what I asked for."

The modiste nodded. "Everything will be taken care of, Your Grace."

Nalyssa watched Pierce leave, a song in her heart.

"My lady, if you will allow us to take your measurements, we will then discuss what you would like to wear to tonight's ball and beyond. His Grace was most insistent that we have a spectacular gown completed for you by this evening."

"Is that even possible?" she asked.

Madame's lips twitched in amusement. "Anything is possible when a duke is pulling the strings, my lady."

As the women fussed over her, Nalyssa found she couldn't agree more.

CHAPTER TWENTY-FOUR

NALYSSA FELT LIKE a fairy princess as Madame Planche stood in front of her. She did not know how the dressmaker and her seamstresses had managed to create such an incredible ballgown in the space of a single day.

"His Grace will be pleased, my lady," the modiste said. "You look lovely. Do not worry. We will begin creating your new wardrobe tonight. It was important to His Grace, however, that we spend all our efforts on this gown. He wanted you to be seen at your best this evening."

"Thank you for all you have done, Madame," she said. "I have never possessed a more beautiful gown, not even when I made my come-out years ago. I cannot thank you enough for the time and effort you and your staff have put into this, as well as working on the rest of my gowns."

"You have always been good to me, my lady, bringing me business over the years. I was happy to do this for you. And I hope you and His Grace will be very happy together."

A warm glow filled Nalyssa. "I think we will be."

The modiste and her assistant left, leaving Nalyssa to do her own hair. She still couldn't quite believe what had happened in the span of a single day. She was worried, though, about the reception she would receive this evening from the *ton*. As she had pointed out to Pierce, not one of the floral arrangements which had arrived were from members of Polite Society. She knew, though, with Pierce by her side that she could brave going into the lion's den tonight.

Going downstairs, she found him already in the foyer waiting for her. He smiled as she came down the stairs, a smile which would always melt her heart. When she reached him, he raised a box and said, "I asked Madame Planche what color your dress would be and matched it accordingly."

He lifted the lid, and Nalyssa saw a magnificent necklace of diamonds and sapphires, accompanied by a matching pair of earrings.

She gasped. "For me?"

He chuckled. "Well, I don't think I would look as good wearing these as you would."

He handed her the box and went to stand behind her, lifting the necklace over her head and placing it around her neck before fastening the clasp. Returning to stand in front of her, he nodded in approval.

"Put on the earrings. This will be the first of many gifts I give to you. For now, we shall call this a betrothal gift." He took her shoulders and kissed her cheek. "Thank you again for agreeing to marry me, my love."

Pierce claimed the box from her again and held it as she put on the earrings.

"It is hard to believe this is actually happening to me," she said.

He placed the box on a table. "It is happening to both of us. We are going to take the *ton* by storm. Come. Mama is waiting for us in the carriage."

They went outside and entered the carriage, where Amanda beamed at them.

"I am so happy for you, Nalyssa. For the both of you. I hoped in my heart that you would find one another."

Pierce settled in beside her and tapped on the roof. The vehicle rolled forward.

"When is the wedding?" Amanda asked eagerly.

"We have not discussed it, "Pierce said, "but I would like to know, because others will also ask that same question this evening." He laced his fingers through hers. "Frankly, I would prefer a quiet wedding at Stonecrest, but I don't believe we should do so."

"What do you have in mind?" she asked.

"I think a certain person explained to her client that a smart wedding at St. George's Chapel should occur once he chose a bride from the list. I would rather purchase a special license and marry you tomorrow, but I don't want anyone to think either of us are being rushed into this marriage. I say we have the banns read starting on Sunday and then wed in three weeks' time. You had told me St. George's books up quickly later in the Season and is quite the busy place after the Season ends." His eyes twinkled. "We might be the first couple of the *ton* to wed in the chapel this Season."

Nalyssa could see the wisdom in his thinking. "Although I, too, would prefer a quiet wedding, a marriage occurring with the entire *ton* invited to it would certainly put a stamp of approval. Yes, we must have the banns read."

"I will arrange for that to happen tomorrow morning," Pierce told her. "I will also reserve the chapel for our wedding."

"That means that Madame Planche should begin work on my wedding dress."

"Oh, I have already spoken to her of it. It is to be a surprise to you."

Tears welled in her eyes. "You have rescued me, Pierce, from my lonely life."

"You have done the same for me, my love," he said, his voice tender as he brought their raised hands together and kissed her fingers.

Amanda clapped her hands in delight. "Oh, to see my son having made a love match is remarkable. *You* are remarkable, Nalyssa. I am grateful to have you as my daughter-in-law, but I will tell you this. I will think of you more as another daughter."

Nalyssa brushed away the tears that fell with her free hand. Pierce pulled out a handkerchief and handed it to her so she could dry her cheeks. The carriage rolled to a halt, and he squeezed her fingers.

"Time to face the *ton*."

They entered Lord and Lady Danby's townhouse, with Pierce in the middle and Nalyssa and Amanda on each arm. The chatter died down as every guest in the receiving line looked at them.

Nalyssa knew enough to hold her head high. She sensed Pierce and Amanda did the same. The silence lingered a moment before a buzz began again. She knew their entrance had created that buzz.

"Stoneham!" a voice cried behind them.

Turning, she saw the Duke and Duchess of Westfield approaching. Once more, those in the receiving line ceased their conversations, the better to hear what happened next.

The duchess took Nalyssa's hands in hers. "Oh, Lady Nalyssa, I was delighted to read of your upcoming nuptials."

"Thank you for the flowers, Your Grace. It meant a great deal to me to receive them from you and His Grace."

Let the *ton* chew on that!

"Oh, we are so pleased for you." The duchess turned to Amanda. "You must be thrilled that your son has made such a wonderful match, Your Grace."

Amanda, gracious as ever said, "I cannot imagine Stoneham wedding anyone *but* Lady Nalyssa. It is a love match, you know."

Those words set the receiving line on fire as everyone began speaking at once.

The Duke of Westfield smiled. "Nothing like tongues wagging. Are you still free to meet at White's tomorrow morning, Stoneham?"

"I am happy to do so, Your Grace," Pierce replied.

"We will talk about anything but wedding plans," the duke promised. "I know how women can become consumed with that kind of thing."

They chatted easily until they reached their host and hostess. The Westfields greeted Lord and Lady Danby and stepped to the side, waiting for their new friends to join them.

"I hear congratulations are in order, Your Grace," Lord Danby said, eyeing Nalyssa with interest.

"Thank you, my lord," Pierce said, introducing his mother and then Nalyssa.

Lady Danby said, "We are so honored to have you attend our ball, Your Graces."

"Thank you, my lady," Pierce said easily. "I cannot wait to dance with my fiancée. I do hope you'll be playing a waltz or two."

"I have told the musicians to do so," Lady Danby said. "Please enjoy yourselves."

They joined the Westfields and as they entered the ballroom, Pierce asked, "Is your grandmother not in attendance this evening?"

"She had a bit of matchmaking to do," Westfield said. "She came early with Lady Fia."

"Hmm," Pierce said. "She seems to keep busy with that, doesn't she?"

The Duchess of Westfield laughed. "I think she may have found a new purpose late in life. Would the three of you please join us for supper this evening?"

"We would be delighted to do so, Your Grace," Amanda replied. "Oh, I see a new friend. If you will excuse me."

"Come, let us make our rounds through the ballroom," the duchess said, linking her arm through Nalyssa's.

"Thank you for your support," she told the duchess. "I will admit I am dreadfully nervous tonight at the reaction of Polite Society to our engagement. They will believe I am unsuited to be Stoneham's duchess."

"I was once thought to be a terrible choice to become a duchess.

But the power of a duke stretches far and wide. Bearing Stoneham's name will magically open doors. Those doors will remain open, once these people see your goodness and kindness, my lady."

They made their way through the room, the Duchess of Westfield paving the way for Nalyssa, making certain everyone they encountered knew that Nalyssa was a dear friend. People who hadn't spoken to her in years suddenly became eager to speak with her, complimenting her gown and jewels and wishing her well on her recent engagement. The last dozen years seemed to melt away.

After they had made a full circle about the room, Pierce said, "It is almost time to begin dancing. Might I have this first dance with my betrothed?"

Nalyssa smiled at him. "You certainly may, Your Grace."

It was a lively country dance. Nalyssa had not danced at a ball in years, except for the dance with Pierce just recently, but every step came back to her. By the time it ended, she was out of breath but so very happy, having not only danced but done so with the man she loved.

Pierce escorted her from the floor. "That was fun. I enjoy seeing you dance." He bent low, his lips brushing her ear. "And I cannot wait to do a different kind of dance with you in my bed."

She knew her face flamed at his words and hoped if anyone looked at her, they would think it was red from the exertion of the recent dance.

"I have heard a waltz will be performed next. I hope you will partner with me for it."

"I can—but two dances is enough, Stoneham. We mustn't dance together after that. It simply isn't done."

The heat in his eyes told her how much he desired her at this moment. "We are engaged, Nalyssa. I want all of my dances to be with you."

As they walked onto the dance floor, Nalyssa spied the Duke of

Linberry leading out Lady Fia Sawyer, whom the Duchess of Westfield had mentioned was a friend. The petite blond had played at the previous night's ball, intriguing Nalyssa. She recalled how Linberry had fretted at supper because Lady Fia had been engaged playing her harp throughout it. She hoped the pair would be able to enjoy themselves tonight.

Pierce took her in his arms as the music began, twirling her about the ballroom. Dancing had been something she had missed dreadfully. Her new fiancé moved them about the dance floor skillfully, and she believed she was the envy of every unmarried woman in the room.

He refused to leave her side, making certain he danced every dance with her. At first, Nalyssa worried about what the *ton* would make of his attention and then decided that she didn't care. She was in love and was loved in return. If Pierce wanted all her dances, then she was more than happy to give them to him.

They waltzed together for the supper dance. This time, the dance was joyous, unlike last night's waltz when she had been conscious of how others might be viewing them. It seemed a miracle had occurred in the past twenty-four hours. Nalyssa said as much as they moved toward the supper room.

"I am afraid I am going to awaken—and find this has all been a dream," she confided to Pierce.

He stopped. "I have had the same worries myself. We need to cast these doubts aside." He took her hands and brought them to his lips, kissing them tenderly. "We have one another now. Nothing—no one—will ever come between us."

She wished she could kiss him now. Too many might turn and see them, however. She would have to be content and wait for his kisses when others were not around.

They went into the supper room and located the Westfields, who were deep in conversation with the Duke of Linberry.

"Shall we go through the buffet together?" Pierce asked.

"I would like that."

Even something so simple as talking about the variety of food before them and choosing what items to put on their plate became magical. Nalyssa felt as if she had been sleepwalking since her father's death and suddenly had been awakened to a glorious life with the most wonderful man. Oh, she knew their life together wouldn't be a bed of roses. Pierce was headstrong and opinionated. The same could be said of her. Still, they loved one another, and she knew they would always find a path in which they could move forward.

They returned to the table, and she saw Linberry was now gone. In his place was the Dowager Duchess of Westfield, with Amanda seated next to her.

"I hope everything is all right with the Duke of Linberry," Nalyssa said.

The duchess smiled a knowing smile. "Oh, it will be. Give him time. Tell us about your wedding plans, my lady."

Both Nalyssa and Pierce shared what they could about having the banns read, starting this coming Sunday, and how they planned to be married at St. George's.

"That sounds lovely," the dowager duchess said. "And what of your dress, Lady Nalyssa? Has the modiste begun it yet?"

"Actually, it is to be a surprise," she shared. "Pierce has worked something out with Madame Planche."

"Won't you go for fittings before the wedding?" the dowager duchess asked, looking confused.

"It will fit," Pierce guaranteed.

"See? My betrothed is being a bit mysterious," she said. "I have learned to trust him, though."

Nalyssa reached for Pierce's hand beneath the table and laced her fingers through his.

"Have you been treated well this evening, my lady?" Westfield inquired.

"Amazingly so, Your Grace. People have, by and large, been quite kind. A bit curious but polite, all the same."

"Having my grandson's blessing, along with his wife's, goes a long way in the *ton*," the dowager duchess said, pride evident on her face as she beamed at Westfield.

"I must thank you, Your Grace, for the role you played in this match," Pierce said to the dowager duchess.

She looked at him, puzzled. "What did Her Grace do?"

"Let us just say that she accompanied me to a few places last night and made it possible to have the engagement announcement appear in this morning's newspapers."

Nalyssa turned to the old woman. "Then whatever you did, I thank you, Your Grace. I am forever in your debt."

The dowager duchess smiled. "I was happy to smooth the way for His Grace. Seeing how happy the two of you are, my lady, is payment enough. You owe me nothing, other than an invitation to your wedding."

"That will be forthcoming, Your Grace," Pierce said. "I will book the chapel tomorrow and then knowing the date, the invitations can be issued. Of course, I know nothing of how a wedding is put together. I will leave that up to my bride and my mother."

"Would you like us to host your wedding breakfast?" the duchess asked. "If you are asking the entire *ton* to your wedding, our ballroom would be able to accommodate them all."

Nalyssa turned to Pierce. "I don't mind having a large guest list for the wedding. For the breakfast, though, I would prefer something more intimate."

"I couldn't agree more. Let the *ton* gawk all they want at the wedding. Having a small, intimate wedding breakfast would be more to my liking." Pierce turned to the duchess. "If you don't mind hosting a small affair, we would be happy for you to do so."

"I think that is wise," the duchess said. "You will be on display for all of Polite Society to see you wed, then you can celebrate your union with more privacy."

They finished with supper, and Nalyssa found herself ready to go. Pierce agreed, and they collected his mother and headed for their carriage. He walked her to her door and saw her inside, giving her a lengthy kiss before releasing her and bidding her goodnight.

Nalyssa allowed Betsy to help her from her finery. She had received numerous compliments on the ballgown this evening. Madame Planche had assured Nalyssa that she would deliver another dress or two tomorrow morning.

After Betsy left, Nalyssa removed the necklace and earrings Pierce had given to her, staring at them for a good while before she returned them to their box. She would wear these jewels on her wedding day as she went to the man she would spend the rest of her life with and pledge her love and loyalty to him.

It was hard to believe how quickly her life had changed. She was to be married. She loved the man who would be her husband and adored his mother and sister. She believed she had a friend in the Duchess of Westfield and hoped that Lady Fia might also become a friend in the near future. The *ton* seemed to have magically forgiven Nalyssa and had embraced her tonight.

After so many years in semi-exile, she had been restored—even elevated—in the eyes of Polite Society. Everything was right in her world.

She only prayed it would stay that way.

Chapter Twenty-Five

NALYSSA'S WEDDING DAY dawned. She was up to see sunrise occur. It had been hard to sleep, due to her excitement.

The past few weeks had been busy ones. She and Pierce had attended numerous *ton* affairs together. It still shocked her how accepted she now was in Polite Society, all thanks to the fact that she was marrying a duke today. It still stung that the *ton* had blackened her name and ostracized her for the sins of her father. Fortunately, she was once again in society's good graces.

She would never forget what had been done to her, being shoved aside as if she had no worth. If she found other women in a similar plight, she would do everything within her power to help them.

Besides her friendship with the Duchess of Westfield, who was now Margaret to her, Nalyssa had also become friends with Lady Fia Sawyer, who had wed the Duke of Linberry. The couple had been the first marriage of the Season, announcing their betrothal on the third day of the Season at a garden party and marrying the next day at the Westfields' townhouse. Nalyssa and Pierce had been invited to attend the wedding and breakfast. They would return the favor today by having the Duke and Duchess of Linberry attend not only their wedding at St. George's but also the wedding breakfast.

Nalyssa had learned a bit of Fia's story and how her new friend had been relegated to an attic room for years, teaching music lessons throughout the week and handing over her earnings to her cousin, Lord Parkhurst, who had inherited his title after Fia's father passed. Fortunately, that was all behind her now, with Fia having wed Linberry. Just as Margaret continued painting after her marriage, Fia's husband was encouraging her to persevere with her music. Fia enjoyed playing and especially loved writing music.

She thought it a bit ironic how she and her two new friends were all women Polite Society had deemed unsuitable. Yet here all three women had wed dukes and risen to the top of the *ton*.

Jenny, who had come to help Nalyssa prepare for her wedding, wrapped a large bath sheet around her former mistress and helped her step from the tub. Once she was thoroughly dry, the maid began helping Nalyssa into her layers of clothing.

Except for her dress.

"Has my wedding gown arrived?" she asked nervously.

"Not yet, my lady," Jenny said. "His Grace assured us it would be here on time."

She couldn't understand why the gown hadn't arrived. Madame Planche had been delivering gowns daily to Nalyssa, slowly building her wardrobe. Every time she had asked the modiste about the gown, though, she was shushed and told not to worry.

"I'll go check again, my lady," Jenny said, holding out Nalyssa's dressing gown and helping her into it.

Jenny had been gone less than a minute when a knock sounded at the bedchamber door. Hurrying to the door, Nalyssa opened it.

And found Pierce standing there.

He looked incredibly handsome. Simply seeing him took her breath away. He stepped into the room and closed the door, turning and handing her a slim box.

"More jewelry?" she asked, seeing his eyes dance with mischief. "It seems as if every time I turn around, you are gifting me with more pieces."

"Many are from the Stoneham estate," he assured her. "But yes, some I have purchased just for you, as I did today's set. Open it. Tell me what you think."

She did so, revealing a stunning diamond necklace and teardrop diamond earrings. A matching bracelet rounded out the ensemble.

Gazing up at him, Nalyssa said, "I have never had anything so grand, Pierce."

"You deserve it, my love. Let's put everything on you."

He fastened the necklace into place, while she put on the earrings. She needed help with the bracelet, and he slipped it around her wrist.

"Now, all I need is a dress to wear to our wedding. I would have thought Madame would have had it here by now. If she doesn't hurry, I will have to choose another gown for the ceremony."

"It's here," Pierce assured her. "It has been for several days now."

"What? No," she insisted. "I would know if it had arrived."

He grinned. "You don't always know everything, my love."

Going to the door, he opened it. Jenny came in, carrying an ivory-colored gown. It had a lace overlay and was elegant and intricate and simply the most beautiful gown Nalyssa had ever seen.

"Place it on the bed, Jenny," Pierce instructed.

The maid did so, then slipped from the room.

"But . . . I need her to help me dress," she complained, even as she stepped to the bed and fingered the gown. "Oh, this is the most lovely gown I have ever seen, Pierce. It rivals the gowns of royalty."

"You think so?" He joined her, slipping an arm about her waist.

"Just look at it. See for yourself. Oh, the lace trim alone must have taken hours and hours."

"It did."

Nalyssa looked at him. "You asked about the hem?"

"I worked on the hem," he revealed. "In fact, I sewed your entire dress, love. If there is one thing I know, it is how to sew. I saw in my mind's eye exactly how I wanted you to appear and created the gown I knew you were meant to wear."

Her throat grew thick with emotion. "You sewed my wedding gown for me? Oh, Pierce!"

Nalyssa burst into tears, clinging to him. "This is the best gift I have ever received. You have designed the perfect gown."

He gave her a soft kiss. "For my perfect woman. Come, we need to dry those tears."

She washed her face first and then patted it dry. "I feel so loved in this moment, Pierce."

"I wanted to show you just how much I do love you, Nalyssa."

"I will wear this gown with pride."

"It should fit without any adjustments needed. I had your measurements from Madame Planche and also one gown which she fitted to you. She kept it and I used it as a guide."

He kissed her. "I should go now. I will see you at the church."

"In my diamonds and wedding gown from the man I love," she said, biting her lip, trying to keep the tears from spilling down her cheeks again.

Pierce slipped from the room and Jenny immediately entered it, saying, "Oh, my lady. It was a hard secret to keep. But His Grace insisted that your gown be a surprise to you."

Betsy also came in to help Nalyssa dress and watched as Jenny styled Nalyssa's hair.

"You are a sight to behold, my lady," Jenny said, awe in her voice. "Lady Penelope is waiting downstairs for you. You are to go to St. George's together."

Nalyssa floated down the staircase as Penelope squealed in delight. "Oh, you look so lovely. Pierce has worked night and day on your gown. Whenever he was not at an event with you, he has been laboring over this dress." She smiled. "I told you he was talented with a needle and thread."

They went to the carriage and entered it, heading straight for St.

George's. Once they had arrived, they went to a small anteroom off the foyer to wait for the start of the wedding. Amanda greeted them, tears filling her eyes.

"I must say that I have watched this gown be stitched together and I knew you would look beautiful in it. But my sweet girl, my imagination did not do this moment justice. You are breathtaking."

They talked for a few minutes, with both Margaret and Fia stopping in to say hello and rave about her dress. When Nalyssa revealed that Pierce had designed and sewn it for her, both women burst into tears.

"I have never heard of a more romantic gesture," Margaret said, dabbing at her eyes with a handkerchief.

"There is an advantage to wedding a duke who once owned a haberdashery and learned to sew from one of his tailors," she told them.

"You may have to let His Grace design all your future gowns," Fia teased.

"It is almost time for the ceremony to begin," Amanda said. "We shall leave you now."

She kissed the three of them goodbye, with only Penelope remaining with her. Her almost sister-in-law would walk down the aisle ahead of Nalyssa and stand up with her during the vows. Pierce had asked the Duke of Westfield to do the same for him.

Penelope opened the door and stepped out. Nalyssa followed, clutching the bouquet Amanda had put together for the wedding. They moved to the entrance of the chapel and the music began. While Nalyssa hung back, out of sight of the guests, Penelope went and stood in the doorway and then proceeded down the aisle. After she had given her friend time to reach the altar, Nalyssa then moved to the center of the archway. She heard the gasps and knew they were for the dress.

Her eyes were not on their guests, however. Her gaze went immediately to the front of the chapel and found Pierce. Even at that distance, she could see the love in his eyes and her own heart swelled with love in return.

She took a handful of steps, smiling broadly, and then her progress halted. Confusion filled her as she realized someone had an arm about her and pulled her back. The strong scent of whisky invaded her as she felt something cold touch her temple.

A cacophony of sounds erupted. Gasps. Cries. Shouts.

The arm banded about her tightened. She was against someone. Someone who smelled of stale sweat and alcohol.

Someone who held a gun to her head.

Nalyssa's eyes darted from left to right, seeing the people in the pews scramble to the edges of the chapel, fear on their faces. She looked forward and saw Pierce moving down the aisle. Their gazes met. Somehow, he would make this right. He had to. They had a future together. Children to make. Events to celebrate. A lifetime of love awaited them.

"Stop!" the man who held her hostage said. "Don't come any closer. Or I will pull this trigger."

Pierce stopped, his jaw tight. He stood a few feet in front of her but seemed an ocean away.

"What do you want, Selkirk?"

"I was Hardwell. *Lord* Hardwell," her captor insisted, his breath hot against her bare nape. "And I should be Stoneham now. *I should be Stoneham!*" His voice echoed throughout the chapel.

With those words, understanding filled her.

And terror.

"Lower the gun, Selkirk," Pierce said calmly. "You don't want to hurt anyone."

"Why not? Have I not been hurt myself? Humiliated? Ruined? I have been the object of gossip. I have lost everything that I held dear. I have not a friend in the world. I no longer have my fortune. My place in Polite Society. I am a no one. With nothing."

Pierce took a small step forward. "You are not penniless. You own Bigby Hall in Somerset. It is a large, profitable estate. Our father wanted you to have it."

"I want Stonecrest!" Selkirk shouted. "I want my birthright. My title. You are a no one. A mere shopkeeper who now struts about, pretending to be a duke."

"I am a duke," Pierce said quietly. "Our father wed my mother. I am sorry for how things turned out, Selkirk. Harming Lady Nalyssa will not change anything. Please. Lower your weapon. Let her go."

Selkirk's arm was squeezing the life out of her. She could barely breathe. And she didn't think he would move the pistol from her temple. Her gaze met Pierce's. A wave of sadness washed over her. They would never be married. Never know happiness.

"I will not, you filthy scrub. You may think me a blunderbuss. I am not."

"If you shoot her, you will hang. All these witnesses will testify against you. You will die, Selkirk, and go straight to the bowels of hell."

A long silence ensued. Nalyssa brought her hands to her captor's forearm, digging her nails deeply into it. It was as if the fellow felt nothing.

"Then take me," Pierce offered, moving another step closer, so close she could almost reach out and touch him now. "I am the one you wish dead. Kill me. Not an innocent woman."

"I know I will hang for my crime," Selkirk said, pressing the cold steel hard against her temple. "But it will be this woman who dies today, *Your Grace*. You love her. And if she dies, a part of you will die. Every. Single. Day. You will forever recall the fear in her eyes. In your nightmares, you will see her lifeless body fall to the ground and regret that you could not save her. I want you to suffer as I have. More than I have. I want—"

Everything happened in a blur—and yet it was almost as if it also occurred at a snail's pace. Nalyssa saw Pierce launch himself forward, his arms thrust out, reaching for the gun. Selkirk turned the weapon from her head and pointed it forward. She realized Selkirk had dropped his arm, and she slammed her elbow into his ribs, knocking him away.

Falling to her knees, she glanced up, seeing Pierce's fingers encircling Selkirk's wrist, forcing the pistol's barrel skyward. A loud shot rang out, the noise reverberating in the chapel.

Westfield jumped into view. She thought he must have left the altar and come along the side wall, slipping behind Selkirk. Both dukes fell to the ground atop Selkirk. Pierce restrained his half-brother as Westfield unknotted his cravat. He slipped it around Selkirk's wrists and knotted it tightly, jerking the man to his feet.

Nalyssa rose shakily, thinking how close to death she had come. How it could have even been Pierce murdered before her eyes, distracting Selkirk, willing to take a bullet for her.

Pierce shot to his feet and threw his arms about her, hugging her tightly. Then his mouth sought hers in a bone-melting kiss, one affirming they were still alive.

He broke the kiss. "Are you all right?"

"He could have killed you!" she accused.

"Better me than you," her groom quipped. Then his eyes softened. "I would die a thousand times over for you, Nalyssa. I love you. I will always protect you."

He turned and she did as well, seeing Westfield hand off Selkirk to two footmen. Selkirk was screaming at the top of his lungs.

Westfield stepped to them. Quietly, he said, "They are taking him to my carriage. You will need to decide what is to be done with him, Stoneham. He holds no title. He can be tried for attempted murder."

"Or sent to an asylum," Pierce replied. "It is an alternative."

By now, she was aware of the many conversations happening at once.

"I am sorry our wedding was ruined," her groom apologized. "We can leave now and try for another day."

"I will not have our day ruined," she said loudly, her voice carrying.

The guests in the chapel fell silent.

Nalyssa looked to the man who held her heart. "I came to this chapel today to marry the man I love. The man I will spend the rest of my life with. The man who will give me children and hold me dear. I will not let Selkirk ruin this day for us."

Pierce beamed at her. "Then allow me to escort you to the altar, my lady."

"Bravo, Lady Nalyssa," Westfield said, hurrying up the aisle before them.

In a remarkably calm fashion, the guests who had sprung from their seats now returned to them as Pierce led her up the aisle, her hand tucked into the crook of his arm.

They reached the front, and he turned so they faced the crowd. "Thank you for coming to our wedding this morning. Lady Nalyssa and I will now exchange our vows with your blessing."

Thunderous applause filled St. George's Chapel.

She leaned toward him. "If you ever do something so foolish again, I might have to kill you myself."

"I suppose I deserve that. I thought while he was rambling that I could draw attention away from you to me. I didn't think he would have time to get a shot off." He smiled down at her. "Nice blow to his ribs, by the way."

"Thank you, Your Grace," she said pertly.

He guided her so they faced the vicar, who wore an astonished look.

"I will see any damage from the gunshot is repaired immediately," Pierce guaranteed. "Now, if you would, we would like to be married."

Somehow, the man found his voice and the ceremony began.

Nalyssa found herself repeating her vows, looking into the eyes of the man she loved and would love, now and forever.

And when they were pronounced man and wife, the kiss her new husband gave her was the best of her life.

Until the next one, of course.

EPILOGUE

Stonecrest—September 1817

PUGH OPENED THE door, admitting Nalyssa. "How was your meeting at the church, Your Grace?"

She untied her bonnet, removing it and her shawl, handing them to the butler.

"It went quite well," she told the butler. "I will have to break the news to His Grace, however, that he is to pay for a new roof for the church."

"I am sure he will take it in stride, Your Grace." Pugh paused. "His Grace is in the nursery."

"Thank you, Pugh," she said, sailing up the stairs, eager to see her husband and three children.

They spent a great deal of their time in the nursery, something they both enjoyed. Their daughter was four and already a handful. Their son, who was two, followed his big sister around, letting her order him about as he kept a sweet smile on his face. The baby, now eight months, was starting to cut his teeth and so was a bit cranky these days. Still, they loved every minute with their children.

Nalyssa entered the nursery, seeing Nanny had just put down the baby.

"How is he?" she asked.

"Better today, Your Grace," Nanny replied.

"Go have a cup of tea," she urged. "His Grace and I will see the other two are put down for their naps."

She watched as Pierce read to the children for a few minutes. Both began yawning.

"Time for your naps," she announced, taking the book from her husband and setting it on a nearby shelf.

"Do you have to take a nap, Mama?" her daughter asked.

"We are all going to take a nap," Pierce declared. "I am worn out from playing with the two of you and Mama is tired from her meeting. Come along."

The children went to their beds and were tucked in. Almost immediately, both fell asleep.

"What did you do while I was gone?" she asked, as they crept from the room.

"What didn't we do?" her husband countered, slipping an arm about her as they descended the stairs.

"Are we really in need of a nap?" she asked. "I, for one, am not a bit sleepy."

He stopped on the landing and pulled her to him for a lingering kiss. Breaking it, he said, "You should be. I kept you up until the wee hours last night."

"I suppose I could at least rest my eyes," she mused.

"Minx," he declared, sweeping her into his arms and carrying her to their shared bedchamber.

Nalyssa nudged the door closed with her foot and then Pierce placed her back on her feet. She wound her arms about his neck.

"Have I told you today that I adore you, Your Grace?" she asked.

"You told me you loved me. Three times, I believe. But no, I cannot recall you mentioning that you adore me."

"Well, I do, you silly goose," she said, pulling him down for a lengthy kiss.

"We should get into bed if we are going to nap," he suggested. "And I find it easier to sleep without clothes on."

Clucking her tongue, she began to untie his cravat. "Anything to get me naked."

He cupped her cheeks. "But I *like* you naked, Your Grace."

"I like getting naked for you, truth be told."

Soon, both had shed their clothes, and they made slow, tender love. As Nalyssa lay in her husband's arms, she mused, "Life cannot get better than this, can it?"

Pierce kissed her softly. "Actually, I think it gets better every day. All thanks to my wonderful duchess."

He kissed her again. *This* was her favorite kiss.

Until the next one came. And all the kisses that would follow it.

About the Author

Award-winning and internationally bestselling author Alexa Aston's historical romances use history as a backdrop to place her characters in extraordinary circumstances, where their intense desire for one another grows into the treasured gift of love.

She is the author of Regency and Medieval romance, including: Dukes of Distinction; Soldiers & Soulmates; The St. Clairs; The King's Cousins; and The Knights of Honor.

A native Texan, Alexa lives with her husband in a Dallas suburb, where she eats her fair share of dark chocolate and plots out stories while she walks every morning. She enjoys a good Netflix binge; travel; seafood; and can't get enough of *Survivor* or *The Crown*.

Printed in Great Britain
by Amazon

26589729R00145